Praise for *This Beating Heart*

'Barnett's well-crafted ba
this novel is no different,
ence that we think more
and especially to the shap

'I found this beautifully told tale of disappointed motherhood moving, but the best bit for me was the lively South London scene Barnett conjures up' Wendy Holden, *Daily Mail*

'An uplifting tale about new beginnings'
Maureen Stapleton, *Heat Magazine*

'A warm, emotional story with brilliant characters'
Deirdre O'Brien, *Best Magazine*

'Barnett writes beautifully about relationships and the possibility of finding a very different happy ever after from the one you were expecting' Mernie Gilmore, *Sunday Express S Magazine*

'Laura Barnett weaves an inspiring story about shifting perspective and finding light in the darkness'
Zoe West, *Woman's Own*

'A compelling read' *Closer*

This Beating Heart

Laura Barnett

WEIDENFELD & NICOLSON

First published in Great Britain in 2022 by Weidenfeld & Nicolson,
This paperback edition first published in Great Britain in 2023
by Weidenfeld & Nicolson,
an imprint of The Orion Publishing Group Ltd
Carmelite House, 50 Victoria Embankment
London EC4Y 0DZ

An Hachette UK Company

1 3 5 7 9 10 8 6 4 2

A CIP catalogue record for this book is
available from the British Library.

ISBN (Mass Market Paperback) 9781 4746 1719 2
ISBN (eBook) 978 1 4746 1720 8
ISBN (Audio) 978 1 4746 1721 5

Typeset by Input Data Services Ltd, Somerset

Printed and bound in Great Britain by Clays Ltd, Elcograf S.p.A.

www.weidenfeldandnicolson.co.uk
www.orionbooks.co.uk

For anyone at any stage of the 'journey'

In the stillness of the house, we hear our blood
pumped by hearts that gall themselves, grow empty:
once, this silence, shared, could draw us close
that now forebodes us with a desperate quiet.

Kona Macphee, 'IVF'

I was having trouble sleeping so in the middle of the night I
walked down to the playground at the end of my street. All the
ghost-children were at play . . . A black-haired boy sat beside
me and whispered in my ear, 'Change doctors.'

Julia Leigh, *Avalanche: A Love Story*

Once upon a time, there was a man and a woman.

The man and the woman fell in love. They walked in parks, held hands across restaurant tables. They moved in together. The woman forgave the man for his obsessive tidiness and secret collection of boxed *Star Trek* figurines, and the man overlooked the woman's grumpiness when tired and tendency to ignore the conspicuous build-up of dust balls.

The man and the woman got married. The woman stopped taking the pills she kept in the drawer of her bedside table, and the man left the last of the little plastic packets on his own side of the bed untouched.

The man and the woman spent a lot of time in bed, and the woman spent a lot of time looking at the calendar on her phone.

Time passed. Each month, the woman bled and cried a little, and the man held her close and told her that it would surely happen soon. It had happened, after all, for almost all their friends and colleagues and cousins and acquaintances, and all the buggy-pushing, sling-wearing people everywhere, on every pavement, every Tube train, in the park the man and the woman still liked to walk in at weekends.

Eventually, the man said, it will happen for us. The woman began not to believe him, but she let him tell her what she wanted to hear, and she let him hold her, because she wanted, above everything, to be held.

It did not happen, not in the way the man said it would. What happened, instead, were needles, and specialists, and blood pulsing on grainy pixelated screens. What happened was life stirring in Petri dishes, under microscopes. What happened was the woman injecting herself, and spreading her legs on hospital trolleys, and losing too many hours on the internet; and the man staring out of windows, waiting, letting his mind go blank until he could admit no thinking at all.

What happened was, not this time. What happened was, let's try again.

Time passed. Two lives quickened into being and were lost. The woman cried, and the man was mostly silent, and did his crying where nobody else could see.

The man and the woman began to shout at each other, and then stop, and then shout some more.

The man said, *No more*. The woman said, *One last time*.

The man and the woman stopped shouting at each other, and the silence this left behind was louder than any sound they had heard before.

The man left, taking half their things with him. His things. The woman stayed, in a half-furnished rented flat with a room she wouldn't enter, a door she kept closed.

This is the story of what happened next.

One

The playground was busy. Four o'clock on a London Tuesday afternoon: low autumn sunshine, rusting drifts of leaves. Crowds at the school gates; grey-haired women in high-vis jackets stopping traffic, waving their small, uniformed charges across the road.

Bev, she was called, the woman outside Wilberforce Primary: she'd been there for years, knew the children by name, most of the parents, too. Even Christina, and she was only there once a week, which hardly counted. But to Bev, apparently, it did. 'Hello there, Aunty,' Bev said with a smile as Christina crossed, gripping the children's hands so tightly that Gabriel complained that she was crushing his fingers, and wrenched free. It was only then, chasing Gabriel towards the park, Leila's hand still in hers, that Christina realised that Bev must have been speaking to her.

'Why,' Leila said, Gabriel still streaking out ahead, 'didn't you tell Bev that you're not really our aunty?'

'Gabriel! Stay where I can see you, please.' Then, to Leila, 'I didn't realise she was talking to me. And anyway, it doesn't matter if she thinks that, does it? I'm kind of your aunty, aren't I?'

'Not really.' Leila, dawdling, drew a line on the pavement

with the toe of her boot. 'Our Aunty Lizzie lives in Sheffield, with Uncle Rob, and Gracie and Oliver and Owen the baby. But we haven't met him yet.'

'I know she does. I know you haven't. But I . . .' Christina wasn't sure what defence to offer in addition, or why; it didn't matter, anyway, as now Gabriel was pushing open the gate to the playground, and Leila was letting go of her hand and running off after him.

She sat on her usual bench under the high, spreading horse chestnut tree, watching Gabriel scale the rope ladder and Leila follow another girl of a similar size – Lina, was it? Christina was sure she'd seen her here before – up the steps to the summit of the slide. When she'd first begun collecting Leila and Gabriel from school, she'd found the playground terrifying – dangers on all sides, everything far larger and higher than anything she could remember from her own childhood. Surely that rough surface wasn't safe; if a child fell off that rope bridge they'd break an arm, or worse. She'd hovered close to the children, not quite preventing herself from squealing out loud each time they attempted one of their simian ascents. This had lasted until one Saturday afternoon when she'd accompanied Jen and the children to the park, demoted to second-in-command; observing Christina's anxious hovering, Jen had insisted they find a bench to sit on, let the kids do their thing. 'We'll keep an eye, but don't worry, Chris – they're not made of glass.'

Oh, but they are, Christina had wanted to say. *They really are.* She watched them now. Leila was at the bottom of the slide, racing back to the steps for another turn. Gabriel had reached the prow of the pirate ship; Christina waved, and he waved back, then dived out of sight.

'How old?' a woman said. Christina looked round: a buggy, a green parka, a blue striped top. Mid-thirties, or thereabouts:

blonde hair, no make-up, but one of those faces that don't need it: wholesome, milk-fed. The baby appeared to be a girl; she stared at Christina, unblinking, from above a red duffel coat, navy tights, tiny shoes buckled with silver stars.

'Six,' Christina said. 'His sister's nine.'

The woman smiled. Her legs were narrow in her skinny jeans, her stomach flat. And the baby, what, six months? Eight? How had she done it? Luck, or breastfeeding, or starving herself? Luck, Christina decided: she had that look about her. Everything smooth, everything easy. Though you could never really tell, could you? No, assumptions could always deceive.

'Such lovely ages,' the woman said.

'Yes.' Christina mustered a reciprocal smile; she was just deciding whether to say more when the woman leant forward, tapped her on the belly. 'And how long,' she said, 'till this little one's ready to meet the world?'

Christina flinched, shook her head. The woman removed her hand. 'Oh God. I'm so sorry, I . . . I shouldn't have . . .'

'It's all right,' Christina said. 'It's fine. Really. Don't worry about it.' And then she stood and turned away, calling Jen's children, telling them it was time to head for home.

'Cow,' Jen said. 'I'd have slapped her round the face.'

'No you wouldn't. She felt bad enough as it was.'

'So she bloody well should have.'

Jen reached for the bottle of wine, refilled Christina's glass. They were in Jen's living room, the kids asleep down the hall, Christina's plate of reheated fish pie abandoned, uncleared, in the kitchen. 'Sod that,' Jen had said when she'd come in, throwing her padded coat over a chair, her hair in a high, loosening bun, her body, as she drew Christina into a tight embrace, smelling of deodorant and cigarettes and the low, musky whiff of drying sweat. 'I'm knackered, and I bet you are too, looking after those monkeys all afternoon. Come and sit with me. There's a posh bottle in the fridge. Chablis, I think. Mum went to Waitrose. Lucky us.'

Christina sipped her wine and said, 'I'm giving this dress to the charity shop. I don't think I can ever wear it again.'

'Oh Chris,' Jen said, laying her head on Christina's shoulder. 'The woman's an idiot. You don't look remotely pregnant.'

The word hung between them for a moment, its presence solid, almost tangible. Jen straightened, looked at her. Christina forced a smile. 'Tell me more about rehearsals. Is it coming together? Is Louis still being a pain?'

Jen waited a moment before replying, still watching her with that searching, clear-eyed gaze. Then she stretched and yawned, arching her back like a cat. 'He wasn't as bad today. Not quite, anyway. It was good. It's kind of . . . coalescing. I hope so, anyway. We've only got two weeks to go.'

'You'll pull it off. You always do.'

Later, they embraced in the hallway, under the ancient, blooming, ceiling water stain: the flat was a dump, Jen was always claiming she was looking for somewhere better, but nothing better ever seemed to appear. Nothing she could afford, anyway. 'Thank you, darling, as always, for today. I'm so grateful. You know that, don't you?'

Christina nodded, retrieved her handbag from the floor, drew it over her shoulder. 'I do know that. But really, it's a pleasure. We have fun.'

'I know you do. They love you.'

Leila earlier, on the way home from the park: taking Christina's hand again, and saying in a high, clear voice, *I wish you were our real aunty. I like you more than Aunty Lizzie.* She smiled. 'I love them too.'

Christina followed Jen to the door, hung back as she opened it. The outside air smelt of damp leaves and, faintly, unemptied bins: it was bin day tomorrow, Christina had wheeled them out onto the pavement herself earlier, after she'd given the children their tea. Her own collection was the following day; she'd have to remember, it had been Ed's thing, it was so easy to forget.

'Have you spoken to Ed yet?' Jen said as Christina stepped out onto the path. Black and white chequers, original, weeds springing up around the missing tiles. 'About . . . Well. What happens next.'

Christina shook her head. 'Not yet.'

Jen leant against the door. She'd taken her hair down: it hung in glossy black coils around her shoulders. Backlit by the hall light, her loose, easy beauty was thrown into stark relief, her face divided by planes of shadow. A drawing by – what was his name? Schiele, Christina thought, or something like that: half mad, wasn't he; German or something, sketched dancers sitting tying their shoes. No, Austrian – they'd seen an exhibition in Vienna that weekend years ago, she and Ed. He'd grown restless, wandered off towards the café, while Christina had stayed, walking from painting to painting, taking the measure of each one: each woman's pale skin and reddish hair, her own particular blend of frailty and strength.

Jen blew her a kiss. 'I'll see you at Emma's on Saturday, right?'

'You will,' Christina said. 'Love you. See you then.'

Something woke Christina in the night. She lay stricken for a long moment, the rush of blood loud in her ears. The sound came again: a rustle, a crunch. Footsteps on gravel, just beyond the French windows. *Shit*. Her pulse redoubled; she could feel her heart thudding in her chest. She reached across the cool expanse of sheet to the empty pillow, felt beneath it for the hammer, gripped the handle in her hand. Its solidity was reassuring; she lay still, forcing herself to breathe. Nothing. A fox, a cat. Breathe.

Nobody knew about the hammer: she'd placed it there not long after Ed had moved out, under the pillow she'd also left on his side of the bed. There had been a spate of burglaries: Mrs Jackson upstairs had urged her to take care. 'Two women alone,' she'd said. 'We can't be too careful.' Christina, without thinking, had opened her mouth to rebut this – she, at any rate, was not alone – and then closed it again. The truth, of course, was that she was. That night, she'd found the hammer in the Ikea toolkit (Ed had left her this, taken the better one with him, the one he'd bought from B&Q), and put it under the adjacent pillow.

That noise again. Crunch, skitter, rustle. *Fuck*. There was definitely something there. Christina's breath stilled in her throat. Finding the light, swinging her legs round onto the carpet. Standing, carrying the hammer. Crunch of gravel. Thud of blood. She crossed the room, switched on the outside light, drew back the curtains, ready for ... what? A face, a body, danger in human form. But there was nothing, no one. Just the off-black London night, the patio slabs set in their bed of gravel, the herbs and rangy geraniums in tubs. Then that sound again, a stirring, and there it was: a hedgehog, scuttling off towards the concealing safety of darker shadows.

Christina lowered the hammer, light-headed with relief. For God's sake. She hadn't seen a hedgehog in years, and never here: her dad had encouraged them into the garden in Carshalton, left out water and cat food, built something he'd called a hedgehog hotel out of a plastic storage box covered with grass and straw. She didn't know whether any had ever moved in, but he'd liked to have it ready for them, just in case. That was just the sort of man her dad had been.

Christina closed the curtains, switched off the light. Sat on the edge of the bed, the hammer still in her hand. Then she placed it on the carpet, climbed back into bed, and lay with the lamp on for a few moments, watching the ceiling, letting her breath grow steady, her pulse slow.

'All well, darling?' her mother said.

Eleven o'clock on Thursday. Christina, at her desk, swivelled her chair away from her laptop screen, towards the wall: the framed graduation photo (Christina, Emma and Jen, in red lipstick and mortar boards, below the high neo-Gothic spires of Whitworth Hall); the bookcase lined with her files and reference books. This, the second bedroom, had survived Ed's departure more or less intact. Only Ed's collection of vintage sci-fi figurines – Darth Vader, Jabba the Hut, ET and others Christina couldn't name, each kept pristine in its box – had disappeared from the bottom of the built-in cupboard where Christina stored the piles of clothes she could no longer fit into, in the belief – optimistic or misguided, she could never quite decide – that one day, again, she would.

'Mum,' she said, 'it's the middle of the day. I'm working.'

'Sorry.' Then, a little pertly, 'You answered the phone, darling. You can't be that busy.'

There was no answer to this. Why hadn't she ignored the call? Boredom, she supposed – boredom, and silence, and habit:

9

the ingrained fear of missing something important, some vital news about Dad. Though, of course, now there was no more such news.

'OK, Mum. What is it? Everything all right with you?'

'Oh yes, darling. Yes. I was just calling to check whether you're still coming for lunch on Sunday.'

Christina shifted back to her laptop, the open Excel spread-sheet, the window beyond. Another fine, washed-clean autumn morning, the oak tree shedding its red and yellow leaves onto the lawn. She'd sweep the leaves up later; she still had all her gardening tools in the shed. They'd agreed that Ed wouldn't touch them: he would have no need of them in America, and anyway, most of them had been her dad's. For as long as she could remember, gardening had been their shared love; she'd had no choice in the matter, Dad had taken her outside with him the moment she'd been tall enough to hold a rake. Long hours together, digging, pruning, planting: all those small acts of tenderness, of care. So much easier, somehow, to do this for a garden than for yourself.

'Yes, I'm still coming, Mum. Why?'

A longish pause. Then, brightly, Sue said, 'Oh, no reason, darling. I was just . . .'

'Just what?'

'Well. You see, I've had this invitation . . .'

'Who from?'

'Oh, a few people from my dance class are going for lunch. There's a new Indian on the high street. They do an all-you-can-eat on Sundays. It really is unbelievable value. But of course, darling, I'd love to see you . . .'

'Mum, it's fine. Go to your lunch. Have fun. I'll come another time.'

'Well, darling, if you're sure. It would be nice to go with them.

The weekend after, then?' Sue paused: Christina pictured her standing in the kitchen, tethered to the phone (her parents had never got round to investing in cordless models), consulting the month-to-view wall calendar. Colin Prior's Scotland: Christina had bought it for her the previous Christmas, thinking of the holidays they'd taken together, the three of them, to Skye, Loch Lomond, Glencoe. But her mother, unwrapping it, had smiled politely and set it aside: too much, Christina had presumed, regretting her choice; too much to remember, too much to miss.

'Actually,' her mother said now, 'I have a cinema trip booked that Sunday. With the dance class. They're showing *The Red Shoes* at the British Film Institute. You know, the place in town, on the South Bank.'

'Yes, Mum, I know.'

Christina couldn't remember the last time her mother had gone 'into town': as far as Christina was aware, the boundaries of her life stretched no further than Croydon, Sutton, Cheam and, on rare occasions, Wimbledon, for the shopping centre, the Common, the smarter coffee shops. Sue had started this dance class in the spring – her friend Helen, a fellow widow, had started going, insisted it had changed her life. And her mother did seem to be changing: these plans, this new brightness, the haircut she'd had over the summer – shorter, jauntier, blonder (they didn't look at all alike: Christina had her father's mousy colouring, his tendency to put on weight, especially around the waist). They'd met for lunch at the Crown, down by Carshalton Ponds, just after she'd had it done. Watching her mother approach, threading her way through the crowded beer garden in her peach slingbacks, Christina had seen her for a moment as others might: an attractive, smiling woman, not the carer, the widow, the one left behind. The thought had cheered her; she'd held her mother to her, told her how wonderful she looked.

'Sounds great, Mum,' she said now. 'Don't worry. We'll find another time. I'd better go. Work, you know.'

'Of course. I'll let you go. Christina?'

'What?'

Another tiny pause. Then, 'You're doing all right, darling, aren't you?'

Christina stared at the spreadsheet, narrowing her eyes until the lines and numbers began to fracture and dissolve. 'Yes, Mum,' she said. 'Really. Don't worry. I'm absolutely fine.'

She stepped out into the garden in the afternoon, retrieved her dad's old rake from the shed. Gardening gloves, her hair scraped back, her ancient kitchen apron on, with its faded blue stripes, its frayed halter attached with safety pins. God knew why she'd kept hold of it; she hated throwing things away, and perhaps that was no bad thing, now that so many of her things – their things – were gone: to storage, to Ed's parents' house, and some, she presumed, to America with him.

Just after three: always, for Christina, the slowest time of day, deadened and dull. It had been different in the office: she'd had distractions then, colleagues, water coolers, tea runs to the canteen. Working from home, there was nothing to leaven the tedium of the client spreadsheets, the expense claims and VAT returns, the emails from panicked theatre directors and gallerists, actors and dancers, asking whether they could expense this dress or that train fare, worrying about whether they were saving enough to pay their tax bill when it came.

Most seemed to wear it almost as a badge of honour, this inability to handle money, the low, rising panic it instilled: *Help us, we are artists, we are not slaves to Mammon.* Jen was impatient with this; she was good with money, she did her self-assessment returns herself, though the broader Arrow Dance finances she left to Christina. Jen's newborn company had been her first client, after university, back when Christina had still had no idea what she wanted to do; she was in recruitment, bored beyond imagining, when Jen had got funding from the Arts Council, founded Arrow Dance, suggested Christina come in to help her with the money side. She'd set up systems, five-year plans, investigated other future sources of financial stability: kept the engine turning over, leaving Jen and her dancers free to think and move and dream. Left recruitment, found other clients in the arts; joined Wright and Marshall, stayed for fifteen years. Gone freelance again three years ago, when it had all got too much: this was after the third round of IVF and the first miscarriage, the one at seven weeks. Their fertility specialist, Dr Ekwensi, had been unable to offer any explanation, just called it one of those terribly unfortunate things. Stress, they'd suspected, she and Ed, stress and long days. And Christina was missing so much work time anyway, what with all the hours they were spending at the clinic, or stuck in traffic getting there and getting home, inching around south London in endless angry rush-hour jams. Patience among the partners at Wright and Marshall had been starting to fray: they had been generous, given her a good severance package. *Stress*. Much better, they'd all agreed, for her to go freelance, establish her own client base again, work from home.

Home. Christina swept, the strokes of the rake rhythmic, soothing. The leaves were dry, friable, easy enough to move from the lawn to the corner of the empty flower bed where she would, she thought, begin a makeshift compost heap, a pile around which she might, one weekend, build wooden sidings. She'd edged the beds herself, not long after they'd moved in:

they'd only taken the flat for the garden, really, which was large for London, for a rented flat, and wild, though Dad had agreed that it had good bones. He'd stood there with her, clutching a mug of tea, surveying the plot while Ed was busy unpacking boxes inside. 'We can clear all this,' Dad had said, sweeping a hand over the scrubby dandelion lawn, the borders choked with nettles and bindweed. 'I'll show you how to edge those borders, neaten them up. It won't take much, Christina – just a few railway sleepers and a bit of elbow grease.'

Right till the end, Dad had looked on the bright side: right till the end, he'd looked for reasons to stay chipper. New treatments, new supplements. Until, in the very last months, when all such approaches had been exhausted, he'd shifted to acceptance. *It's all right, I'm comfortable; I'm ready, I've loved the life I've lived.* Dad's bright, brittle courage, his refusal to fall into despair. She was like him: Mum had always said so; Ed, too. Like Dad, she had refused to fall; like Dad, she had refused to give up.

She stood on the lawn for a moment, rake in hand, breathing, shielding her eyes from the sun. *One last try.* The treatments had cost them so much – their savings, their marriage, everything – but there was still one chance left. Her last chance: it wasn't the same for her as it was for Ed, he had to see that, even now. There had to be a way to reach him – to cut through the layers of exhaustion and resentment, bridge the gulf that had opened up between them, year by year, round by round, until here they were, their marriage over, their possessions divided, their lives five thousand miles apart.

Two

Sixteen today.

Isla's dress was tight-fitting, drawn around her slender frame in bandaged tiers. Bare arms and legs, though the temperature had dipped that morning, and the sky outside was heavy, pigeon grey. Heels, hooped earrings, her mother's curls caught in a high, cheek-tightening bun. Isla leant forward to embrace her, and Christina caught a heady whiff of floral perfume.

'Happy birthday, lovely.'

Christina handed her the gift bag – a Mac voucher, and a triple-wick candle, wild fig, from one of the posh shops in Dulwich – and Isla grinned, displaying her perfect Colgate teeth. Those months when they'd first come through: Isla's sleeplessness, her inconsolable grizzling. Emma's exhaustion – she had never, she said, known tiredness like it, not even in their first year at Manchester, when she'd used to pull an all-nighter at least twice a week. Christina had come over to hold the baby, rock her, wheel her around the Common, give Emma an hour or two to rest. They'd been in their twenties then: Emma was a trailblazer, the first of them to stake a claim to motherhood. 'Looks like a total fucking nightmare,' Jen had said to Christina privately, and she'd agreed. It had been years, in each case, before either had changed her mind; before motherhood had become, for

Christina, the treasured end point, the mirage, always staying just out of reach.

Isla placed the bag on the console table, among its many replicas. Yellow for Selfridges, purple for Liberty's, Tiffany's telltale duck-egg sheen. Above the table, doubled and refracted by the broad, gilt-framed mirror, two rose-gold balloon digits swayed, beside an oversized champagne glass filled with silver and gold bubble balloons. Emma and Pete made money these days, serious money, their other friends did, too: Christina knew this, of course, had known it for years, but that money was rarely spread out for all to see.

'Thanks, Aunty Chris,' Isla said. She had developed a distinct mid-Atlantic drawl. There had been those years she'd spent in New York with Emma and Pete, but it wasn't just that, her friends all seemed to speak that way: Christina had met some of them and heard them on FaceTime when Isla was meant to be working on quadratic equations (she came to Christina for maths tutoring a couple of times a month). 'Shall I get you a glass? Mum's around somewhere.'

'Chris.' Emma, emerging from the kitchen, where the other guests had already gathered, their voices drifting through. 'You shouldn't have. Look at all this stuff. She's spoilt beyond all measure.'

They hugged, kissed each other on the cheek. Years ago, they'd used to laugh at people for doing that – *so pretentious* – until, gradually, they'd realised that they'd started doing it too, and so had everyone they knew. 'Sweet sixteen. Couldn't let it pass unnoticed, could I?'

'Don't know about the sweet. But thank you.'

Isla didn't seem to be listening; she was watching the living room through the glass partition wall, where a hermetic teenage gathering had formed. All those new-minted young women in their dresses and heels, the boys in T-shirts and jeans, their hair artfully mussed and smoothed. Music pulsing from the wireless sound system – something shouty and bassy, alien to Christina's ears. Young people's music. Her own sixteenth might as well have been a century ago. Christina had still been a goth: she'd worn her best white make-up, fishnets and leather skirt, played her new Cure and Siouxsie and the Banshees CDs to a cheerful gathering of fellow weirdos. Mum had swallowed her disappointment that Christina had refused to wear the green taffeta party dress she'd bought for her, and served sandwiches with the crusts removed, cheese and pineapple on sticks, miniature sausage rolls. Dad had played the amiable off-duty schoolteacher, refilling glasses of Coca-Cola and asking Christina's friends about their plans. *And which of you, then, is intending to apply to university? Any of you set your sights on Oxbridge?*

Christina smiled. 'Off you go, Isla. Have fun. Your mum'll get me a drink.'

'There's cake and stuff in the kitchen,' Isla said vaguely, turning away.

'You look good,' Emma said. 'New dress?'

Christina shook her head. 'You know this one. I've had it for years.'

Emma widened her eyes, mock innocent. Of course she knew. 'Oh. I don't remember it. Works with the lipstick. Anyway, we're all hiding in the back. Jen's not here yet. Let me find you a glass.'

Emma and Pete's house was broad and handsome, with white columns either side of the front door and clipped bay trees in square terracotta pots. Big, airy rooms, high ceilings, everything open-plan. Many, many shades of grey: Ed, on their first visit, had joked under his breath that it must be like living inside John Major's wardrobe. He had a talent for that, Ed – making light of things, trying to make her laugh. He'd succeeded, too, for as long as he could.

The kitchen spanned the rear: an enormous island marooned in a sea of antique oak, huge black Crittall doors framing the garden, with its limestone paving and its outdoor kitchen and its drifts of lavender. Emma gave Christina a glass and melted away; Christina hung back, absorbing the scene, summoning the courage to step in. Smart strangers – school mums, she assumed, or colleagues of Emma and Pete's; names she might know, attached to faces she did not – stood in groups, holding wine glasses, eating small morsels from slabs of black slate proffered by Sarah, the live-in nanny, and a skinny, anaemic-looking man in clear-framed glasses: Sarah's German DJ boyfriend, she assumed. Some faces were familiar – Emma and Pete, of course; and Pete's brother David; and Emma's mother, the Honourable Lydia Dalrymple-Scott, holding court on the yellow velvet sofa, waving what looked like a dry martini. A few stray teenagers drifted by, solemn emissaries from a taller, leaner species; their younger siblings ran in and out from the garden, thunder-footed, laughing, flushed from their assaults on the high-sided trampoline. Here was Alfie among them, throwing his arms around Sarah's waist (Sarah's, not Emma's, Christina noted; though Emma, across the room, didn't seem to). Turning, he saw Christina and ran over.

'Aunty Chris! Did you see me bouncing just now? I went higher than *everyone*!'

Christina bent down, kissed the top of his seven-year-old head. His black curls smelt of soil and coconut shampoo. 'I didn't see, Alfie. Let's go outside, and you can show me again.'

'Not so fast.' Jen, appearing from the hallway in a green silk jumpsuit, waving a bottle of champagne. 'Hi Alfie, I love you very much, but Aunty Chris is staying here with me.'

Alfie shrugged, blew them a kiss, and stampeded away.

'Thank God you're here,' Christina said. 'I'm not sure I can remember how to do this.'

Jen looked at her, her head on one side. She'd put her hair up, applied hot-pink lipstick; twin leopard-print hoops dangled from her ears. How Christina loved her; Emma, too. How lucky she was still to have them, when the rest of her life had shrunk to fit inside so small a frame.

'It's easy,' Jen said, and she linked her arm with hers. 'Follow me.'

Later, they sat together at the kitchen island, the three of them, among dirty plates and glasses smudged with lipstick and fingerprints, Isla's cake demolished to crumbs and jam smears and slivers of rose-gold frosting.

The birthday girl herself had left hours earlier, with her entourage, for a party somewhere: a rave, it sounded like, under a railway arch in Peckham. 'Midnight,' Christina had heard Emma saying in the hallway as they'd gathered there, Isla and her girls and boys, like so many twittering, preening parakeets. 'Home by midnight, please. Don't drink too much, and don't, for God's sake, *take anything.*'

Christina had smiled to herself, remembering Manchester, their own nights under railway arches, sweat dripping from curved red-brick roofs. Was this what motherhood required: the erasure of your own youthful fearlessness, the inevitable transformation into someone who bore a dangerous resemblance to your own mother? Christina wasn't sure she could do it. Slipping back towards the kitchen, towards her half-full glass of wine, she had wondered with misplaced drunken logic whether this could, on some unconscious level, be a part of the reason why the opportunity to be a mother had been denied her. Perhaps she would simply fail at it, fail miserably. Perhaps the universe knew this, and was for this reason refusing to allow her the opportunity to try.

'Brie?' Emma said. She had brought out a platter of cheese, together with biscuits, grapes, three plates, three silver cheese knives. Pudding wine, too. This was the sort of woman Emma was now: a woman who kept an open bottle of Sauternes in the fridge, and a set of thin-stemmed crystal glasses in which to serve it. But then, Christina thought, remembering their house in Levenshulme in second year – 'the Mansion', everyone had called it, after the vanload of tweed and velvet furniture Lydia Dalrymple-Scott had sent down from the castle in Caithness – perhaps this was simply the sort of woman Emma had been waiting to be. We all had costumes we stepped into, disguises we assumed. *Emma, the wealthy solicitor, wife and mother of two. Jen, the acclaimed choreographer and single mum. Christina, the . . .* Actually, she didn't want to go there. Not now.

'Go on then.' Christina had reached the stage of drunkenness when everything seems slightly watery, off-kilter, as if viewed through a thick pane of glass. Emma cut a slice, laid it on her plate. Christina, examining her knife, said, 'I don't think I've ever knowingly owned a cheese knife. But then, I don't really own anything any more, do I? Well, not much.'

She laughed. The laugh came out sounding brittle, thin. She put the knife down, speared a square of cheese, aware of Emma and Jen exchanging looks across the creamy marble. There was a silence, punctuated by the low burble of the television from the basement den – Pete and David were down there watching *Match of the Day* – and the whirr and gurgle of the dishwasher. Sarah had filled it earlier before heading out to a club in Hoxton with the snow-white German DJ.

'Hey C,' Jen said, and Christina braced herself: she generally called Christina 'C' when she was about to say something she knew she might not want to hear. 'Have you spoken to Ed yet?'

Christina shook her head.

'Or to the clinic?'

Christina let a further silence roll out across the room. She cut herself another piece of cheese. 'Not yet. No.'

'Chris,' Emma said, 'I really wish you'd have a word with Joanna. I know you both want to do things your own way, no lawyers, keep things civil – and that's great – but I wish you'd let Joanna give you some advice. She's a specialist. I mean, if Ed says no to what you're asking, then . . .'

If Ed says no. Christina closed her eyes. The night landscape behind them spun a little. Flares in the darkness, jagged shapes. She opened them again. 'I'm going to talk to him. I am. Soon. Of course I am. I have to. And then . . .' She looked down at her left hand, stretched her fingers wide, as if spanning a piano chord. She'd played piano as a child, had reached Grade 5. Her wedding ring was still there; she hadn't had the courage yet – the courage or the honesty – to take it off. 'And then, I guess, we'll see.'

Sunday came with leaden skies, and rain, and a pea-souper of a hangover, of the sort Christina hadn't experienced in years. She'd been careful since splitting up with Ed, aware of the pull of alcohol, its deadening draw, and she'd avoided the stuff through the years of treatment as one of the few things she could actually control in the whole endless, cyclical charade. Since Ed had left, she'd vowed not to allow herself to become a cliché. The childless, lonely almost-divorcée, pickling her liver in a rented flat. An occasional gin and tonic to mark the day's end; the odd glass of wine, a few more than that on her evenings with Emma and Jen: this was all she usually allowed herself, and from the way she was feeling now – God, hangovers were brutal past forty – this would seem to be no bad thing.

She called Dinah, regretting her arrangement to visit, put in place after her mother had cancelled, when the prospect of another empty Sunday, alone in the flat, had been too much. But her aunt wasn't there: Christina remembered, too late, the swimming club, her long-standing Sunday-morning dip. More than a dip: Dinah, at seventy-eight, was a Trojan, even swam in the Channel on New Year's Day. She'd made it into the papers more than once, in her swimming cap and one-piece (not for her the muffling cosiness of a wetsuit), a link in a chain of fellow swimmers. Christina couldn't cancel now: it would be midday before Dinah was back from the beach, and she'd have already got something in for lunch. No, there was no other option: she'd have to shower, find Nurofen, drink a strong black coffee and then get herself in the car, hoping she was sober and alert enough to drive.

The weather was brighter on the coast: the sky was clearing, the clouds rolling off across the Channel, the damp, lingering scent of rain merging with the spray carried on the air. Gulls wheeling, the taste of salt, the safe promise of the sea, the same as it had ever been and would always be: it cheered her, all of it, as it always had. She found a space in the car park and walked the minute or two to her aunt's terraced house. Faded white stucco, the blue paint at the windows peeled and cracked: shabby now, compared to its neighbours, with their smart paintwork and olive trees, but Dinah didn't care much for such things, she never had. Her interests lay elsewhere: in books, in ways of thinking and living, in the intricacies of her research. *Anthropology*: a word whose meaning Christina had learnt early, absorbed eagerly into her rapidly expanding childish lexicon. 'The study of people,' Aunt Dinah had told her, 'and what could be more important, really, than that?' ('Lots of things,' her mother had said when Christina had reported this back to her – unaware, then, of the trickiness that defined her mother's relationship with her sister-in-law. There had been some early schism – Christina learnt this later. Dinah had refused Sue's invitation to be a bridesmaid at the wedding and then hadn't even attended, had been on a field trip in Latin America – Guatemala, perhaps, or Honduras, Christina wasn't sure. 'Like housework, for one thing. And emptying the fridge once in a while, before you give yourself listeria.')

'Christina,' her aunt said now, opening the door. Her hair was still damp, drawn into a black and silver plait that snaked across one shoulder. She wore a striped jumper, unravelling in places at the hem, and one of her many pairs of utility trousers, with their essential pockets. ('Are you aware, Christina, of how few items of clothing for women actually have pockets? This is a feminist issue, you know.') Her feet, in their usual Birkenstocks, were bare: Dinah never seemed to feel the cold. 'You look dreadful. Are you ill?'

'Thanks a lot. I'm hung-over. It's clearing a bit now, though.'

'I should hope so. It's after midday.'

Dinah stepped aside and Christina followed her into the little hallway, with its bare splintered floorboards and assorted litter of unexamined post. 'Come through. You'll be wanting coffee, I expect. I'm just back from a swim. Haven't done a thing about lunch yet. You can give me a hand.'

Radio 3 was on in the kitchen (Dinah disdained Classic FM, Sue's favourite station, considering it the lowest common denominator). '*Private Passions*,' Dinah said, switching on the kettle. 'You don't mind if we listen for a bit, do you? It's a good one.'

'Not at all.' Christina didn't mind: this was one of the things she most enjoyed about her aunt, her dislike of small talk. No *How was the journey? Are you busy with work at the moment? What were you up to last night?* No, Dinah preferred to keep conversation for bigger, important matters, and if you weren't forthcoming with those, then silence was just fine, too. Driving back to London after their first meeting seven years before, Ed had said, 'I'm not at all sure whether your aunt liked me. She doesn't ask a lot of questions.' Christina, rejecting an instinctive defensiveness of her aunt (they'd been at that very early stage when it is so easy to be charming, and kind, and to put the other person first at all times), had reached for his hand, and said, 'She definitely liked you. She was just sizing you up. Next time you see her, she'll be asking you what you think of the international development budget.'

This hadn't quite happened, though. Dinah had been friendly enough with Ed, who'd made a big effort with her after that (he had actually taken to reading *The Economist* in preparation for their trips to Whitstable). But Christina could sense a certain impatience in her aunt's tone; observe, in her manner towards him, a certain ongoing reserve. Dinah had never criticised Ed, not aloud – not even recently, since the separation, when she might have felt more at liberty to do so. But once, during the fortnight Christina had spent staying with her the previous year, after the second miscarriage – the worst days of all – she'd come and sat on the end of the bed in the spare room, where Christina was lying under Dinah's handwoven Guatemalan bedspread, and said, 'Are you sure, Christina, that this is really what you want? To have a baby, now? With him? I think the body sometimes knows things that we don't.'

Christina had been furious; later that day, she'd packed and left with barely a word. She hadn't told Ed exactly what Dinah had said, only that she'd been horribly tactless, implied that somehow losing a precious, longed-for pregnancy at twelve weeks could be anything other than the horror it had been. Three months: Christina's second pregnancy, and the only one they'd told everybody about, the only one in which she'd allowed herself to begin to relax. She'd redecorated the box room as a nursery – they'd given up on the dream of buying a flat by then; the treatments had cost thousands, had eaten their savings in hungry gulps. She'd bought a cot, toys, an assortment of miniature clothes. Ed had wanted to wait – he'd said it was tempting fate – but she'd gone ahead anyway, she just hadn't been able to stop herself. They'd waited so long, and now their child had been growing and moving and living, until suddenly she (it was almost certainly a girl: they'd paid for an early scan) had stopped. A heartbeat lost, a tiny body expelled. An unkept promise; a daughter they'd both loved, as deeply as anyone or anything they'd ever known – though they hadn't known her, not really, and now they never would.

The rift between Christina and Dinah had remained, a painful severance, for several weeks, until Dinah had called to say how sorry she was, how deeply sorry, how she would take the words back at once if she could. 'Forgive your clumsy old aunt,' she'd said. 'I didn't mean it. How could I? I'm a stupid old woman. Fit for the knacker's yard. I really am so sorry.' And so Christina had forgiven her; how could she not?

They made omelettes for lunch. Christina cracked the eggs, grated cheese, shredded ham while Dinah prepared a salad. They ate in the garden, under the ancient vine-covered pergola, leafless now, its branches gnarled and intricate. Dinah brought out blankets, and the sun emerged, warming the wooden table and chairs with their Jackson Pollock spatterings of seagull muck. Their talk was of everything other than the personal, though they were there between them always, the shadows, the ghosts. Christina's father, John. Iris, whom Dinah had loved for thirty-five years and lost. Ed. The vanished children.

Later, they walked along the seafront towards Tankerton, past the brightly coloured beach huts on their wooden struts, most of them shuttered for the season.

'Your mother called me the other day,' Dinah said.

Christina watched the side of her aunt's face: her plait, her long, aquiline nose. 'Mum called you?'

Dinah strode on. 'She did. She said she's worried about you. About this plan you have.'

'Which plan?'

'You know exactly which plan, Christina.'

Christina looked away: to the huts, the escarpment, a man walking a spaniel on the high stretch of grass above. Below, on the beach, was a family in matching waterproofs, the mother and daughter in yellow, the father and son in navy blue. The daughter, running seawards in her red wellingtons, looked about five – the age their oldest child would have been, Christina's and Ed's, had the first round of IVF been successful. They might have had two children by now; three even. They might have still been together, living in a house they owned: a house with wood floors and high, corniced ceilings and a big old rambling garden, roses and apple trees, a sweep of lawn. A nursery, filled with life, with discarded clothes and books and toys. A child sleeping in the cot: a boy, hair sticking damply to his face, thumb tucked into his mouth; a girl, lying on her back, her eyes tight shut, the monitor carrying the steady aspirated rhythm of her breathing to them both downstairs.

'It can't all have been for nothing,' she said. 'This can't be the end of it. It just can't.'

Dinah said nothing, just reached for her arm, tucked it inside hers. Together, they walked on.

Three

They had met when Christina was thirty-six and Ed was forty-two: late, by any standards. He'd been married before. Not for long: it had turned out that his ex-wife didn't want children. Christina had imagined this might have been a conversation they'd have had before going through all the faff and rigmarole of a wedding, but of course she had never said so, not aloud.

What did Christina care, anyway – she wasn't dating Ed Macfarlane, not back then. No, he was with Ana, one of Jen's dancers: Spanish, tiny, saucer-eyed, with a handspan waist like that of a Disney princess. Filthy mouth, though. 'He is a good fuck,' she'd told Christina; they'd been in a pub round the corner from Sadler's Wells after a show. Ed was at the bar; Christina had met him earlier, would do a few times while he was with Ana, haunting the fringes of Jen's circle. A 'professional nerd', he'd called himself when they were introduced: he worked in tech, designing and beta-testing apps, and did stand-up about science and computers. Nerd stuff. 'Very good fuck,' Ana repeated. 'But he wants kids. Keeps talking about them. Broody as a – how do you say? – chicken. A hen. I don't know if it will last. But for now' – Ana shrugged, speared an olive with a stick, popped it into her perfect rosebud mouth – 'is OK.'

It hadn't lasted. A few months later, Jen had sent Christina a text. *Ed Macfarlane wants your number. What do you think? Shall I give it to him?*

I thought he was going out with Ana.

Not any more, it would seem.

Christina had said no: she was seeing someone at the time, a friend of Pete's, he worked for the same bank. She'd been quite into him, for a while – dazzled perhaps, despite herself, by the cash he'd splashed around on their early dates, the dinner at Nobu and drinks on the terrace at the Coq d'Argent. He'd had a flat on the river, at Butler's Wharf: not a penthouse, but almost, with a balcony, a view of the water, the Gherkin, Tower Bridge. But the sex had been unexciting – energetic but bland, like a run through a nondescript landscape, without anything interesting to snare the view. And on their fourth date, he'd taken her to a dizzyingly expensive Thai restaurant in Knightsbridge with a stream flowing through it – an actual stream, teeming with actual koi carp – and insisted, at the final moment, that they split the bill. It wasn't that Christina had minded paying her share – she earned decent money at Wright and Marshall, could have owned a flat by now if she hadn't minded living in a shoebox in Mitcham or Elmers End. It was that she'd realised, handing over her debit card to pay £150 for a meal that she hadn't chosen or particularly enjoyed, that she didn't find this man even the slightest bit interesting. She'd ended things the next day; she struggled, now, even to remember his name. Ah, that was it: Steve. She wondered if she'd ever known his second name.

Ed's email had arrived soon after that. His name in her inbox, still innocuous then, uncharged by lust or familiarity. For a second or two, she'd struggled to place him. Ah yes – Ana's ex, the nerdy stand-up with the square, black-framed glasses that had, she could just recall, made him look like a slightly shorter, dumpier version of Louis Theroux. He'd asked for her number; now, it seemed, he had taken matters into his own hands:

Hey, Ed here. We met ages ago. You won't remember. I was going out with Ana. Well, I'm not, now. In fact, I'd really like to take you out sometime. So I guess I'm hoping that you do remember me, and that I don't therefore sound like a total weirdo stalker.*

Memory jog: I'm the nerdy stand-up guy who looks like a shorter, dumpier version of Louis Theroux. Anyway, write back if you do remember. Delete this if you don't. **

* Your email address is on your website – something to think about in case you do ever get approached by a total weirdo stalker.

** Actually, write back either way. Go on. You know you want to.

Of course she'd written back. They'd met at a pub in Balham. He lived in Streatham then, she in West Norwood; she imagined he'd suggested this as neutral ground. He'd been at the bar when she entered, his back to the room; she'd worried, beforehand, that she might not recognise him, had asked Jen to provide a minute description, looked at the photo on his website a few too many times. But she'd known him right away: his height, his hair, the shape of him, the set of his back in his pale blue denim shirt. He'd turned, seen her – those glasses; that lopsided, quizzical smile. He was wearing a black T-shirt under the shirt. *Nerd*, the T-shirt announced in tall white print.

'In case you didn't recognise me,' he said, pointing to the slogan. 'Just covering all bases.'

She'd smiled back, gone over to him, ordered a glass of house white. A few nights after that, in bed, he'd asked whether she wanted children, and she'd said yes without hesitation. A few weeks after that, they'd begun discussing names. And a few months after that, they'd begun a process which had seemed to them both, back then, so simple, so natural, like reaching out and plucking an apple from a tree.

Eight a.m. in San Francisco, 4 p.m. here. Christina sat at her desk, her mobile in her hand. Rain again today, dreary, sleeting London rain. The grass was sodden, covered with fresh wet leaves, the paving slabs slick. The leaves she'd swept onto the bed had drifted, scattered; it had been windy overnight. She'd have to get out there again with the rake when the shower eased. That was the trouble with gardening: the tasks were infinite, never complete. But that was its comfort, too.

Was eight too early to call? She no longer had a grip on Ed's routine. He'd never been an early riser – would have slept until midday if she'd let him, which she had sometimes, especially after one of his comedy shows – but everything was different in California, wasn't it? People got up early, ate avocados, ran to the office in skin tight Lycra, showing off their muscles. Actually, no – of that she could be certain, there was no way Ed would be running to the office. He hated running, had made a whole skit out of it, said it was the human equivalent of dogs chasing sticks. Pointless activity, energy expended for no reason. And anyway, his office was too far from his apartment to permit a run: thirty minutes by car along a six-lane freeway. She'd looked it up on Google Maps. Checked out his apartment block on Street View, too: red-brick, small barred windows, a row of tall, sombre conifers. Modern. Nothing special. The company was paying – that was the only reason he was still contributing half the rent on the flat, at least until January, when their tenancy was up. Then, she knew, he was planning to move – Haight-Ashbury or Fillmore, one of the older neighbourhoods, with those fine Victorian houses, the Painted Ladies. That's what he dreamt of, she knew, though it would be further from the office. Ed loved old buildings, history, wooden floors, and he'd read *Tales of the City* too many times. There was so much she knew about him: the way he thought and felt and voted, the taste of his skin, the small wheezing sounds he made, sometimes, when he was sleeping. You couldn't just erase all that knowledge overnight, or even over three long months of separation.

She'd had another email from the clinic that morning. *Dear Mr and Mrs Macfarlane, I am following up, as arranged, on your conversation with Dr Ekwensi last July. Would you like to book an appointment to discuss ongoing treatment?* Christina hadn't replied. She hadn't told them yet that she and Ed had separated: why should she, it was none of their business. Except it was, of course, wasn't it? It was their business, when half his DNA, and hers, was sitting in a frozen embryo in a refrigerated unit somewhere in their building, a unit she had never seen, nor wished to see. She pictured scientists in white coats, goggles, cryogenic clouds of steam. *Frankenstein, Dr Strangelove.* The strangeness of it all, the freakishness. She didn't want to think of their baby in a place like that. Not that it was a baby yet, but it wasn't *not* one, either. The possibility of a baby. Their baby. Her baby. Her last chance.

Her finger hovered over his name. His name, his new American number. She pressed the small green phone icon, awaited the connection. Her heart thudded. Ridiculous: he'd been her husband, the man she'd known more intimately than any other. He still was.

'Christina?' Ed sounded breathless. She waited. 'I'm just out for a run. Is everything OK? Are you OK?'

A run? Really? For God's sake. 'Yes, I'm fine,' she said carefully. 'Fine.'

'Oh good. Good. It's early here, you know.'

She swallowed. 'It's not that early, Ed. I thought you'd be at work by now.'

'I'm heading to the office in a minute. There's a meeting. I'll be staying late.'

Silence. She watched the rain run down the windowpane; the shower had gathered pace, but there was bright light behind it, it would surely pass.

'I see. How are you doing, then?'

'I'm OK. Busy, but OK. Settling in. It's all strange, you know, new, but it's good. It is what it is.'

'Yes.'

'The money's coming through OK? For your rent, your bills?'

How long was it since they'd last spoken: a month, six weeks? *Your rent, your bills.* He hadn't described them as that before. The shift felt pointed, brutal. *What's yours is no longer mine.* As if it was her fault they'd signed a contract with a six-month break clause that neither of them could afford to bail out of. As if it was her fault that she still had some shreds of dignity. As if any of it was her fault. And yet it was, wasn't it? It was her body. Her failures. Her . . .

She drew a breath, exhaled slowly. *One. Two. Three.* She opened her mouth to speak, but in the fraction of a second before she did, he said, 'Look, Christina. It's good to hear from you. I'm glad you're doing OK. I'm glad we can be . . . civilised about all this. But if it's nothing important, I'd really like to finish my run.'

Christina closed her mouth again. The rain was coming down harder now, sluicing the glass. But behind it, that broadening patch of brighter, bluer sky.

'Sure,' she said. 'Finish your run. Let's talk another time.'

The shower ended as suddenly as she'd predicted, chased by a fierce, low-hanging sun. Nothing much to do with the rest of the day: nothing but staring at spreadsheets, or sending emails, or cleaning the bathroom, all while wondering why she was such a coward, why it was so difficult for her to say what needed to be said. Because it *was* difficult, that was why. Because she had no idea what Ed was going to say. Or perhaps she did. They'd had the argument so many times – her need to go ahead with this last transfer, his point-blank refusal to do so. It was the wall against which their marriage had crashed and breathed its last. Absurd, really – she both knew it and didn't know it, didn't want to know – to think that the argument might end differently now that they were no longer together. It was crazy, really, what she was asking of him, what she wanted to ask. And yet. And yet. And yet what else was there for her to do? Give up. Accept that she was forty-three, divorcing, childless, living alone in a half-furnished rented flat that she could no longer afford to pay for on her own. Accept that the probabilities Dr Ekwensi had mentioned at their first appointment, the success rate of around 25 per cent – though of course, the doctor had added, elegant in silk, her nails lacquered postbox red, nobody liked to talk in statistics – had not fallen in their favour. And the 25 per cent had only applied to their first attempt; who knew what her chance of success – of a 'live birth', to use the brutal term, one Dr Ekwensi never said aloud, but which was printed all over the

35

clinic's medical literature – might be now. That was where hope crept in, wasn't it? Hope, the most pitiless thing of all.

Nobody ever talked about the failures, did they? And yet there were so many like them, surely: legions of them, the silent majority, the 75, or 80, or 95 per cent. The people for whom medical intervention wasn't enough. The people left to write the epilogue to their own story.

Once, waiting at the clinic for one of their early appointments – an internal scan, probably; Ed hadn't been with her, she'd been sitting skim-reading a novel, drinking ice-cold water from a plastic cup – Christina had seen a couple emerge from the room she was shortly to enter. The woman had been crying: long, gulping sobs, her face red, contorted. The man had glowered at the room, put his arm around her, steered her away. Christina had returned her gaze to the page, read the same sentence over and over; told herself, as the doors closed behind them, that they were strangers, that she didn't know them, that none of it had anything to do with her.

She went out, up the steeply sloping road to the Triangle: three narrow local high streets, joined at sharp angles, choked by eddying traffic.

Crystal Palace had changed so much in the years since Christina and Ed had arrived: these isosceles streets now had coffee shops and homeware boutiques tucked in alongside the bookies and Chicken Cottages. There was a sourdough pizza restaurant, and a deli selling only pickles and local ale. The pub that, when they'd first moved in, had sent its drinkers spilling out onto the pavement on Saturday nights, trailing snatches of tuneless karaoke, had been painted a smart grey, issued with stripped-pine tables and mismatched chairs. The Sauvignon Blanc cost £7.50 a glass. She'd sat in there many times drinking it with Ed, remembering the original Saturday-night punters with their beer flushes and their cigarettes, wondering aloud where they all went drinking and singing now. She'd found an answer eventually: an old-style pub close to Sydenham station with a dartboard, a karaoke machine. She'd passed it one night recently, on her way back from an evening with Emma and Jen; heard the music, seen the same old drinkers and felt cheered, somehow: by human resilience, by the remarkable ability of people to adapt, to change.

The day Ed had moved out she'd spent with Jen: gone into town on the train, seen a film at the Curzon Soho (*Mary Shelley*, suitably gloomy, though Christina had hardly absorbed a single frame), then for cocktails at the Savoy – a first for both of them, though not the treat it should have been. She'd been restless all day, restless and sad; over their second round of martinis she'd begun to cry, and Jen had discreetly paid the bill and taken her home. Ed was gone by then, anyway: gone, as per their arrangement – their civilised arrangement, their unmediated division of assets – with approximately half their stuff loaded into a van. She had walked into the flat as if into the scene of a crime. They'd agreed their list – she knew what he was taking – but the place had still looked so bare, so ransacked. Two kitchen chairs left, of the four they'd bought online with the round oak table, in a matching set. The coffee table gone. The shelves in the living room half-empty, dust coating the spaces where Ed's books had been.

'You can't stay here tonight,' Jen had said, and Christina had agreed. They'd gone back to the station, got onto another train. A gorgeous summer evening – the sun still warm, the pavements radiating heat. The summer had seemed to be taunting her, with its promise of happiness, love, ease. Jen's mum had made a discreet exit, and they'd sat for a while on Jen's scrubby, weed-infested patio while Leila and Gabriel slept on.

'You'll recover from this, Christina,' Jen had said. 'I know it doesn't feel like it now, but you will.'

Christina had looked at her, and known she was talking about Ariel: the night he'd left, when Leila was three and Gabriel just six months. They'd done for her then, Christina and Emma, what Jen was doing for her now: closed in, formed an impenetrable line of defence. And so Christina had reached for Jen's hand, that summer evening in Jen's garden, and held it, and tried her hardest to believe her.

There was a place on the Triangle, tucked away down a back street behind the supermarket. An old warehouse, or a stable block; a collectors' market now, a place for lost things, records and crockery and tea dresses. Silverware and glasses. Discarded furniture and long-forgotten books.

They'd come here most weekends when they'd first moved to Crystal Palace: Christina for novels and clothes, Ed mainly for LPs (he loved the classic American comedy recordings, Lenny Bruce and Steve Martin and Tom Lehrer plonking out his cerebral piano tunes). Christina hadn't been in for ages. There was the painted sign now: *Collectors' market. Open today.* Surely not for much longer – it was almost five – but perhaps it was worth a look. Something to do, to help divide the day from the evening, when she had nothing else on but going home, maybe calling her mother or Dinah, texting Emma and Jen, permitting herself that one crisp, delicious G&T. Ed had

38

left her the television – she'd insisted on that – and now that he was gone she didn't have to sit through any more inscrutable seasons of *The Wire*. That was one thing to celebrate, at least.

Christina turned, followed the steeply descending street, past the handsome row of cottages, like something transplanted from a Kent village brick by brick, tile by tile. One was for sale now – freshly painted, white shutters, winter pansies in window boxes. She stood for a moment, admiring it, then veered left. There was no way she'd be able to afford to buy a place like that, not without a hefty chunk of savings, and the treatments had swallowed them all. Into the courtyard, the old, sagging, gap-toothed building rising before her. The door was open. She stepped in.

'Sorry. We're just about to close.' A woman, looking up from behind racks of clothing: a few years older than Christina, perhaps, with cropped greyish hair and a purple leather jacket. Plum lipstick, a small silver ring through her left nostril. South London accent laced with the melody of somewhere calmer, greener. Kent, perhaps, or Sussex.

'No problem. Sorry. I'll come back another day.'

The woman's face softened. 'Pop in for a bit if you like. Usually takes us all a bit of time to get packed up.'

'Thanks.' The woman nodded. Christina walked on, past crates of records, shelves of dusty china. A man in a green army-issue anorak sat behind a fanned tabletop arrangement of local photographs. The war memorial, covered in commemorative wreaths; the piano tuner's, long demolished to make way for the supermarket; the Crystal Palace, that great construction of glass and wrought iron that had once drawn people to this dusty suburb from miles around. There they were, in another of the photographs, rising from the tiled belly of the train station: men with hats and moustaches, slender-waisted women in long dresses, fringed shawls. It had burnt down in the 1930s; all that was left were the foundations, and a couple of weird stone sphinxes, and a collection of anatomically improbable dinosaurs, much loved by children and dog walkers and hungover Sunday couples. Ed and Christina had been among them once, walking off their Saturday nights, gloved hand in gloved hand, watching other people's children play.

She moved on, up the narrow stairs. Stuff everywhere, floor to ceiling. Glass bottles and toast racks and Toby jugs and one of those life-size plastic doll heads she'd had as a child, had used to practise make-up and hairstyles. Her mum had bought it for her – her seventh birthday, or perhaps her eighth. She didn't think Leila or Isla had ever had such a thing – who, these days, considered teaching a girl to put on make-up a priority? But times had been different then, of course, and that had been her mother all over, anyway: she'd always, Christina knew, longed for more of a girly girl. 'Why don't we book a spa day?' she'd said more than once in the months since Ed had left. 'Just the two of us. Get a massage. Lounge by the pool. Might do us both good.' Christina had been grateful for the offer – it went with the new hairstyle, she'd decided, and this feeling that Sue was changing, emerging from the long, dark tunnel of her grief. And yet she hadn't yet set a date for the visit; it seemed impossible, somehow, to sit with her mother on twin reclining chairs, pretending that all was well, that her life hadn't collapsed around her, leaving her with nothing to do but pick up the fractured shards.

Here was the bookstall. Not large – two tall shelving units either side of a grimy window, conjoined by a pair of tables. Books arranged alphabetically, pile upon pile. Fiction. Biographies.

Music. Children's. Music playing, a CD player under the table, but nobody around. David Bowie. 'Heroes'. They'd had that at their wedding. Lambeth Town Hall and a party upstairs at the Prince Regent in Herne Hill. Ed had done the playlist; she'd sat up half the night with Emma and Jen putting supermarket flowers into jam jars. Her dad teary as he accompanied her down the registry office aisle. Would there ever be anything, she thought with a low, clawing tug of sadness, that didn't remind her of Ed, or her father, or both of them at once?

She was beside the children's books now. The stack wasn't large, the books mainly old. Vintage, Christina supposed, though decrepit seemed more apt. She rummaged, thinking of Leila or Gabriel, of something to surprise them with the next time she collected them from school. From the middle of the pile she drew out a copy of *Grimms' Fairy Tales*. A turreted castle, a pinkish sky, a dark-haired woman in a smock, birds feeding from her outstretched palm. Strangely familiar, as were the dwarves gathered at her feet, with their caps and beards and bulbous reddened noses. Why? The answer emerged slowly: Aunt Dinah had had a copy, hadn't she, had kept it on the small white bookcase in the little room where Christina had slept as a child. There'd been a few other books and toys on there, too, for Christina to play with when she came: a threadbare teddy, missing an eye; a farmyard with a set of miniature animals. Cows, pigs, sheep; a low white picket fence, a painted duck pond. God, she hadn't thought about any of that in years.

'One for the kids, is it?' a man said.

Christina looked up from the book. He had emerged from nowhere, or perhaps only downstairs: tallish, broad-framed, wiry black-grey hair. She didn't recognise him from before, but it had been a long time since she'd last come in. 'No.'

He shrugged. 'Fair enough. Better kept for adults, anyway, I reckon. It's dark, that stuff.'

North-eastern, though not strong enough for Newcastle: Sunderland, perhaps, or Durham. She said nothing. The man settled himself on a stool. His fingers tapped absently against the table's edge; the CD had moved on. Roxy Music, she thought, though she couldn't recall the name of the song.

The book was £3.50. A lot, perhaps, for such a battered old copy, but Leila might be old enough to enjoy it, might not find those dark Teutonic tales (the man was right: they'd haunted her own dreams) too frightening. She reached into her handbag for her wallet, then realised she had no change. The man watched her, his fingers still drumming on the wood. 'Don't take plastic, I'm afraid,' he said as she slid out her card. 'Haven't got round to getting one of those little wireless things. I should, I suppose. Nobody carries money any more.'

'No.' The book was still in her hand. She put it back on the pile. 'I'll go up to the cashpoint, then,' she said, knowing that she'd do no such thing; that when she got back up to the high street the moment would have passed, and she'd walk on home.

'Don't bother,' the man said. 'Take it. Pay me next time.'

She looked at him. The man looked back, his gaze level, clear. His eyes were brown, darker than Ed's – a deeper patina, mahogany rather than pine. There were wrinkles at the corners, multiple and complex as a spider's web.

'Well. Thanks. Are you sure?'

He nodded. 'You don't look like the thieving sort.' He smiled. 'Are you?'

'No.' She retrieved the book, slipped it into her bag. 'Thank you. I'll come back tomorrow.'

'Whenever.' She walked on, towards the next stall, towards the exit. From behind, she heard him say, louder over the dying strains of Bryan Ferry, 'Mal, all right? If I'm not here, ask for Mal.'

Four

In her mind, the conversation went something like this.

She found a good time to call: midday Ed's time on a Saturday or Sunday, which meant 8 p.m. hers, but no matter, she'd have dinner first, and a small glass of something to steel her nerves. He'd be up and about, breakfasted, maybe out for a stroll – a farmers' market, perhaps, or browsing a bookshop. There was a famous bookshop in San Francisco, wasn't there, beloved of William Burroughs and the Beats? She was sure he'd mentioned this more than once as one of the prime reasons for why they should both move there, why this year-long transfer was such a fantastic opportunity for them both. 'You can work from anywhere, can't you, Chrissy?' (Ed had been the only person on earth allowed to call her this). 'It'll be good for us. A change of scene. A fresh start.'

But she hadn't wanted one: the only fresh start she'd wanted was this final chance to have a child. So no, she had not been persuaded, not by the City Lights bookstore (yes: that was the name of the place), nor the Painted Ladies, nor Alcatraz, nor the Golden Gate Bridge. Christina had been persuaded by none of it, and now Ed was there alone.

Perhaps it would be better if she caught Ed at home. She'd ask how he was, how work was going: his team was partnering with a Californian tech giant on DigiBeat, the smartphone app he'd designed to help children and young adults manage type 1 diabetes. (His nephew Henry had type 1: the fact that Ed had, early in their relationship, expressly set out to design an app to make Henry's life a little easier was, she'd reflected since, one of the primary reasons she'd fallen in love with him.) She'd ask what his Silicon Valley colleagues were like, how the British contingent was fitting in. She'd ask how Ed's parents were doing (she'd exchanged a couple of phone calls with his mother Liz since the break-up, but the conversations had been stilted, un-enlightening); whether he'd seen any good stand-up, was still thinking about trying an open mic. He'd ask a few reciprocal questions, and they'd talk reasonably, calmly, like the reason-able and calm human beings they surely still were, or could be.

And then she'd come out with it: present her argument, state her case.

Ed, there's something I'd like to talk to you about.

Yes. The embryo. The last one.

You see, I'd really like to . . .

Yes, I know we're no longer together, but . . . Well, the thing is that I . . .

Yes, I know it's your decision, too. Of course it is.

Yes, you did say you were done with it all, you made that very clear, but you see, it's not that simple for me, is it? Even if I met someone down the line – no, I'm not saying I've met anyone, I'm really not in that headspace yet, I can't imagine ever being in it, really. But what I'm saying is, even if I met someone, it would be too late for me, wouldn't it? I'm forty-three years old. I have to get real about things. This is it, for me. What? Yes, I know you're fifty. But men can be fathers when they're seventy, can't they? You've got lots of time. As much time as you could ever need. And we both know, the problem wasn't yours.

46

. . .

I want it so badly, Ed. You know how badly I want it. It's broken me, really, the whole thing. The cycles of hope and loss. Please do this for me. Please let me do this. It might not even work – let's face it, it probably won't – but at least then I'd know I'd given it everything I had. Every last thing.

What? No, I'd pay. Of course I'd pay. How? Let me work that out. I don't know. A credit card. And if it worked – well, then we could cross that bridge. There are plenty of parents in stranger situations than that.

Silence at his end of the line. The click and whirr of Ed's brilliant lightning brain. And then . . . *No. Are you mad? Have you completely lost the plot? This is a ridiculous, impossible thing to ask. Or, Chrissy, this is a lot. You must know this is a lot. I'll have to think about it. Give me some time to think.*

She could only in her most luxuriant fantasy allow herself to imagine him answering in the affirmative. And so, for now, she kept the conversation there, in her imagination, which at least permitted the bright, shining possibility of his saying yes.

Her mother had a new top: fine navy and white stripes, subtly displaying the smallness of her waist (she had always been tiny, birdlike, a fact that had, through Christina's teenage years and beyond, caused Christina a not inconsiderable degree of pain). She had paired the new top with jeans (had Christina ever seen her mother in jeans before?) that weren't skinny, exactly – the transformation wasn't quite as extreme as all that – but certainly straight-cut, ending in wide turn-ups. Beneath the turn-ups she wore nude popsocks (these, at least, were familiar), and navy flat-soled pumps.

'Per Una,' she said when Christina, confronted with the outfit at the door, told her how good she looked. 'You don't think it's a bit ... well, young for me? Not mutton dressed as lamb?'

'Not at all, Mum.' Christina leant in for a hug. 'No. You look like that amazing lady in the back of the *Guardian* magazine – you know, the model in her seventies. The one with the long grey hair. Looks fabulous in everything.'

'You know I don't read the *Guardian*, darling. And I'm not at all sure about long hair after fifty.' But she was smiling, ushering Christina through.

'In that case,' Christina said, 'I'd better start planning for a pixie haircut, hadn't I?'

Sue waved a hand, dismissive. 'Don't be silly. You've got years to go yet before the big five-oh.'

Not so many really, Christina thought, but she kept the observation to herself, settled on one of the pine chairs. The kitchen wasn't the one she'd grown up with – her mum and dad had had it done about a decade ago, ripped out the 1990s pine units and laminate worktops, gone for something tidily modern, white, soft-closing cupboards and too-bright ceiling lights – but its shape and contents, like those of the rest of the house, were as familiar to her as her own skin. There was the Colin Prior calendar, beside the ancient black coiled-cord phone; there was the slender, blue-glazed vase on the windowsill, an anniversary gift from Dad, now filled with long-stemmed irises; there was the mug tree by the toaster, with her father's favourite ... Actually, the mug tree wasn't there, nor Dad's old mug, the one Christina had made for him on a potter's wheel when she was twelve: a lumpen, hideous thing, but his favourite ever since the day she'd brought it home.

'Where's the mug tree, Mum? Where's Dad's mug?'

Sue was standing beside the stove, holding a ladle, looking at her phone. Looking up, she said lightly, breezily, 'Oh, it's in the cupboard, darling. But I got rid of the mug tree. I've been having a little clear-out. Just a few things. Helen lent me that book – you know, that Japanese lady. Marie Kondo.'

'Oh.' Christina looked down at the table. She was forty-three years old, she was damned if she was going to make a fuss about a missing mug tree, but still, it stung, that small loss, among all the others.

'I'm making risotto, darling. A recipe I found online. I thought we might eat in the dining room, have a glass of wine. Just a small one. I know you've got the car.'

The dining room? Wine? Her mother didn't usually drink more than a glass or two, certainly never in the day. And they hadn't used the dining room in ... Well, she couldn't think how long. Rarely since Dad had died, if at all.

'Sounds lovely, Mum. I'll set the table, shall I?'

The dining room had been renovated at the same time as the kitchen. In Christina's childhood it had been a dark, lugubrious place, with heavy brown velvet curtains and a mahogany G Plan table, chairs and sideboard her grandparents had bought as a wedding gift. Now the curtains were white linen, patterned with fine gold thread, and the walls a pale primrose yellow; the table had been replaced with a new one from John Lewis, pale oak, with six matching chairs. The G Plan sideboard was still there; Christina reached into the top drawer for the cutlery, the mats. There was a card on top of the sideboard, beside her dad's ancient turntable. Navy stripes on cream card, *thank you* stamped across it in embossed gold letters. Inside (she couldn't help herself), the message ran, *Dear Sue, Thank you so much for a wonderful evening. The supper was excellent, the company even better. With every hope of more such evenings, R x.*

R? Who was R? Christina arranged the mats, the cutlery, the coasters, the gold ironed napkins. Mum had had a friend at school, hadn't she, named Rachel? They hadn't been in touch for years, but she'd come to the funeral – perhaps they'd picked up where they'd left off. Or perhaps it was someone from the dance class: her mother was spending more and more time with them all, had gone for dinner with some of her fellow dancers on the South Bank after *The Red Shoes*. Yes, perhaps it was someone who'd been there; but then why would she – or he, but surely it was a she – be writing to thank Sue, and only Sue, for her company?

'Who's R, Mum?' she asked when they were settled with their plates of risotto and their diminutive glasses of Chardonnay.

Her mother patted her mouth with her napkin. 'R?'

'The card on the sideboard.'

Her mother laid down her fork. 'R. Yes. Well, it's funny you should ask, Christina, because there was something I wanted to talk to you about.'

The phrase rang in Christina's ears with eerie familiarity. *Something I want to talk to you about.* She had still not made the call. 'Oh. Well, of course. Go ahead.'

Sue picked up her napkin, folded it in two and replaced it on her lap. Then she said, 'R is Ray. He's a . . . friend of mine. A new friend.'

'From your dance class?'

Sue nodded. She was looking down at her plate. When she lifted her face she was smiling, her features illuminated, her expression suddenly girlish, almost shy. 'We met there. We've been spending some time together outside the class, too. He's . . . Well, he's a widower himself. He understands how it is. He used to be a teacher too, actually. History. A private school: you know St Mungo's, out in Epsom? We've had a few little clashes about that, but we ... get on, I suppose. Enjoy each other's company.'

Christina sipped her wine. So her mother was moving on, as everybody had to, eventually. And why shouldn't she? Who wanted to spend the rest of their life alone? 'This is great news, Mum. Why didn't you tell me before?'

'Well, because I didn't . . . I wasn't sure whether . . .' She was flailing; Christina put down her glass. 'Mum. I'm forty-three, not fourteen. I don't want you to live in some sort of state of purdah forever. If you've met someone – a friend, or whatever he is, whatever he might be – then really, that's wonderful.'

Her mother nodded again. Her eyes, fixed on Christina's, were damp, her liner and shadow seeping into the fine creases on her upper lids. 'I'm so glad you think so. I wasn't sure whether I . . . Well, I didn't want to go on about it, about being happy like this, about having met someone, when you're ... Well. Still missing your dad. And when you've been through so much.'

The words settled heavily on the table between them. Grief – for the failed IVF, the lost pregnancies, the end of her marriage; and for her father, too – had made her solipsistic, Christina knew. Self-centred and sad. It did that: it squeezed out everything, everyone, until there was room only for yourself, and your own problems, your own pain and anger and resentment. Christina hated this. It was one of the things about the whole sorry business she hated above all. 'Look at you, Mum,' she said. 'I haven't seen you this happy in years. You deserve it. You really do.'

'Chris,' Jen said, 'when you watched Ed do stand-up, did it ever make you cringe?'

They were sitting in their usual Tuesday-evening positions on Jen's sofa, drinking tea rather than wine: Jen was knackered, had an early start the next day, and Christina had the car. She considered the question. Those rooms above pubs, the dado rails and flocked wallpaper; the foil curtains, the glitter ball, the guy who'd almost always been on before, making angry, razor-line jokes about consent. Ed hadn't been like that – he was a good comic, he was actually funny. He wore his nerd T-shirt (it had turned out that he had a whole drawer of them, that they were basically his stage costume), he made a load of jokes at his own expense, and then somehow turned his wit on science, physics, the extraordinary laws of the universe. Others did it better, perhaps, and certainly to larger crowds, but Ed had something, it was true. And yet, honestly, Christina had cringed inwardly a little every time she'd sat there and watched him perform. Not because he was bad, but because she couldn't bear to watch the faces of the other punters trying to work out whether he was any good, whether to award him the approbation of their laughter. After a couple of years, she'd stopped going to all but the most important gigs; but by then there'd been fewer important gigs to go to anyway, and recently they'd all but petered out. 'Nobody,' Ed had told her, 'wants to go and sit in a pub and watch a sad guy stand there and cry about the fact that he and his wife just lost another baby.' Which was not, in all honesty, an argument with which Christina could disagree.

'Yes. It did, a bit. I couldn't bear waiting to see what people made of him, whether he would sink or swim. Why do you ask?'

Jen shrugged. She was curled into the nook of the sagging sofa, her hair loose around her shoulders, her feet bare beneath her leggings. Her toenails still bore the ragged traces of scarlet polish. 'Dan doesn't want to come to the show. He says he wouldn't enjoy it, that he'd just be too stressed, watching to see what other people thought. Worrying for me, you know.'

'Well.' Christina weighed the most diplomatic response. Dan was a new thing: she'd only met him once, at Jen's birthday drinks in Brixton Village. He'd seemed all right – bit straight, a civil servant, did something in the Cabinet Office. Not Jen's usual type. He hadn't met Leila and Gabriel yet. Christina wasn't sure he ever would. 'Does he have any interest in contemporary dance?'

'Beyond me, probably not.' Jen reached for her mug, took a sip. The mug was pink, with the words *World's Best Mum* picked out in glittery pink letters. Leila's choice for Mother's Day; Christina had taken the kids shopping, helped them choose gifts for their mum. Gabriel had selected a T-shirt that said *My Mum's a Rock Star*. It was one of Jen's favourites: she still wore it often, to rehearsals; even, she'd admitted, on the odd date, to get the whole 'I'm a single mum' thing firmly out of the way.

'It's weird that he won't come, isn't it? He should be there.'

'Yes,' Christina said. 'I think he should.'

They sat for a moment in silence, pondering the implications. Darcey, Jen's ancient arthritic cat, sloped into the room, stared up at them through snake-like amber eyes, and then leapt inelegantly onto Christina's lap. She favoured Christina; she was, Jen asserted, a grumpy old cow with the people she actually lived with. Especially the kids. Christina buried her hand in the cat's fur, then stroked her head, pushing down on her ears in the way she loved. Darcey's eyes narrowed to slits. A great shuddering purr rose up from her belly. 'Remember that Eddie Izzard gag?' Christina said. 'About cats drilling?'

Jen smiled, leant back against the sofa. She looked tired. She always looked tired: beautiful but tired. No wonder, with a full-on career and two kids. Too stubborn and too hard up to accept anything other than piecemeal help. Emma had suggested, more than once, that Sarah collect Leila and Gabriel from school as well as Alfie – had offered to add a little extra to Sarah's pay from her own pocket – but Jen had refused. 'You have to understand, Em,' she'd said, 'that I have to handle things my own way.' It had been tricky between them for a while after that; Christina had been scrupulous not to take sides, though she'd known that she'd back Jen if she had to: they all knew it, that was simply how things were.

'How's your mum doing, Chris?' Jen said now.

'Good, actually. She's met someone.'

Jen sprang forward, put her mug down on the table. 'What? Like, a man?'

'Yep. His name's Ray. They met at her dance class. It's early days, I think, but she looks totally different. Happy.'

'Wow.' Jen nodded. 'Good for her. That's great, isn't it?' Then, studying Christina's face, 'Is it?'

'Yes. It's great. Of course I don't want her to be alone. It destroyed her, everything with Dad, looking after him, losing him so slowly. And I know she worries about me. I'm hardly a daughter she can be proud of. Divorcing. No grandchildren.'

Gently, Jen said, 'She is proud of you. I know she is. Don't be so hard on yourself, C. None of it is your fault.'

'I know.' Christina nodded, met her friend's kind brown-eyed gaze. Jen squeezed her wrist. After a second or two she said, 'By the way, what were you thinking giving Leila the Brothers Grimm? She's traumatised. She's woken up twice the last two nights with nightmares about being locked inside a castle and forced to spin straw into gold.'

'Christ. I'm sorry. I should have thought . . .' Stupid. The kind of mistake a mother would never make. But Jen was smiling. 'Nah, don't be silly. She could do with mixing a bit of grit into

54

that imagination of hers. Far too many rainbows and unicorns in there, as far as I'm concerned. I mean, she'll be coming to the show, won't she, and the story of Judith and Holofernes is hardly *Paddington 2*, is it?'

Christina smiled back. 'No. Well, that's all good then.'

Jen gave her wrist another squeeze, let go. 'Yes, C. It's all good.'

Christina usually did her food shopping on weekday afternoons: the supermarket was quieter, less likely to be thronged by smug families. (Of course she knew they weren't actually smug – at least, not most of them – they just seemed that way to her.)

On Friday, she loaded her bags into the car (lazy to drive up, perhaps, but she couldn't carry everything now she lived alone: laundry liquid weighed the same, whether you were one half of a couple or not), and then went for another walk around the Triangle. Passing the sign for the collectors' market, she remembered that she'd never actually paid that guy – what was his name: Mal? – for Leila's book. Once more she turned, passed the lovely little cottage with its *For Sale* sign. She had cash on her today, luckily: she'd taken some out on Tuesday, on her way to collect Leila and Gabriel, to buy them hot chocolates at the playground café.

The market was busier today. She found the bookstall, waited for a young couple ahead of her to move on, make space in the narrow gap between the tables. Early twenties; perhaps they'd taken the day off work. They looked happy, easy with each other. She was blonde, not skinny, kind of a Marilyn; he was a boyish reed of a thing, all elbows and knees. He picked up a book – the title, Christina saw as she came closer, was *The Unbearable Lightness of Being*.

No Mal. She walked on. The next stall was all glass – shelf upon shelf of it, ceiling to floor. Carafes and tumblers and champagne coupes. There was a man next to the shelves – large, red-cheeked, balanced improbably on a high, narrow-seated stool.

'Mal around?' Christina said.

The man looked up at her through small blue watery eyes. 'Out with Ziggy,' he said. Then, into the puzzled silence, 'The dog.'

'Oh. Right.' He went back to the magazine in his lap: porn, she wondered wildly for a moment, but no, it was more of a catalogue. Hard to tell what for from upside down, but the thing in the photograph looked distinctly like a porcelain doll.

'I've got some money for him,' Christina said. 'I owe him for a book.'

She opened her palm, displaying the coins, and the doll man shrugged. 'Leave it on his stall, if you want. By the cashbox. I'll keep an eye.'

'Thanks.'

Back at the bookstall, she drew her wallet from her purse. The young couple had disappeared; there was a white-haired man by the music pile reading a biography of Chopin. She peered down into the wallet, seeking the dirty-bronze flash of pound coins.

'Here she is, then.' Mal, in a battered leather jacket, a striped scarf. A dog on a lead beside him: medium-sized, black and white, with a long-nosed, intelligent face. A collie, perhaps; she was no expert on dogs. Her dad had loved them; he'd grown up with Yorkshire terriers, would have loved one, but Mum had put her foot down: too messy, she'd always said, too

56

much work. Ed's parents had two golden retrievers, Lassie and Ovid: sweet, lumbering, affectionate creatures, but prone to leaving gifts of slobber and yellow hair across furniture and clothes.

'Not a thief, after all,' Mal said. 'I was starting to wonder.'

'Sorry. I did mean to come back sooner.' She handed over the coins.

'Cheers.' He was smiling. 'You're all right. I'm only messing.'

The dog was looking up at her: deep-brown eyes, pink tongue half lolling from his mouth. His expression was disconcertingly alert. He seemed to be telling her something. Christina bent to his level, ran her palm across his soft fur. 'This must be Ziggy.'

From this angle Mal was foreshortened, his legs tree trunks, his face a looming stubbled moon. 'How do you . . .?'

She unfolded herself, drew herself up to her full height. 'The guy at the next stall. I asked him where you were.'

'Oh.' Mal glanced across at doll man, who had returned his attention to his catalogue. 'Sinclair. Right. Yes. This is Ziggy. He likes a walk after lunch.'

'He's lovely. Looks very intelligent.'

'Yep. Raised him from a puppy. Got him off a book dealer mate of mine. Probably whelped in the back of a van. Anyway, he's clever all right. Sometimes I look at him and get the feeling he's a two-year-old in a dog costume.'

Ziggy was sitting now, staring up at Mal, seemingly fully aware he was being discussed. 'Down, Zig,' Mal said. 'Under the table. Good dog.' The dog slunk away, lowered himself to the floor, rested his head on his paws.

The man with the white hair and the Chopin book had been watching all this; now he stepped forward, offered Mal a £5 note. 'Three pounds, it says in here. Bit much, isn't it? They've got books in the charity shop for fifty pence . . .'

'Still,' Mal said mildly, 'they probably don't have this one.' He took the money, reached for his cashbox, drew a key from his pocket. A Scrabble tile keyring; M, three points. 'Thank you. Just a second.'

Christina took her cue. 'Cheers, then.'

Mal looked up at her. So, from under the table, did the dog. 'Right. Cheers. Come back sometime, if you like. I'll look out something cheery for you. Lots of lost children and goblins.'

Lost children. Yes. 'Great. Thanks. Bye, then.'

Five

'She's been like this for weeks,' Emma said.

'Like what?'

'Sullen, withdrawn, always on her phone.'

Christina scanned the crowd for Isla, found her perched on the metal bench seat that ran around the perimeter of the room, eyes glued to her iPhone screen. They were in the foyer at Sadler's Wells, awaiting Jen's opening night. Leila and Gabriel had seen the dress rehearsal earlier; Jen had worried that it would be too frightening for them, but apparently they'd got bored halfway, wandered off to the foyer to watch cartoons on the lighting technician's phone. They were at home now, being tucked up in bed by Jen's next-door neighbour. Jen's parents were here, waiting at the bar, with Pete and his brother David; she knew others here, faces Christina recognised from other Arrow Dance performances. Critics, too. Quite a crowd; there'd be a party afterwards, in the upstairs bar. Jen was freaking out backstage, as she always did. *TELL ME IT'S GOING TO BE OK*, she'd demanded of Christina by text five minutes previously. Christina had immediately written back, *It's going to be OK. More than OK. You know it will, you silly thing.*

'Looks like a typical teenager to me.'

Emma looked at her, her lips narrowing. She seemed about to

say something, and then to think better of it. Before she could stop herself, Christina said, 'You were about to tell me that I don't understand. Not being a mother myself, and all.'

'No I wasn't.' Emma fiddled with her necklace, a thick gold cord that snaked around her neck and plunged down her bare décolletage. Her dress was incredible, a floor-length orange waterfall. Only Emma could get away with such a colour, such a gown. Christina had bought a new dress from one of the shops in the Triangle for the occasion – a tiered maxi, navy with white flowers. With her cropped leather jacket, her black ankle boots, she'd felt good, almost like her old self; but beside Emma she knew she faded into insignificance. The frumpy friend, the foil to the heroine. Every story had one.

'You know I'd never say that, Chris. Or think it, even.'

Christina nodded. 'I know. I'm sorry. I'm hungry, and I need a drink.'

Emma smiled vaguely, shifted her gaze to the bar, the tension between them not quite dissipated, not quite addressed, but dispensed with for now, for Jen's sake, for the sake of the evening. 'Me too. They're taking an age, aren't they?'

Later, as they settled into their seats in the upper circle – Christina was between Emma and David – the moment in the bar returned to her, another hairline fracture in the surface of her relationship with Emma. There was no pretending these cracks didn't exist – they'd been there for a while now, she couldn't quite say when she'd begun to notice them. They'd been friends, the three of them, since freshers' week, had bonded over too many vodka jelly shots in the union bar. Jen had known Emma first – they lived in the same halls in the Northern Quarter; Christina was in another building, closer to campus – and Christina had been a little wary of her initially, a little unsure. Emma had seemed so elegant, so self-assured; she'd been privately educated, had attended a boarding school somewhere in the Scottish Highlands, a place with turrets, and lacrosse, and a beagling club.

'*Beagling?*' Jen and Christina had chorused all those years ago when she'd informed them of this. 'What the bloody hell is that?'

Hunting hares with dogs, Emma had replied; and yes, she'd found that just as weird and disgusting as they did. In sixth form, she'd staged a protest – sabotaged the hunt with a few other troublemaking misfits – and been suspended for the remainder of the term. Her father – an eminent geneticist, emigrated from Nairobi to Edinburgh in the mid-1960s – had suggested moving her to the local college, but her mother had held firm. Every female Dalrymple-Scott had been educated at the school for at least six generations. 'But not one of them,' Emma had said, 'looked like me, did she? I bloody hated the place. I mean, how many black girls do you think they'd had before me? Two, that's how many. Two, in three hundred years.'

Christina had relaxed around Emma after that; they'd become a trio, inseparable, had moved to the Mansion in Levenshulme the following year. Stayed close through the remainder of university, through their scattered early-twenties years. But then Emma had gone into the City, met Pete, started earning a salary that had begun to carry her far from Christina and Jen's scratchy, hand-to-mouth existence.

It wasn't money, though, that had caused this new shift in their relationship; Christina was sure of it. The change had been subtle, but she thought it had begun when Isla was born. Some women, she had decided over the many years of being one of the only childless women in the room – if not the only one – changed entirely when they became mothers, and some re-tained at least the architecture of their former selves. Jen was in the latter camp; Emma, she feared, was in the former. It seemed to Christina now – wrongly, perhaps; she'd never actually dared to voice these thoughts aloud to Emma, or even to Jen – that when Emma looked at her, she didn't see a complete person but a fraction of one. A childless woman. A woman who could never, until she had carried a child to term, held that child in her arms, fed it and burped it and rocked it to sleep, soothed its nightmares and brushed its teeth and bought it a first pair of shoes, understand what it was to handle the real, flesh-and-blood stuff of living.

'Penny for them?'

David, smoothing a hand over his programme in the seat beside her. He was wearing a blue paisley-patterned shirt, holding a plastic tumbler of red wine. Only David could use a phrase that had surely last been uttered in 1942.

'Just a few things on my mind,' she said. 'How are you, anyway?'

He shrugged. 'Not too bad. Can't complain.'

What was his second wife's name? The first one, Sylvie, had been French, the second English – Louisa, was it? Yes, Louisa De Montfort. Christina had met her twice, as she recalled – she and David had only been married for a year. A haughty, angular woman with a long, strong-chinned face – 'a face like a horse', Emma had said, and it was true, there had been something equine about her, some restless racehorse grace. Hedge funds, she'd worked in, and that had amused Christina: she had pictured Louisa clearing hedges, those clipped box jumps, high-kicking her fine equine ankles. And it was true: David hadn't been as bad before his second divorce. Still a bit awkward, but not so . . . Well. So miserable. So lost. But then Christina, of all people, should know how that felt.

The performance transported her, as dance always did. Jen had talked her through the concept, played her the music, shown her the paintings she had taken as inspiration, but it wasn't the same as seeing the show first-hand.

Ana – birdlike, Spanish Ana, Ed's long-ago ex – was Judith, the Jewish woman who seduced the enemy Syrian general Holofernes, then beheaded him while he slept. Louis, who was French-Algerian and built like an Olympic weightlifter (which, if you thought about it, was more or less what he was), was Holofernes. The stage was entirely dark, but for stark uplighting, casting the dancers in blocks of light and shade; Jen had taken the Caravaggio painting as inspiration, and another by Artemisia Gentileschi, a painter Christina had never, to her shame, heard of. Jen had shown her both paintings on her phone. In Gentileschi's version, two women were at the scene of the murder: Judith, grasping the general by the hair while she plunged a sword into his neck; and another unknown woman holding him down. Jen wasn't, she'd explained, interested in gore, or even violence, but in the power dynamics that underpinned the story: the powerful man brought down by a woman too easy to subjugate, too easy to dismiss.

Christina understood why Jen had hesitated about letting the children see the show; all this bloody history, however, had been spared them, and it floated from Christina's mind now, too, as she watched the dancers. There was no sword, no blood: the violence was implicit, the dynamic between Ana and Louis more sensual than murderous. Jen had slept with Louis a couple of times, not long after he'd joined the company – an overlap she generally avoided, due to the potential for uncomfortable fall out. But there had been none of that. The dancers were all very relaxed, very bohemian; some had partners, some didn't, and those who didn't (and, Jen suspected, some of those who did) fell in and out of each other's beds like characters in a Regency romp. 'Is it something about being so physical?' Christina had asked her once. 'Being so inside the body?' And Jen had laughed, waved her cigarette and said, 'More about being half-naked most of the time, I reckon.'

Louis was half-naked now: his chest was bare, his powerful legs clad in what looked like leather breeches, though Jen had confirmed that they were not leather but a fabric that resembled it from a distance, as leather had been too expensive. Ana wore a full-body leotard, with a diaphanous gown over the top that followed the contours of her body as she moved. The chemistry between them was tangible; Christina watched, unable to take her eyes from them, from the sinuous interwoven movements of their limbs. A memory returned to her, vague, formless, a feeling more than a moment. The memory of how it had felt, not so very long ago, to meld her body to another's; not to comfort, or console, or in the vain hope that the act might result in the child they had both so longed for, but in response to the plain, unadulterated demands of desire.

The opening-night party burbled on, with chatter and wine and small unidentifiable canapés, laid out on the bar and quickly, too quickly, devoured. Christina was starving by now. She knew she should have eaten something before she came, but it had taken her an hour and a quarter to get here from south London, and she'd actually been busy all day: one of her clients, a small but prestigious opera festival in Suffolk, was being audited. She hung back, disappointed, having missed her chance: the platters had already been cleared as by an advancing swarm.

'Too late,' Ana said; she'd appeared at Christina's elbow, her face scrubbed, bare of make-up, her leotard and gown exchanged for a plain black sack of a dress that would have looked nun-like on anyone else, but on Ana looked positively sexy. 'I have a banana in my bag if you like.'

She pointed at the voluminous bag hanging from her shoulder. Christina smiled, shook her head. 'It's OK, I'll get something later. Thanks, though. You were amazing.' She leant forward, kissed Ana on each cheek. (See? Everybody was at it now.) 'I couldn't take my eyes off you both.'

Ana's gaze glittered. 'Couldn't take your eyes off Louis, more like.'

Christina felt the colour rise in her cheeks. 'Oh no, it really wasn't . . . I didn't mean it like . . .'

Ana laughed, tapped Christina on the shoulder. 'Only joking. We all know that he is – how you say – sex on a stick. But I'm married now, you know? Did Jen say?'

She lifted her left hand to Christina's face, displaying an engagement ring with an enormous sapphire flanked by two diamonds; on her right there was a slim wedding band. 'Wow. Congratulations, Ana. Jen didn't say, no. Really, that's wonderful.'

'Thanks.' Ana beamed; it must be a new thing, Christina thought. Nobody still looked like that, surely, after two years of marriage, three, four. Or perhaps some people did. 'His name is Justin. He is a doctor, you know. A surgeon. Nothing to do with dance. Look, he is over there, talking to Pepe.'

Christina followed Ana's gaze to a far corner of the room, beside the window, where a medium-height, mild-looking man with thinning blond hair was deep in an animated discussion with Pepe, another of the Arrow dancers. 'Also,' Ana leant forward, lowering her voice, 'this is secret, I am not supposed to be telling people yet, but I am pregnant. Nine weeks. I say to Justin, what does it matter, telling people a few weeks before three months? But he is insisting. He is very proper, my Justin. Very English.'

And yet you're telling me now, Christina thought, but she smiled, of course she did, she pegged the smile to her face and let it float in the breeze for all to see. 'Ana, that's wonderful. Really. Congratulations. I am so happy for you.'

'Thank you.' Ana's gaze intensified, and then she said, 'I have always liked you, Christina. Always, I have. I was very happy when you got together with Ed. It seemed . . . I don't know, just right.'

The smile was faltering, slipping from its tethers. 'Well. I guess it wasn't.'

'No.' Ana reached for her shoulder again, gripped it, let it go. 'I am very sorry for this, Christina. I am.'

Christina was saved from providing an answer to this by Jen, who had been circling the room all evening, radiant in her green jumpsuit, her pink lipstick, her new silver snakeskin heels. 'Ana, I need you. Come and meet this man over here. *Telegraph* critic. He wants to tell you how good you were.' To Christina she mouthed, 'Sorry, Chris. Can you hang on a bit longer? We'll go for something to eat in a bit.'

They would, Christina knew, but not for hours yet: there were too many hands to press, too much post-show energy to work off. They hardly ever seemed to get hungry, anyway, the dancers: it was true what people said, they did mostly seem to live on caffeine and cigarettes. (Not Jen, though; no, Jen could eat for England.) Christina wandered back to the bar, rather at a loss; Emma and Pete had left a while ago – Isla had school the next day – and she assumed David had gone with them. Most of the other faces she'd recognised appeared to have melted away; she busied herself at the bar, ordering another glass of wine (the free stuff had run out), promising herself it would be her last.

'Can I get you that?'

She turned: David. The wine had stained his lips purple; Christina fought the urge to reach over, dab his mouth clean with her sleeve. 'I thought you'd gone back south with the gang.'

He shook his head. Like Pete, he was a tall man – both were more than six foot – but David carried himself like a shorter one: round-shouldered, slumped. Emma had said he'd been suffering from depression. Poor man. 'Thought I'd stick around for a bit. It's early yet, isn't it?'

Christina looked at her watch: just after ten. Yes, still early, though she was often thinking about going to bed herself around now, permitting herself just one more episode, one more chapter of her book. The barman brought her drink, and David ordered another glass for himself; when the barman returned, she let David pay. Why not? He worked in shipping – she was vague on the exact details – but he earned more than she did, of that she had no doubt.

They moved away from the bar, drifted over to the window, close to where Ana's husband Justin was still talking to Pepe. 'The thing about being married,' she heard him say, 'is that you don't know how good it is until you're in there yourself, you know?' Beyond the window, the night-time north London street glittered in the darkness.

'You're looking well,' she said to David, flailing to open a conversation he clearly had no intention of initiating. She watched him straighten, drawing himself up to his full height. He looked different when he smiled: younger, almost boyish. She remembered now – she hadn't thought of this in years – that there

67

had been a time, ages ago, when he'd made something of a play for her. There'd been a party, Pete's thirtieth perhaps, at which they'd got chatting; afterwards, he'd asked Emma for Christina's email. They'd gone for lunch near his office in Farringdon, one of those warren-like City pubs. Christina had thought it kindest to tell him, as he'd walked her back to her own office (sweet), that lunch had been lovely, but she wasn't interested in anything further. David had coloured, but parried, insisted that he'd only been intending to get to know her as a friend. For a while, she remembered now, she'd struggled to forgive him for that small sting. But that had been so long ago, almost fifteen years; they were different people now, he'd been married twice since then. Two divorces. Christ. And she hadn't yet managed to get one off the ground.

'Do you really think so?' he said. 'This shirt's new. I wasn't sure about it, but the woman said – I use one of those personal shoppers now, you know, they make it so much quicker, so much easier – she said it was a good colour on me. Louisa used to help me with things like that. My wife, you know. My ex-wife. I think you met.'

'We did.'

He looked at her, and there was something so naked in his stare, so raw and pure and vulnerable, that she had to look away. She couldn't do it, she realised, she just couldn't do it: stand here at a party with David like the two wounded people they were, comparing tales of how badly they'd been hurt, exchanging their inventories of loss.

'I'm sorry,' she said. 'I just remembered that there's somewhere I really need to be.' An improbable excuse, but she didn't care; she left her wine unfinished on the ledge beside him and edged back into the party, looking for Jen, looking for the lift, looking for the way home.

Dinah's head bobbed on the waves, one of three strung close together like tethered buoys; or a trio of seals, slick in their neat swimming caps. Dinah was the only one not wearing a wetsuit; even her fellow swimmers, Petrina and Ruth, had raised eyebrows at this. 'It'll be freezing, Di,' Ruth had said – a large woman in her late sixties with a shock of dyed-red hair. 'Are you sure you don't want to borrow one? I've got a spare in the car.' But Dinah had shaken her head, stood regal and goose-pimpled in her plain black one-piece. 'I'll be fine. We won't be too long anyway, will we? Just a quick plunge.'

Christina sat on the beach and watched them, warm in her padded coat, her scarf. It was a fine, bright winter Sunday, low shafts of sun shattering on the water. Across the shingle, a pair of toddlers of about two, by Christina's estimation, were busily loading stones into buckets, two sets of parents keeping close watch from a few feet away, gulping down cups of take-away coffee. She sent a smile in their general direction. There had been a time, during the years of treatment, when it had been difficult for Christina to be out in the world, among the families, the children, the newborns, plump-cheeked in their pram suits, their knitted hats. Had there ever been so many children, she'd asked Ed: she'd never noticed them before, really, and now they were everywhere, swarming across climbing frames, screaming in cafés, staring goggle-eyed at the stone dinosaurs in the park. There was a term, wasn't there, for the phenomenon by which you learnt a new word or concept, and suddenly you saw it everywhere, in every paragraph you read?

'Yes,' Ed had confirmed. 'The Baader-Meinhof phenomenon,

after the German leftist group. Some researcher noted that just after he'd learnt the name of the group, he saw it two or three times in one day.'

She'd stared at him. 'How do you *know* things like that?'

He'd shrugged. 'Told you I was a professional nerd.'

Well, this had been something similar, she'd decided: they'd started trying, and failing, to have a child, and suddenly she'd seen children everywhere, all the time. It had been different with her friends' children, of course – with Isla and Alfie, Leila and Gabriel, and the others – she knew and loved them, loved their parents, too (well, apart from Jen's errant Ariel, the Israeli choreographer, handsome as the very devil, who'd skipped back to Tel Aviv and never returned). Still difficult sometimes, yes – standing there at Alfie's christening, for instance, as pretty much the only woman in the church not holding her own infant in her arms – but different.

Take the clinic: the two hospital departments were in the same building, antenatal and fertility, those who had and those who did not have. Antenatal was on the first floor, fertility on the third. She had travelled up to her appointments (more often than not, alone: Ed had come when he could, but his work was less understanding, and his role in the whole affair limited, after all) in the company of women at various stages of pregnancy, clutching their maternity notes to their swollen bellies.

'It's needlessly cruel, isn't it?' she'd said to Ed. 'I mean, surely they could have installed two different lifts.'

He'd looked at her for a long moment. 'Chrissy,' he'd said, 'I think the whole world seems cruel to you, to us both, right now.'

Dinah and the other swimmers were still in the water; they hadn't gone far, were keeping close to the shore, within their depth, bobbing and turning to keep warm. (They knew the rules, the advice; they were not novices.) One of the toddlers, a cherubic boy in a bobble hat and earmuffs, blond curls creeping down over his collar, reached into his bucket for a handful of stones, sent them skittering across the beach towards her. He stared at her as he did so: *Look*, he seemed to be saying, *I exist, I am powerful, I can make these stones move if I want to*. She smiled at him; his mother, drawn from the adult huddle, looked across with an apologetic grimace. 'So sorry. He's at that throwing stage. He didn't hit you, did he?'

'No,' Christina said. 'No, I'm fine. He's fine.'

The mother offered her a quick smile, then took the boy by the hand, drew him back towards his friend, or his sibling (it was hard to tell the gender of the other child in its voluminous yellow padded suit). 'Come on, Wilfie. It's getting chilly, isn't it? We're going to head back to the car.'

Christina watched them go. The clinic had called the day before: the unfriendly receptionist, the one Christina liked the least. She'd recognised her voice, though it had been a while since they'd last spoken. There'd been a call she couldn't forgive her for – an early bleed, five weeks, months before she would actually miscarry, but still she'd been afraid, of course she had, bleeding that early was never a good sign. This woman had answered the phone, told Christina that nobody was available, that she could come in if she wanted, but the list was full, she'd just have to wait. Christina, desperate, had said, 'But I think I might be losing my baby.' And the woman, brutally, unforgivably, had said, 'That happens to a lot of women. Keep an eye on the bleeding, call back if it gets heavier. I can't just move you to the top of the queue.'

So there this awful woman had been on the phone yesterday, asking to speak to Mrs Macfarlane. Dislike had risen in Christina, an unreasonable, avenging anger. 'It's a bad time right now,' she'd snapped. 'A very bad time.' And then she'd hung up. Childish, of course, childish and ostrich-like; she couldn't bury her head in the sand forever. In a few months she would be forty-four: her own potential for success was diminishing by the hour, the minute, dropping even lower from what was surely the lowest possible starting point, given her age, her miscarriages, the rounds that hadn't resulted in a pregnancy at all. 'We need to remember,' Dr Ekwensi had said at their last appointment, 'that two of your treatments *have* resulted in a pregnancy, and that we have another embryo in storage. That is an important mark in your favour. I think, if you both take some time, allow yourselves to grieve this loss – which is enormous, I know, I can hardly imagine how you must be feeling – then, well, you can consider trying again.'

She was lovely, Dr Ekwensi, she'd made up for that awful receptionist. Very beautiful, with her flawless skin, designer dresses, perfect nails. An advertisement, almost, Christina had thought illogically at their first appointment, for the perfect human, the ideal test-tube baby: illogical, of course, because the babies were not made to order, eugenics was not practised here. Perhaps all doctors in private practice looked like her; Christina and Ed had no idea, this was the first time they'd paid for anything medical in their lives. 'She looks like that,' Ed had said, 'because of random genetic luck, and because she earns a fortune from the savings of people like us.' But still, it was easier to like beautiful people, wasn't it, everybody knew it: it was easier to trust them, easier to offer them your faith in your cupped hands.

Her aunt was coming out of the water now, her body rising, dripping, from the waves. Her skin was red, her grin infectious. 'Christina,' Dinah called, her voice travelling up the shingle towards her, 'it's wonderful out here. Next time you must come in with us.'

'Perhaps,' Christina called back, and with the affirmation came a sudden rolling wave of optimism: perhaps she would swim next time, perhaps she would. Perhaps Ed would agree to this final round. Perhaps, this time, she would carry to term. Perhaps, in roughly ten or eleven months – next summer, for goodness' sake! – she could be down on this beach with her own newborn, her own tiny perfect boy or girl. Perhaps. Perhaps. Why not? Good things happened every day: people, good and bad, got what they wanted, what they'd been longing for. Sometimes, surely, the odds were just stacked in your favour.

That evening, Christina sat at her laptop. She was going to write to Ed; she didn't, she'd realised on the drive home, have the courage to make the call, didn't think she could bear to hear a flat refusal over the phone.

She opened her email. She hadn't looked since Friday: she preferred to turn email off on her phone at weekends, so as not to be bothered by clients panicking out of hours. There, at the top of her inbox, sent on Friday evening (Friday morning his time) was his name. *ed.macfarlane@bigbrightideas.co.uk*. Subject line: *Meeting up*.

She opened the message, stared at it for a few seconds, the words swimming before her eyes. Ed was coming to England in a few weeks. His dad's eightieth: the weekend in the house in the Lake District, did she remember? (She did – she'd helped Ed's mum Liz choose the Airbnb back in the spring, though she had, as it happened, forgotten that the trip was now imminent.) Of course, Christina wouldn't be coming – well, of course not – but could they meet while he was over? He'd be staying with his parents for ten days in total, around the Lake District trip; he could come into London from Bath on any day that suited her. *I think it's important that we do this, Christina*, he wrote. *There's a lot we need to talk about.*

Well. Christina could count on one hand the times in her life that she had been properly blindsided – the call her mother had made to tell her that Dad was gone; each moment the sonographer had told them, gently, so gently, that the heart no longer seemed to be beating. *A lot we need to talk about.* Yes. She could raise the whole business with him then. She wasn't sure whether the prospect filled her with fear, or something closer to relief. Both, perhaps, she thought, sitting in her dark study, her desk lamp throwing a pool of light across her laptop screen, her mug of tea cooling beside her.

Six

'So what do you think Ed wants to talk about?'

'I don't know, Mum.' They were in the snug of a country pub near Epsom, waiting for Ray; he'd made the reservation for twelve-thirty, Sue had explained, suggesting he give mother and daughter some time to catch up before arriving at one. 'The divorce, I imagine. We need to kick things off sometime, don't we?'

Sue gave her a long, assessing look. 'Perhaps he's having second thoughts. Time apart, you know. It can work wonders.'

Christina's grip tightened on the stem of her glass. Her mother adored Ed, and didn't comprehend the break-up, not fully; how could she, really, when she'd been married to Dad for forty years, when they'd never argued – not as far as Christina knew, anyway – about anything more substantial than wallpaper patterns or where to go on holiday. Dad had seemed to have more insight; she'd sat with him once, not long before the end, just sat beside his bed and talked. A few months since the third round of IVF, the first miscarriage: she'd been exhausted, wrung out, the cracks had already been starting to show, though she'd tried to hide them from her father, to stay cheerful, not wanting to burden him. John hadn't been fooled. 'Takes a toll, love, doesn't it?' he'd said, reaching for her hand. 'Sadness, loss. It takes a toll on a marriage.'

She'd brushed his comment aside – 'Oh, Dad, don't worry, we're fine' – but they hadn't been, had they? And yet she struggled, even now, to articulate exactly what it was that had gone wrong. The best description she'd found was that it had felt, by the end, as if they had been hollowed out from the inside: that their need to be parents had eclipsed every other need, every other ambition, and their ultimate failure had left them with nothing else to say to each other, nothing else to aim for. A ragged hole where their love had been. 'It's like I don't even know you any more, Chrissy,' Ed had said the morning he'd left, when they'd sat together at the kitchen table – beyond shouting, beyond arguing, just tired, more than anything, tired and sad and admitting defeat. 'It's like I don't even know myself. I can't live like this. I just can't.'

'I know,' she'd said, not looking at him. 'I know.'

Now, across the pub table, her mother set down her gin and tonic and said, 'Do you ever think that you might be letting go of things too easily? I mean, I know you've been through a lot, the two of you – believe me, I do – but marriage isn't something you just let fall at the first hurdle.'

'Mum. For God's sake, I . . .' But Christina was saved from saying more by the arrival of Ray, or the man she assumed must be Ray: a smiling, grey-haired seventy-something in a pressed cornflower-blue shirt, coming noiselessly towards them.

'Oh,' Sue said, her cheeks colouring; she really likes him, Christina thought, and her mood softened. The smiling, grey-haired man reached their table, and they both stood. 'Oh, please don't get up. Hello Sue.' He leant over to kiss her on the cheek. Then, turning to Christina, extending his hand, 'You must be Christina. I'm Ray. It's really good to finally meet you.'

Christina swept away the last traces of her irritation, mustered a smile. 'Good to meet you too.' And it was: she liked him, or would do, anyway, as she got to know him; she could tell she would. A soft, kind, intelligent man who had suffered deeply and come out the other side. According to Sue, his wife's decline had been cruelly drawn-out, far slower than Dad's: MS, Ray had cared for her for years. Christina could see it in Ray's face, in the way he carried himself: gently, as if afraid of breaking, each movement measured and precise.

'So,' Ray said as he settled on the third, empty chair, 'what have I missed?'

Sue looked away. Christina lifted her glass. 'Oh, nothing much. Shall we order? Ray, what would you recommend?'

He looked from mother to daughter, perceiving, perhaps, the small breach, the argument that hadn't quite caught light. Took up the menu, and said, 'Well. It is Sunday, so perhaps we really ought to try the beef . . .'

She was restless all week, restless and anxious, plagued by worries to which she couldn't quite put a name. Each night she woke several times, lay there silently in the darkness, the hammer still a foot or so away from her, under the pillow. It was crazy, really: she should put the thing back in the cupboard, she had no use for it, if a burglar did break in – a burglar or worse – was she really going to smash him over the head with an Ikea hammer?

No hedgehog shuffling broke the quiet beyond the patio doors – perhaps it had moved on, unenticed by her makeshift pile of leaves. (She hadn't got round to building the compost bin, suspected she probably never would. What was the point? She'd be leaving the flat in a few months anyway; to go where, she didn't know.) Only the usual London night-time stirrings: the thrum of a passing car, wind rustling the trees, a high, receding siren wail. She pictured Mrs Jackson asleep upstairs; her neighbour's bedroom was directly above. They'd been invited up once for tea, not long after they'd moved in. The flat was a replica of theirs, with dark red walls, white wallpaper embossed with black velvety fleurs-de-lys. Stuff everywhere: books and ornaments and magazines and coats and hats and framed photographs of beaming children; of their mothers, elegant in wrappers and headscarves; and of the late Mr Jackson, preserved for posterity in his Transport for London uniform on the day of his retirement after forty-seven years of service. Ed, noting none of this, only the similarity of the layout of the flats, had made a joke about the bedrooms, about trying to keep down the noise. Christina had cringed; Mrs Jackson, across the room, hadn't even pretended to smile. They hadn't been invited back. She had been polite to Christina ever since, remote and polite, but had barely bothered to acknowledge Ed. He could be tactless sometimes; it was as if he had no understanding of the subtleties of human interaction. 'I'm a scientist,' he said, 'a tech geek, you can't blame me.' But she had blamed him in the end, hadn't she? She had, just as much as she knew he had blamed her for her own faults, her own failures.

Christina lay in the dark in her bedroom – their bedroom, until just a few months ago – eyes open, watching shadows shift across the ceiling. The day was beginning to lighten; it was almost morning, almost time to get up, get on, fit a shape to the formless hours. That was all you could do sometimes, wasn't it? Get up, get dressed, and find a way to carry on.

Ed was flying from San Francisco overnight on Wednesday; on Friday, he told her by email, he'd travel up to the Lake District with his parents.

Isabel's decided to come, he wrote, *which means the usual drama, the usual me-me-me. And Zach's making a fuss about not having decent Wi-Fi. God knows what it's going to be like.*

She didn't know what he wanted her to say; he loved his family, she knew he did, even his tricky sister, just as she'd thought she'd loved them, too. The whole clever, eccentric Macfarlane clan, presided over by his parents Liz and Toby in their gorgeous cream-coloured house near Bath. She'd loved visiting; they'd all drunk like fish, put away more in an evening than her parents would in a month, sitting around the enormous farmhouse table eating scratchy, thrown-together meals, cold meats and cheeses and artichokes bought from the expensive deli in town, the dogs milling at their feet. Politics and world affairs and good-natured arguments: it had all come up there, around that table, and she'd sat there drinking wine and loving it, loving him, loving that she was a part of this now – a part of this looser, more elegant life, this intellectual ebb and flow. But emotional affairs, it seemed, they handled less adroitly: the whole family had been cold with Christina, at least as Christina had seen it, throughout the years of treatment, hadn't even acknowledged either of the miscarriages aloud.

'Oh, that's just Mum and Dad,' Ed had said. 'They're no good with stuff like that.'

'What,' she'd snapped back, 'you mean stuff like the deaths of their unborn grandchildren?'

'Christina,' he'd said then. 'For God's sake. I know it was awful – of course I do, I was there, it was awful for me too. But you have to stop taking it out on everyone else.'

79

For this reason, then, and the fact that she hadn't heard a thing from any of his family other than Liz (that one stilted phone call; a card on her birthday, with a photograph of the dogs – *they miss you* – and a voucher for L'Occitane) since Ed had left, she wrote back saying only, *I'm sure you'll have a great time. Back Sunday evening, then, right? Shall we meet on Monday? A late lunch somewhere? I have a meeting at Jerwood Space at one. We could do the South Bank, if you like? The BFI café?*

It was her mother, perhaps, who'd made her think of the place – her visit to the *Red Shoes*. That, and the fact that she'd been trying, since Ed's first email, to think of somewhere neutral, somewhere with no particular emotional resonance. The BFI was such a place: they'd been there once or twice, maybe, but never for anything special, anything momentous or memorable.

Sure, he wrote back. *3 p.m.?*

I'll see you there.

He would. She'd walk in, and he'd be there. Her estranged husband. A moment that meant nothing and everything. A scene for which she would be sent no script.

The weekend was quiet – no visit to Dinah; no scheduled meet-ups with Emma and Jen, who were tied up with the children. ('You can come to Leila's under-10s football match in Brent-ford,' Jen had said, 'if getting up at six on a Sunday sounds like your idea of fun.') Even her mum had plans – the dance class were seeing *Strictly Ballroom* on Saturday, and on Sunday Ray was taking her to the RHS gardens at Wisley. Christina had almost asked if she might tag along – she loved Wisley, they'd gone there often with Dad – but no, she wasn't going to be a forty-something third wheel, gatecrashing her mother's date.

And anyway, Isla was coming round for tutoring on Sunday afternoon; that was the one firm plan in her calendar.

The weekends were hardest when you were single, over forty, and without children: those were the hours when you felt the difference between yourself and what seemed like the entire rest of the world most keenly. She tried hard not to think about the Macfarlanes, up in the Lake District, in the Airbnb she'd helped his mother find. About the champagne they'd no doubt open on Toby's birthday, and the conversations they'd have around the table; the family that had been hers, and from which she was now excluded, all their lives spinning on without her.

On Saturday afternoon she went up to the Triangle, sat for a while in a café with an almond tart and a pot of Earl Grey, rereading Isla's GCSE textbook. She had chosen one of the tables closest to the door – a little burst of chilled air rushed over her each time the door was opened, but it had been the only table left. The fourth time this happened she looked up, resisting a rising irritation, and saw Mal. Same leather jacket, same wild pepper-and-salt hair; no Ziggy, they didn't allow dogs. There he was outside, tied to a lamp post, paws neatly tucked, eyes trained on Mal. How wonderful it must be, she thought, to have someone in your life – something – that would not rest unless they knew where you had gone and when you would return. Mal ordered a latte, the coffee machine whirred and hissed. It struck her, perhaps for the first time, that this was what she had longed for most through the years of trying, what she still longed for: a person, a being, to whom she mattered more than any other. Not from choice – a lover's promise, even a husband's, easily broken, easily withdrawn – but from the tie of blood and flesh and bone.

'Mal,' she said.

He turned. A fractional moment in which she worried that he might not know her, recognise her – but if he hadn't, he hid it well. 'Well, if it isn't my book thief. Swotting up, are you?'

She looked down at the book. 'Oh – I help a friend's daughter out sometimes. She's doing her GCSEs.'

'Wish I'd paid more attention in maths.'

'Me too. Especially as I'm an accountant.'

Surely the most boring words ever uttered by anyone, anywhere, but he managed to look interested. Not everybody was able to do that. 'Don't suppose you fancy sorting my finances out, do you?'

The barista handed Mal his coffee in a takeaway cup, and he thanked him, moved a little closer to Christina's table, out of the way of the woman behind him in the queue. She'd opened her mouth to say she'd be happy to take a look – what other polite response could there be? – but he added quickly, 'Only kidding. I've got a guy. I wouldn't wish his job on anyone. Talk about the loaves and the fishes.'

Christina smiled, closed the book. 'Tough going at the market?'

'Always. But that's not all I do. I take photographs. Weddings, mainly. A few projects of my own when I have the time.' He reached into his pocket, drew out a card. Dark grey type on off-white. *Malik Osman. Photographs & Books.*

She picked up the card. The font was familiar – like the one they used on the Tube. Helvetica, wasn't it? 'Malik?'

He shrugged. 'I only tend to use my full name for work. And when I visit my mum.'

She turned the card over. There were two numbers on the back – a mobile, a landline – and an email address: *ziggyplaysguitar@gmail.com.*

'Does he?' she said.

'Does he what? Who?'

'Ziggy. Does Ziggy play guitar?'

'Ah.' He stood there smiling at her, half angled away from her table, towards the door, where the dog was waiting, staring in with his soft brown trusting eyes. 'Only when he's in a really good mood.' And then, after a beat, 'Take care, then, Christina. I guess I might be seeing you.'

Isla was meant to be coming for two hours on Sunday, from three till five. Emma called in the morning, regretting that she wouldn't be able to drive her over. 'Sorry C, Alfie's sick – some sort of tummy bug – and Pete's got a rugby thing. She'll have to take the bus.'

She was forty-five minutes late in the end – 'the bus took *ages*,' Isla said, though Christina strongly suspected she hadn't set off on time – and then wanted a coffee, so it was almost four before they actually sat down to work. They sat in Christina's office – Isla at the desk, Christina perched on the edge of the Ikea daybed she and Ed had bought for guests – working through a chapter of Isla's textbook. After twenty minutes, Christina remembered exactly why she had never wanted to follow her parents into teaching: was there anyone, she wondered disloyally, less rewarding to teach than a bright, privately educated teenage girl who just couldn't be bothered? Gabriel could focus for longer, Christina thought, and he was only six. To be fair, though, he didn't have a mobile phone to distract him as obviously and repeatedly as Isla's was doing now.

'Shall we turn that off for a bit?' Christina said, after setting an exercise for Isla to work on alone. 'Or I could take it with me, if you like. Give it back when you're done.'

Isla looked up briefly from the screen. Her hair was in a high ponytail, curls exploding in a cloudburst at the crown of her head; her eye make-up was smudged and blurred, as if she hadn't quite bothered to remove last night's kohl. She smiled without warmth. 'No, I'm good, Aunty Chris. I'll just keep it on silent. Just give me a few minutes, yeah?'

Christina allowed her fifteen – made herself another coffee, sat drinking it at the kitchen table, trying not to think about Ed, about the next day. Failed: remembered, too clearly, the day he'd left, the last conversation they'd had here, in this room, at this table. Neither of them had slept much: Christina in the bedroom, Ed on the sofa. A summer's morning, soft, incongruously golden. She'd made coffee then, too. They'd sat drinking it, both knowing what was to come; when he'd spoken, it had only been to voice what she had not been brave enough to say. She'd respected him for that – loved him for it, a little, even as she'd acknowledged silently that it was true, it was over, she could take no more of this, their marriage was past-tense. 'I'll go to my brother's,' he'd said, and that was what he'd done. 'Whatever we do next, Chrissy, let's just promise we'll keep things civilised, all right? We loved each other for a long time. We did our best.' Yes, she'd said. It was true. They had loved each other. They had done their best. She had seen him to the door, and then, only then, once he was safely gone, had she allowed herself to lie on the bed – their bed – and shatter into fragments, send them scattering across the room.

When she returned to her office, she found Isla – inevitably – glued to her phone. 'Isla,' she began, 'I really did think you would . . .' But when the girl looked round, her expression was so sour that Christina faltered. 'Are you all right?'

Isla shrugged. She put the phone down, swivelled the chair round to face the room. 'I think you're lucky, Aunty Chris.'

'Lucky?'

Isla nodded, her brown-eyed gaze steady, unflinching. 'I don't ever want to have kids. They spoil everything.'

Christina sank down onto the bed. Not cruelty, surely, just the brutal, blinkered solipsism of youth. 'What makes you say that?'

Isla watched her for a moment. Neither of them spoke. Soap opera horrors hovered at the fringes of Christina's mind: secret pregnancies, doctors' offices, whispered conversations. Isla was sixteen, after all: anything was possible. Did Emma know? Ought she to press her, draw her out? She took a breath. 'What is it, Isla? Are you . . .?'

The younger woman's face crumpled in disgust. 'Ugh. No. I'm not *stupid*.'

'Of course you're not. I just . . .'

'Forget it. Please. It's nothing. I don't even know why I said it.'

Christina sat on the bed, helpless, out of her depth. Emma at Jen's show: the way she'd looked at Christina, as if to say that she didn't have a clue, not really, she wasn't a mother, she couldn't *know*. Perhaps Emma had been right. Perhaps Christina didn't, couldn't, know.

Isla shifted on the chair, turned back to her laptop. 'I did the equations. They were quite easy, really, after you explained it to me. You can have a look if you like.'

'Good.' Relieved, really; relieved that the moment, whatever its source, had sped off into the past. 'OK, let's see.'

Seven

Monday arrived with grey skies and rain. Christina hesitated in the hallway, unsure which coat to choose. Her bulky navy overcoat, which kept out the wet but made her look like Michelin man; or her grey trench, a size too small these days and no more than splash-proof, but a good deal more chic. The mirror was decisive: the trench. She'd take an umbrella to keep off the rain. Her hair was freshly washed; she'd taken trouble with her make-up. Beneath the trench she wore her best cashmere jumper, her most flattering jeans. None of it should matter, but it did, of course; Jen and Emma understood. They'd had a three-way WhatsApp conversation through most of the previous evening about what she should wear, Christina in her bedroom, photographing outfits for their dissection. *Perfect*, had been the unanimous verdict on this one. And the jumper was new, too: better, they'd all agreed for reasons they hadn't quite been able to define, that she should wear something Ed had never seen her in before. Something she felt good in. Something that made her feel like her best, most powerful self.

Here was Jen now, buzzing in her pocket. *Good luck today, C. Whatever happens, keep your cool. Love you xxx*

Later, Christina would look back over this message and wonder whether Jen had known something she didn't, or at least possessed some sort of sixth sense. But, for now, she smiled, tapped out a quick reply – *Thanks darling xxx* – and walked, huddled under her umbrella, to the station. Changed at Balham, rode the escalator down into the mouth of the Underground. Took the Northern Line to Waterloo, sitting in the middle of the carriage, closing her eyes as the Tube train roared and swayed. Was this fear or excitement, or some strange, pulse-quickening hybrid of the two? Almost as if it were a date she was heading for – and it was, in a way: she was only meeting her husband for lunch. A thing she had done so many times, in so many places, over the years they'd been together. Not so very long, really: seven years, a pebble in the ocean compared with Emma's relationship with Pete – twenty-three years, they'd been a couple now – or her parents' four decades. And now here she was, on her way to meet Ed, to discuss neither the easy mundanities of married life – weekend plans; what to cook for dinner – nor, if they could help it, the painful complexities of their shared losses. To ask Ed a question, and be ready for his answer, whatever it might be. And it was true: finally, she decided, stepping out onto the crowded concourse at Waterloo, she was ready.

The meeting first, at Jerwood Space: a choreographer, a friend of Jen's, setting up a new dance company, wanting her advice. She got through it, though it felt for most of the hour that she was outside her own body, had somehow split into two, leaving one half of herself talking to a distractingly attractive Cuban named Rodrigo about the intricacies of tax planning and the other half wandering the South Bank, watching the clock tick towards three o'clock.

And then, almost too quickly, it was done: the two halves reconciled, walking together through the rain to the river. She was early, she was always early. Stood for ten minutes under the dripping bridge, pretending to examine the stalls of second-hand

88

books laid out on trestle tables under protective plastic sheets. Found herself thinking of Mal, of his market stall, of his dog, Ziggy. *Malik Osman. Photographs & Books.* Two pairs of kind brown eyes, watching hers. The thought cheered her. It was one o'clock now. She furled her umbrella, stepped inside. Mouth dry, heart pounding. Ridiculous. It was only the man she had married. It was only the man she had loved, suffered with, let go. The thought struck her, really for the first time, despite her mother's assertions, despite Emma and Jen's tentative questions, that Ed really might have wanted to meet in order to tell her that it had all been a terrible mistake: that he still loved her, still wanted to make a family with her, whatever the cost, however difficult it continued to be. Her pulse was accelerating now; it suddenly seemed so possible, even probable, that this was what Ed was going to say – how could she, really, not have considered this, and the response she would give in return? What would she say to him? She didn't know, she didn't know. It was over, she knew it was, and yet . . . They were still married. They'd been through so much. She stood still in the middle of the restaurant, looking around, unable to see him, unable to breathe.

Her phone, ringing in her bag. She rummaged, couldn't find it, knelt down to empty the bag's contents onto the floor. A waiter stepped around her, saying irritably, '*Excuse* me, madam.' For God's sake. Why hadn't she kept the phone in her pocket? He wasn't cancelling, was he? Surely he wouldn't, surely he wasn't that . . . Here was the phone, tucked between the pages of the book she hadn't bothered to open on the Tube. He hadn't left a voicemail, had sent a text instead. *You didn't say which restaurant – I'm in the one at the back. E.*

No kiss. Traces of an old, long-established irritation: her scattiness, his organised scientist's brain. Reality returned to her, colour-saturated fantasy shifting to grey. She was in the restaurant at the front; she'd forgotten there were two. She threw her stuff back into her bag, kept her phone in her hand as she hurried on through the cinema foyer to the other restaurant. Another room, another jumbled assembly of heads. People eating, drinking, sitting, standing, walking. *Can I help you, madam?* Yes, I'm looking for my ... I'm trying to find my ... Ah, yes, there he is, over by the window. Yes, that's him. Thank you. I can take it from here.

He looked different: she saw it right away.

His hair was shorter, for one thing – before he'd left, he'd started letting it grow quite long – and he was wearing clothes she didn't recognise. American clothes: a checked shirt (plaid, they called it, didn't they?), in place of a cardigan, over a burgundy T-shirt. New glasses, too, with fine tortoiseshell frames; they made his face look longer, somehow, longer and younger. Perhaps he'd lost weight. But no, there was something else: a loosening, a softness. Ed looked lighter, she decided, sitting down across the table from him. He looked as if a hundred-pound pack had been lifted from his back.

'Hi,' he said.

She met his eye. She breathed. It was just Ed Macfarlane, after all. Nothing to be afraid of. She'd loved him once. Perhaps, if things had gone differently, she still would. 'Hi.'

'You look good,' he said.

'Liar. But you do.'

He didn't deny it. 'Thanks.'

They ordered: pasta for Ed, a Caesar salad for Christina, who wanted the cheeseburger, but felt obscurely that she needed to show him that she had changed too, or was in the process of changing. They talked about nothing much. His father's birthday, the whole Macfarlane clan. 'Mum and Dad send their love,' he said. 'They specifically asked me to pass that on.'

Bit late for that, she thought, but she managed to say out loud, 'That's kind of them. Thanks. Give them mine, too.'

He wasn't drinking – had ordered a Coke before she arrived – so she did the same, sat sipping a rose lemonade. On they went, bumbling around, making conversation, skirting anything resembling an issue. Politeness, its easy runnels, the English default mode. Her mother would be proud, Dinah horrified. She had no idea, she realised then, of what Dad would say if he were here. *What a shame*, perhaps. He'd just look at them both, and shake his head sadly, and say, *I'm so sorry for you both. How unfair it is. What a dreadful shame.*

Their food arrived. After the waiter had departed a silence fell across the table between them, and they each leapt to fill it at the same time.

Ed: 'Christina, there's something I really need to . . .'

Christina: 'Ed, I'm glad you got in touch, because I really wanted to . . .'

Both trailed off, stared. Was it then that she noted the change in his expression; had she really seen no fear in his face until then? He isn't a cruel man, she'd think later; he hates hurting people more than anything in the world. He must have been so very nervous, knowing what he had to say.

And then she'd think, well, he should have been nervous. He should have been quaking in his new American hi-tops. Which, by the way, make him look like a fifty-year-old man pretending to be a child.

But then, in that moment, she only lifted her fork, speared a strand of lettuce, and said before lifting it to her mouth, 'It's all right, Ed. You go first.'

And he had, hadn't he: he'd gone first, and she'd let him, and after that she'd never had a chance to say what she'd come to say.

She retraced her route through the cinema, stumbling back through the foyer, the front-facing restaurant, out onto the riverside. The rain had stopped, the sun was out: a feeble winter sun, reaching down under the bridge, resting on the second-hand bookstalls, on the faces of the out-of-season passers-by, closing their umbrellas, taking down their hoods, pausing to watch the restless, steel-grey Thames. She paused too, leant against the nearest stretch of wall, watched a passing riverboat, low-slung, its red hull carving the water. Too tired, suddenly, to carry on; too exhausted to be anywhere but here, clinging to the solid brick embankment as to a raft.

She had left Ed sitting at the table, his half-finished plate of pasta in front of him. She hadn't finished her food either. There she'd been, eating her salad like the fool she was, offering him his cue.

'All right,' he'd said, laying down his fork. 'There's no easy way to say this, Chrissy, so I'll just come right out with it.'

What had she imagined, in that moment? So many things. He was hiring a lawyer, was planning to take her to the cleaners (let him: she had nothing, almost nothing). He was ill. One of his parents was ill. Something had happened to his nephew Henry. He was going to stop paying his portion of the rent and bills, force her to see out the remainder of the tenancy unaided. Many things, she'd imagined, of various degrees of disaster, but none of them, not a single one of them, had even slightly resembled what he'd actually gone on to say. And yet, as soon as he'd said it, even through her shock, the sudden searing pain of it, she'd been aware of a feeling of inevitability. *Well, of course this. Of course. Why didn't I think of this? Why didn't I come prepared?*

At least he'd been direct. At least he'd said it all at once, offered her the blunt truth, fast and brutal. At least he hadn't tortured her with slow, drip-fed revelations. Yes, perhaps there was that to be grateful for.

She replayed his statement in her mind. Something rehearsed about it, she thought now. The script she hadn't been given in advance.

Chrissy, I've met someone.

Her name's Marianne. She's from Milwaukee. We work together. It hasn't been going on long, but it's serious. She's pregnant. Eight weeks, so it's early days, but I had to tell you in person, it didn't feel right not to. And no, it wasn't planned. We haven't been together long enough to plan anything. An accident, but one we're both happy about, both trying to make sense of. We only found out a couple of weeks ago – I'd have told you sooner otherwise. I wanted to tell you in person. I felt I owed you that at least. I'm so sorry, Chrissy.

Ed was sorry. Sorry.

An accident, but one we're both happy about.

We only found out a couple of weeks ago.

We only.

We.

Christina hadn't been answerable for what had happened next. She hadn't owed anyone an explanation: not Ed; not the diners who'd heard her cry out, not the waiter who'd hovered at a discreet distance from the table, asking madam if everything was all right. No, everything was not all right, not all right at all. She'd had to go. She'd stood up, stumbled out, not quite trusting her legs to carry her. But they had. They'd carried her away, and he'd at least had the decency not to follow. And now she was standing here, watching the river, knowing that at some point she would have to move, make her way back to the station, to the flat, to the relentless onward flow. But for now, for a while yet, she was just going to stand watching the water, letting time shift on without her.

Eight

Her dad had loved many things – gardening; Scotland; fig rolls; Euler's identity, a mathematical equation he'd considered as beautiful as poetry. And walking.

The habit had started young – he and Dinah had grown up in a village in Kent, not far from Whitstable, and had famously had to walk the two miles to school and back in all weathers, the family being too poor, as Dad had told it, to own a car. (Dinah saw things differently – 'We had a car,' she said, 'our dad was just too much of a selfish bastard to bother to drive us to school.') Their mother Christina – Christina's grandmother, from whom she'd acquired her name – had died when Dinah was ten and John five; their father Stanley Lennox had indeed, by all accounts, been a bit of a bastard, or perhaps just a man made bitter by grief and disappointment. He'd died when Christina was four; she couldn't remember him, but even Sue had observed once that she really wasn't missing much. 'He didn't even turn up to our wedding,' her mother had told her when Christina was in her teens and starting to see her family as individuals, with their own particular histories, rather than just a generic, featureless backdrop to her own existence. 'Went out and got so drunk the night before that he fell in a ditch and broke his arm. To be honest, both your father and I were more than a little relieved.'

So perhaps it had been not the lack of a car that had caused John to traipse out across the fields from an early age, but the desire to spend longer and longer periods away from the house; whatever its source, anyway, Dad had never lost his love of walking. Her mother had shared his interest, at least at first – they'd met, according to the well-worn story, on a UCL rambling trip to Dungeness, had felt the first stirrings of romance under the long shadow of the nuclear power station. But Sue's had waned over the years – something, as Christina understood it (neither her mother nor her father had ever been precise about this), to do with the difficult time she'd had giving birth to Christina, some shadowy, nameless damage she'd sustained. Their family holidays had almost always been to self-catering cottages in wild rural locations – Dartmoor, the Forest of Dean, the Isle of Skye – but Sue had usually stayed behind, let John and Christina go out walking for the morning or the afternoon, sometimes the whole day, Dad carrying foil-wrapped sandwiches, a thermos and an Ordnance Survey map. These were among her loveliest memories of her father: those hours together, Dad matching his longer pace to her shorter one, crossing gorse or heather or hill; sometimes, if they were very lucky and the location allowed, being rewarded by a sudden, diamond-cut vista of the sea.

Was it for Dad, then, that Christina decided, on Tuesday morning, to put on her trainers, get out of the house and walk? Dad, and the fact that it felt as if the walls of the flat were closing in on her. She'd slept badly: she might not have slept at all, but suspected she'd probably managed an hour or two, had spent the rest of the long night awake, her mind refusing to settle. She'd had four missed calls from Jen the previous evening, another couple from Emma. (She'd learn, later, that Ed had texted Jen, asked Jen to look after her; though he had not, at least, been specific about why.)

She'd sent them both a text – *Thanks for checking in. I'm all right. Don't want to talk about it just yet, but I'll be in touch soon, I promise* – and then turned off her phone. Jen didn't need her to pick up Leila and Gabriel from school the following day – she had some time off now that the show was finished. And Christina hadn't felt ready, not then, not yet, to speak to her friends, to package up what was happening, what Ed had told her, and offer it to them, to anyone. She hadn't wanted, not then, not yet, to turn this into a subject for discussion: more pain to unpick, more grief to process, to make sense of. Oh, grief was the wrong word – a child was going to be born; she would not allow herself to make this an occasion for grieving – but she could, she would, grieve the fact that her own would surely never, now, be born. For Ed would never agree to it now, would he, the last treatment, her last treatment – the chances of him agreeing before had been slim, she'd known that really, just hadn't wanted to admit it, but now they had dwindled to zero. It was over. All of it. Her marriage, her last chance of being a mother. All of it was gone. Had been for months, really – longer, if she were truly honest – but this had never seemed as starkly, bleakly obvious as it did now, on this chilly, grey-roofed Tuesday in December.

She walked. Down the hill, over the roundabout, along the wide, leafy streets of Dulwich, with their broad detached houses, their scrubbed brickwork, their lovely tended gardens and shining brand-new 4x4s parked on weedless driveways. A working day: only the occupants who didn't work would be in, or those who, like her, worked from home. She passed a woman of about her own age, blonde, lithe, a yoga mat slung over her shoulder.

Watched the woman turn onto one of the weedless driveways, put a key in the lock, open the door. A brief flash of grey walls, a framed painting (a real one, no doubt, watercolour or oils, no prints in a house like this), small coats hanging on hooks. Children's coats. The woman had children, of course she did: five of them, no doubt, and a chocolate Labrador. Didn't work, didn't need to work. Did yoga, picked up the kids from school in the 4x4, met friends for lunch. Nice husband, still worked out too, still looked good. A good life. A lovely life, everything sorted, her to-do list neatly ticked off. *Marriage*. Tick. *Children*. Tick. *Money*. Tick. Maybe she'd never wanted her own career, or maybe she had one too, maybe she was a CEO or a West End actress: who knew? The woman closed the door. Christina wanted to shout after her, *Do you know how lucky you are? Do you wake up, every morning, and thank God, or luck, or whoever you believe in, for everything you have?*

She walked on, past the school, its red-brick turrets, its sheets of rolling green lawn. Her entire salary, these days, wouldn't pay a year's fees. That was something, then: no children meant no school fees to pay. Not that she and Ed would ever have sent them private, even if they could have afforded to. That was how she'd been brought up. Her parents had both been teachers, Dad maths, Mum history, until she'd had Christina; went back to a bit of supply work once Christina was a teenager. Always in the state sector: her parents had both hated private education with a vehemence they'd rarely expressed towards any other political cause. Christina had been shocked, really, when Emma and Pete had decided to send Isla, and then Alfie, to private schools. Shocked, and more than a little disgusted, though she'd never said as much aloud, not even to Jen (she hadn't needed to: she'd known, without asking, that Jen had felt the same). Another crack, another fault line. Strange, really, that she and Jen were still friends with Emma: she was so different, she inhabited another world, and always had. The same world as that woman with the yoga mat, the original art; perhaps they knew each other, moved in the same circle; perhaps that woman's daughter was in the same class at Isla's school.

Isla on Sunday, looking up from her phone. *I think you're lucky, Aunty Chris.* Do you, Isla? Do you really? Lucky only, perhaps, to have met Ed when I did. I was thirty-six, I wanted children, Ed was there. He wanted children, too. It wasn't just that – we loved each other, we really did, though it's hard to remember that now, today, so deep is my anger, my sadness, my disbelief – but our age was part of it. Love, yes, but timing also, and luck, or the lack of it. And then, eventually, an ending, a severance. And now he's met another woman on the other side of the world, before we've even embarked upon divorce. Now he's fathering a child, just like that, the way I'd always known he could if he wasn't with me, not carrying my failures, my lack. The way so many people do, every day, everywhere: they get pregnant, for good or ill, on a whim, by accident, I'm pregnant, keeping the baby, not keeping the baby, either way, it's so easy isn't it, not rocket science, just biology, the simplest, most natural thing in the world. No, Isla, not for me. Not for my freakish failure of a body.

She walked. She'd reached Dulwich Park now. Stopped. Found a bench. Sat down. Realised that there were tears coursing down her face; perhaps they had been there for a while, perhaps she just hadn't noticed them. *Are you all right?* An older lady, her mum's age, passing with a white cockapoo on a lead. A soft face, plump, creased with concern. Yes, yes, I'm all right. Well, I'm not, of course, but for your sake, and for mine, let's just pretend.

She saw Ziggy before she saw Mal, the black and white collie streaking across the grass, chasing a ball thrown by a man's out-stretched arm. Well, just *a* black and white collie, at first: it was only when she saw the rest of the man – tall, broad, bearded, a leather jacket over a navy jumper – that she recognised him, recognised them both. Strange to see them here: not their usual stomping ground, she presumed. But then it wasn't hers, either. And presumptions were almost always worthless, weren't they?

Christina stood up, turned to go, hoping Mal hadn't seen her – he was still a good distance away. But it seemed he had: she heard her name carried on the air between them. She looked up; he was waving, smiling. Ziggy darted towards her across the grass, dropped the ball at her feet. She knelt down, rubbed the dog's rough fur, felt his warm animal pulse through his skin.

'Hello again,' Mal said as he approached. 'We've got to stop meeting like this.'

She smiled, couldn't help it. Politeness – acknowledgement of the small joke – and the fact that something about his smile demanded reciprocity. She hoped it wasn't too obvious she'd been crying. 'Shouldn't you be working?'

He shook his head. 'Always a slow day, Tuesday. Market's closed, weddings are thin on the ground. Ziggy and I like to drive around, mix it up a bit with his walks. He gets bored easily, as do I. And you?'

'Something of a slow day, too.'

Ziggy, lying panting on the ground, shifted his gaze from Christina to Mal and back again.

'We were just going to grab a sandwich,' Mal said. 'Fancy joining us?'

'No,' she said, too quickly. 'No, I'm . . .'

He looked away, offended, perhaps, by the speed of her refusal. 'Busy. Not hungry. I get it.'

'No, it's not that, I'm just . . .' How to explain it to a stranger, when she hadn't yet said the words aloud to anyone? Impossible. She couldn't even try. 'Having a bad week. One of the worst.'

Mal nodded again. His gaze was gentle, still; she met it for a moment, felt a sudden, absurd desire to tell him everything, everything about her, about who she was, and wasn't, and would never be. Crazy. She didn't even know the man. He'd think her even madder than he no doubt already did, sitting here on a park bench with tear stains drying on her cheeks.

'I'm sorry to hear that,' he said. 'I've had a few of those in my time.'

He leant down, retrieved Ziggy's ball from the ground. The dog leapt to his feet, poised for action, tongue lolling from his mouth. 'Sorry, Zig, not now. Got to go and get lunch.' Mal pocketed the ball. 'Listen, maybe this isn't the moment, and maybe this isn't at all something you'd be into. But there's a walking group I run, a local thing, we go out every few weeks, try different routes, around London and out in the country, too. Kent, Sussex, Surrey. Sometimes further, make a weekend of it. I set it up a few years ago, when I was having a really tough time myself, and it helped. I can't really tell you why – not now, anyway, not here – but it really did.'

She nodded. It was something she could imagine, understand. 'My dad loved walking.'

He smiled. 'So did mine. He was, for many years, the only Pakistani member of the Durham City Rambling Club. Took me with him most weekends – Mam wasn't bothered. Anyway, we're on Facebook – Crystal Palace Walkers – and we usually meet for a drink in the Wheatsheaf, second Thursday of the month.'

'I'll check it out.'

'Do,' he said, watching her face for a moment, two, and then angling himself away from her, shifting his gaze to a row of distant trees. Embarrassed, perhaps, ashamed of having told her, a stranger, about something that clearly mattered to him and might not matter to her at all. A kind act, a kind man. Intelligent, too, she thought, the word floating into her mind of its own volition. Intelligent, and kind, and perhaps more than a little lonely.

'Thanks, Mal,' she said. 'Really. Thanks for the invitation. I'll . . . I'll see about coming along sometime. I love walking, actually, I'm just a bit . . .'

'Busy,' he said flatly. 'Sure. No worries. I know how it is. Take care of yourself, all right?' And then Mal turned and loped off in the direction of the café, Ziggy darting and barking at his heels.

Nine

Christina was losing, again, the ability to sleep. She saw it like that – an ability, a skill, that could be lost as easily, as suddenly, as it had been acquired. Actually, acquiring it hadn't been so easy, according to her mother: she'd been a terrible sleeper as a baby, hadn't slept through the night until she was eighteen months old. This had been Sue's warning, offered as soon as Christina had confirmed that, yes, she and Ed wanted children. *Prepare never to sleep properly again.* A warning offered with a smile, a knowing look: you won't mind, of course, you'll love the child so much, you'll be prepared to sacrifice everything for it, even your own sanity. This was what everybody said: friends, colleagues, even the midwife she'd seen at her first pregnancy check-in. 'Let's hope you're not too attached to your sleep,' she'd said, not looking up from her computer screen. A gentle, soft-featured woman; she had five kids of her own, she'd told Christina later at that same appointment, hardly knew where she found the time to breathe. 'Because Baby is going to make sure you don't get much more of it from now on.'

But you didn't need a child to stop you from sleeping. It had happened to Christina before – at school, when she was doing her GCSEs; at university, around the time of her final exams. Again in her twenties, after she'd got together with Joe, her first proper boyfriend. For almost two years she'd been convinced that this was it – the real deal, marriage-and-kids-the-lot – and then had her assumptions brutally severed when he'd dumped her for a nineteen-year-old student nurse. Again when she and Ed had started IVF – the tablets, the injections, the scans – and lost the first pregnancy. Again when Dad was dying; again when they'd lost their daughter, and again when it had become clear that their marriage was lost, too. So yes, she was not unused to bouts of insomnia, to waking in the darkest portion of the night and lying there, as alert, as electric-brained, as if it were the middle of the morning. But it was still shocking each time it happened, she was never any better prepared. Hope, that dangerous flicker (*perhaps I'll drift back off, I'll just lie here, I'll just keep my eyes closed and try to focus on my breath*) replaced, eventually, by anger (*why is this happening?*), fear (*how will I get through the day?*) and finally, resignation (*oh sod it then, I might as well get up*).

For several nights – or several almost-mornings; she refused to allow herself to look at her phone or at the clock on the kitchen wall – she got up sometime before dawn, wandered the dark flat in her pyjamas and dressing gown. She'd read some-where, over the years – she'd read everything, tried everything: even tablets, which had knocked her into a deep, tranquillised slumber but made her feel like a zombie the next day – that it was better not to turn on too many lights if you had to get up in the night, to try to keep reminding your brain and body that it was time to sleep. She settled on the sofa, switched on the one lamp that was left – they'd had two, Ed had taken one of them – and tried to read. She was halfway through a book she'd read about on one of the fertility forums (infertility forums, she'd always thought they should be called, really, but they were not): a memoir by a woman for whom IVF had also not, in the end, resulted in a full-term pregnancy; who had lost her relationship to the process, too. A beautiful book, an eloquent writer; a woman who, like Christina, had been sad, and angry, and lost, and perhaps still was.

One of those nights, after she'd woken, disorientated, from a brief, obliterating sleep on the sofa, the book splayed across her chest, Christina closed the book, stood up, walked out into the hall. The darkness was less absolute than it had been – greyish, shifting, edging towards dawn. Her eyes adjusted quickly. The coat pegs, the cheap doormat, the laminate floor. She and Ed had dreamt, once, back when they'd thought it would all be easy, of the house they'd buy – not large, but old and beautiful, with floors they'd sand and varnish themselves. It had remained a dream. Here was the rented hallway, the space where the shoe cabinet had been; hers were lined up there now, toes to the skirting board, trainers and boots and a pair of high-heeled courts she'd once worn to the office, hadn't bothered with in years. Should get rid of them, really, along with so many other things. Things to get rid of, things to acquire. A sequence of doors, left open, admitting the distinct, shaded darkness of the rooms beyond: the living room behind her, the kitchen to her left; beyond it, the bathroom; beyond that, the second bedroom, her office; ahead, the main bedroom, to which she should return, try to dive back into sleep. Around the corner, to the left, the third bedroom, the box room.

She stood in front of the closed door. From somewhere out on the street came the low purr of a car engine starting, the thrum of its tyres on the road. Then nothing. She breathed. She pushed open the door.

A small room, dim even in daytime, as there was only one window, and this one looked not out over the garden but sideways, into the cobwebby passage that divided the building from its neighbour. A framed prospect of shabby London brick; a portion of frosted window through which, late in the evening, you could see shadows moving – the couple next door in their bathroom, shifting from shower to toilet to sink. Christina had actually worried about that – not the shadows, but the brick; the unappealing blankness of it. The lack of natural light. *Will it harm the baby, do you think? Should we think about swapping the bedrooms round? I could just about fit my desk in here.* Ed staring back at her from behind his glasses, gentle in his reply. *Christina. Please. It's still too early. Don't do this. Don't do this now.*

Oh, but it wasn't, wasn't it? She was pregnant again, the fifth round had worked, and it was different this time, she was sure. She felt different: nauseous most of the time, and a couple of times she'd actually been sick – once in the morning, once in the afternoon. Her breasts were tender, swollen. One day she'd taken such a violent dislike to the taste of coffee that she'd thrown away an entire Starbucks cappuccino. The barista had seen her do it; she'd asked if everything was all right with the drink and Christina had looked at her, a skinny young woman with tired eyes and a ragged mop of black hair, and said, 'Oh, it was absolutely fine – it's me – I'm feeling so sick. I'm pregnant, you see.'

It was the first time she'd ever said the words aloud: she hadn't dared to with the first pregnancy, it had still been such early days. She'd beamed at Christina, this woman, this stranger. She'd nodded. 'I was just the same with my first,' she said, her accent heavy, guttural – Polish, perhaps, or Ukrainian. 'Couldn't keep anything down.' She hadn't looked old enough to Christina, but there it was, she was a mother, and she was looking at Christina and smiling, and Christina realised, in that moment, that she was almost a mother, too. She had graduated.

Finally, she was a part of that mysterious female sect: the pregnant woman, the mother-to-be.

She'd decided, that very afternoon, that they should decorate the nursery. White, with one wall grey – a warm grey, if such a thing were possible (it had turned out that it was). Across one corner, the corner in which they would place the crib, she would create a mountain range, just like one she'd seen online: a rising sierra made from masking tape and paint and an angled decorator's brush.

Ed had still been against it – said it was bad luck, too soon, they should at least wait until after the twelve-week scan – but when she'd threatened to do it herself anyway, he'd reluctantly agreed. It had taken them a weekend. They'd filled and scraped and sugar-soaped and primed and rolled. She'd ordered a cot online: new, a good one, the one that most Mumsnet readers recommended, though the baby would sleep with them at first, of course, she was going to order another crib for their bedroom, one that attached to the bed. They bought a changing table and a daybed, and Christina made her mountains: measured the tape, used the ruler and the spirit level, held the brush as steady as she could.

The room looked good. Even Ed couldn't deny it, though he was still reluctant, though he'd stood there on the Sunday evening, shaking his head, saying, 'I just hope we've done the right thing.'

Of course they had. That first bleed had passed without damage, and not been repeated; they'd had their early scan, they knew they were having a daughter, and that she was growing well. Eleven weeks, then twelve – almost into the second trimester, nearly past the danger zone. And look at how lovely it was: three white walls, one grey. A white crib. A daybed. A mountain range. In a few months, Christina would be sitting on that daybed with their baby in her arms, nursing, feeling the sweet weight of her, loving her even through the dead weight of her exhaustion, an exhaustion that she'd bear with gratitude because she was here now, wasn't she? She was here. This was her room. This was their baby's room.

Three white walls, one grey. The dry, musty smell of a room left unaired. Christina turned on the ceiling light, with its cloud shade; the bulb made the contrasts greater, the shadows sharper. There were fine traceries of cobweb in each corner. Dust on the skirting boards, the windowsill, the empty crib. She'd cut her finger building it. Ed had been in the kitchen making tea, the Allen key had slipped; she'd noticed only when a smear of red had appeared on the white post she was screwing into place. Red on white. A seeping stain. She'd tried to read nothing into it; she'd found a plaster, she'd wiped away the blood.

An omen, or no such thing. Just a silly accident. She didn't know. She didn't care.

She was standing in the middle of the room now. The ghost room. And she the ghost now, haunting this empty, silent space.

By day, there were conversations. Everybody had a view on what was happening, and what she should do next.

'Sort the divorce,' Jen said. 'What matters is you, and whether you still want to be a mother. It's not too late yet, Christina. Talk to the clinic. There are other ways.'

(*I know there are, Jen. I'm thinking about it, all right? I'm thinking it all through, or trying to, but I'm tired, I'm really, really tired.*)

'I've spoken to Joanna,' Emma said. 'She'll see you whenever you're ready. She agrees that it's very important that you talk to her, that you get the financial side of things sorted out properly, even if you go DIY for the divorce. There's too much at stake now.'

(*I'll give her a call, Emma. I will. I guess you're right.*)

'I can't believe it,' her mother said. 'I just can't believe that Ed would do this. You're still married, after all. Do you think you should fly over there, Christina? Fly over, and talk to him, and see whether you can't work something out? I mean, what do we even *know* about this woman? Do we even know she's telling the truth?'

(*Of course she is, Mum. For God's sake. You watch too much EastEnders. This is happening. My marriage is over, really over, like I told you it was, and we can't just stick our heads in the sand.*)

'A selfish man,' Dinah said. 'Selfish and immature. I knew it from the moment I met him. Wasn't he married before?'

(*He was, Dinah, and I know you did, and I can't disagree with you. Not right now.*)

She sleepwalked through the days, exhausted, feeling as if she were missing a layer of skin. Scraps of these conversations, all this advice, rang in her ears like fragments of familiar songs. In one moment one of them would ring louder than the others, and she'd seize it, settle on that as the best course of action; in the next, another would pick up the refrain, and she'd move with it, distracted, her skittish mind incapable of reaching a resolution: a fly buzzing against the windowpane, unable to find its way out.

Joanna wasn't at all what Christina was expecting. In her mind, she'd pictured someone brittle, hard-edged – lacquered hair, armoured in expensive tailoring – but this woman was younger than her, late thirties maybe, small and soft-spoken, wearing an ivory cardigan over what looked like a vintage tea dress, white flowers on a wash of pale green. Her office was chaotic: piles of papers, teacups, a pair of framed posters of Penguin book covers on the wall: *Swallows and Amazons*, *Pride and Prejudice*. Nothing like Emma's floor – Emma had met her in the lobby, brought her up, offered her a coffee in her office before taking her down to meet Joanna – with its floor-to-ceiling windows and ultra-modern furniture. In one corner there was a small woven basket of toys: a plastic tractor, a stuffed mouse, a copy of *The Gruffalo* just poking out behind the mouse's ear. For the children, Christina presumed: the children who sat in this room, transporting themselves off to other worlds while their parents dismantled the world they knew.

'I know,' Joanna said, taking the armchair as Christina settled on the sofa, 'it's a mess in here. I'm sorry. I keep meaning to tidy up.'

'I like it. I imagine it helps put people at their ease.'

'Perhaps.' Joanna smiled, adjusted her glasses, which sat a little lopsidedly across her nose. 'So Emma's told me something about your situation. But why don't you tell me exactly where you feel you are.'

How to sum it up; how to hold up the end of a marriage, with all its intricacies and silences and dark, unexplored shadows, for inspection? How to explain the exhaustion of failure, of wanting something so much, for so long, and having it slip repeatedly from your grasp? And now this: Ed's wish granted, his new start. Christina tried. She did her best. When she had finished, Joanna sighed and said, 'I'm sorry. That's really tough.'

Christina said nothing. She had slept very badly again; a curtain seemed to hang across her vision, gauzy and shimmering. It was almost pleasurable, in a way, tiredness. It was almost, like drunkenness, a way of padding the sharp edges of reality. And that could do with some padding right now, it really could.

'Here's the thing, Christina,' Joanna said. She was leaning forward, her expression sharpening. 'I don't work like the lawyers you may have seen on television. Most of us don't – the good ones, anyway. We don't exacerbate conflict, just to wring as much money out of people as we can. To be honest, if there's any conflict at all, it tends to come from the clients themselves. People are often very angry with each other, sometimes for good reason. But you don't seem angry, Christina. Are you?'

Christina sat back. The sofa was shallow, and not as comfortable as it looked. She sat forward again. 'Yes. No. I don't know.'

'Divorce is a horrible word, isn't it?' Joanna said after a while, her pale blue eyes sincere behind her glasses. 'There's a term we use here. We talk about an "elegant disengagement". A euphemism, perhaps, but one I find useful. It speaks to the fact that it's possible to keep a legal separation civil, simple, affordable. Especially, forgive me, when no property or children are involved.'

Silence. An eruption of laughter from somewhere out in the corridor: another department, Christina presumed, one that didn't involve raking over people's private pain.

'You said Ed was married before?'

Christina nodded. Joanna readjusted her glasses. 'And how did they manage things? Do you know?'

Christina nodded again. She'd met Hannah once, at a drinks thing early in her relationship with Ed; they'd stayed friends, of a sort, which had seemed incredible to Christina at the time. Hannah had never had children, as far as Christina knew. Some years ago, Ed had mentioned that she'd moved to Hong Kong. Perhaps Christina ought to get in touch with her on Facebook, ask if she wanted to form a club. *The Ed Macfarlane Ex-Wives' Support Society.*

'I think they did it themselves,' Christina said. 'Without lawyers, I mean.'

'Well.' Joanna smiled. 'I do, as I said to Emma, feel it's important to ensure that everything is neat and tidy. People don't often realise that, without a formal financial agreement – what the court calls a consent order – either party can be vulnerable to claims later on. But clients do sometimes prefer to sort the actual divorce themselves, to keep down costs. You can file online, either of you, once we've worked out the appropriate facts. I can help you with that. I'd say, from what you've told me, that the process would be pretty simple here.'

'Simple?'

'Yes. I'd advise that you agree between you that you be the petitioner, and that you divorce him on the grounds of adultery. You are separated, but you're still legally married. So I think, in the circumstances, even the most stringent judge would accept that.'

Christina nodded. The curtain shimmered in the breeze. None of it was quite real; none of it, she decided, was really happening. 'And the embryo we still have in storage? What are my options there?'

Joanna's smile slipped a little. 'Christina, you should know – and your clinic will confirm this, too – that both of you need to consent to continue with treatment. Ed can withdraw his consent at any time until the embryo has been transferred to the womb, although he will need to do it formally. If he does this, a twelve-month cooling-off period begins.'

'And after that?'

Joanna laced her hands together in her lap. Kindly, softly, she said, 'And after that, Christina, if Ed still doesn't consent, any remaining embryos will be destroyed.'

She took the train south, the grimy commuter service wheezing out of Victoria, crossing the river, passing the old power station, with its coterie of cranes, their red warning eyes blinking in the darkness.

Five o'clock, and already night had fallen. It was the middle of December now, just days to go until Christmas. She was going to her mother's; Ray was coming too, not for lunch, but for the evening, just a glass of sherry and a mince pie in front of the *Strictly* Christmas special – he didn't want to intrude, Sue had said, though Christina had assured her mother that he wouldn't be intruding. In fact, she'd have liked Ray to come; she preferred the idea of his company to another Christmas Day spent just the two of them, their old, long-standing trio lopsided, the gaps and silences too long, made too noticeable by the enforced festivities.

Perhaps she should have arranged to go to Dinah's – her aunt ignored Christmas, always had; Christina could have done so, too. Or she and Jen could have taken Leila and Gabriel out for lunch – a Chinese restaurant in Soho, maybe, paper hats and dim sum, walking through the empty central London streets while everyone else sat indoors stuffing their faces with turkey and bread sauce. But no – Jen was going to her parents', Emma's mother Lydia was coming to them, Christina was going to Carshalton. And it had to be better than last year, which they'd spent separately, she and Ed: he'd gone to Bath for Christmas, she to her mum's, both of them pretending that there was nothing remiss in this, nothing at all strange about a married couple preferring the company of others to their own little rubber-stamped unit of two.

The train rumbled on. Across the carriage, a child, perhaps five or six, lolled sleepily against her mother, clutching a glossy theatre programme. *Goldilocks and The Three Bears*. She mumbled something about Father Christmas – Christina didn't quite catch what – and the mother laughed, smoothed the daughter's hair away from her face, and said, 'You'll just have to wait and see.'

Christina turned away, watching the window: her reflection, her shadow-self, was superimposed over the narrow terraces, the blur of fence and glass and brick. She wouldn't think about what Ed was doing for Christmas: whether he, *they*, were staying in San Francisco, or coming to England. A new face at the big old farmhouse table, a pregnant woman from Milwaukee who, according to her Facebook profile (yes, Christina had looked her up online, though only the most basic information was public), liked running and French bulldogs. A woman with long, highlighted hair and eyes of indeterminate colour that were, in Christina's not exactly unbiased opinion, slightly too close together. She wasn't especially pretty. She looked nice. She looked like exactly the sort of woman Christina would chat to at a party, in a GP's waiting room. Brief eye contact, a shy twitch of a smile. *So how long have you known Emma and Pete? Yes, I think Dr Collins must be running late again.*

At Gipsy Hill she stepped from the train, paused to stroke the little black and white cat that haunted the platform – she wasn't a stray, had a collar and a Twitter account, just seemed to enjoy the station, all the attention, the toing and froing – and climbed the hill towards home. Passed her street, and carried on, unwilling to face the empty flat, the empty evening. She'd found Mal's walking group on Facebook; earlier in the day, on her way to meet Joanna, she'd had a notification on her phone – *Crystal Palace Walkers Christmas drinks! TONIGHT, The*

Wheatsheaf, 5.30 till close! Hadn't thought she'd go – she was so tired; surely she should get another early night, try to catch up on her sleep – but why not: it was somewhere to go, something to do. And she saw him sometimes in her mind, another of the shifting images conjured by her restless, unsleeping, small-hours brain. Ed, and Marianne, and her father, and yes, for reasons she couldn't quite begin to explain, Mal, the book man, the photographer. Not attraction, exactly – no, she wouldn't call it that – but something. Yes, something, though she had acknowledged this aloud to no one – not Jen, not Emma, not her mother or Dinah; not even, really, to herself.

The Triangle was busy: the Christmas lights were on, bright globes of light strung between lamp posts, the restaurants filled with early-bird families, the pubs spilling post-work drinkers out onto the pavements. The only one that didn't look packed was the Wheatsheaf, a small pub set back from the road behind a stretch of cobbles. She'd never been in before, had always found it a bit forbidding, with its peeling paintwork and luminous handwritten signs – *grolsch, £3.99!* – and the wall-mounted TV that always seemed to be on. She stepped inside. The usual smell of beer and dirty carpet and, faintly, something sweeter, spicier: *try our new thai menu!* a blackboard read, in that same handwriting, careful lower-case, a heart placed jauntily above the 'i'. Busier than she'd thought – most of the tables were full, but it didn't take long to see them, to see *him* – a group of ten or so, over in the corner, four round tables pushed together, crowded with pints and glasses of wine. Mal at the centre in his leather jacket and a Santa hat; he was talking to a woman on his left, laughing, sharing a joke. Christina hung back for a moment, staying close to the bar, suddenly shy; observing, too, the way that Mal seemed to exert a subtle magnetic draw, the way the others in the group appeared to lean towards him, to be listening to what he was saying, even as they were talking among themselves. Ed had been like that, too – charismatic, if not exactly handsome, at least not in a conventional way. But she was done thinking about Ed: she had to be, for God's sake, he was certainly done thinking about her.

Ziggy spotted her first. She was ordering herself a glass of wine, hadn't seen him under the table, but the dog, it appeared, had seen her: here he was, nosing her legs in greeting, then sitting staring up at her, tongue lolling, his tail thumping the carpet. She knelt down, leaving her wine on the bar, making a fuss of him, stroking his long black muzzle, the velvet hair between his eyes.

'Joining us, are you, book thief?'

She looked up: Mal. His face, watching hers under the bar's yellowish light. Smiling. His gaze warm. 'Thought I might, Santa.'

He did look ridiculous in that hat; both ridiculous and – the thought struck her quite suddenly – cute. No, that wasn't the right word: he was too crumpled, too frayed at the edges, to be cute. 'Good. Come on, then. Ziggy and I'll introduce you.'

The group shuffled round to admit her; names were given, smiles and greetings offered, glasses lifted to meet hers. A mixed bunch: three men including Mal, four women excluding her, various ages and ethnicities. South-east London in microcosm, she supposed; more were expected later, Mal said, the Facebook group had thirty members, though not all of them turned up to every meeting, every walk; this was the A-team, the solid core. 'Hardcore,' said the woman on Mal's left, the one he'd been joking with earlier. Angie, her name was; she looked vaguely familiar, cropped greyish hair, plum lipstick, a small silver ring through her left nostril.

'That's right, Ange,' Mal said. 'You are, anyway.' To Christina, he added, 'Angie's the fittest of all of us. Walked the South West Coast Path last year. Runs her own gardening business, too.'

'*And* the stall, Mal. Don't forget that. Perhaps our new recruit likes vintage clothes.'

Christina nodded. 'I do. But most of them don't seem to like me. They made women smaller in the 1950s, I think.'

Angie spluttered into laughter. 'You're right, love, I reckon they did. You're fine as you are, anyway. Gorgeous, isn't she, Mal?'

Her eyes were bright with mischief; Christina felt her cheeks colour. Mal, next to her, lifted his beer and said, 'I couldn't possibly comment.' And then a moment later, almost under his breath, so that Christina, afterwards, wasn't sure if she had heard him correctly, if he had even said this at all, 'Yes. Yes, she is.'

She stayed all evening. Stayed until the bar, and everyone in it, was swaying slightly, until she'd consumed five glasses of cheap Sauvignon Blanc and a few handfuls of salt and vinegar crisps, the foil packets split at the seams and shared among the group. She talked to Angie; she talked to Paul and Deanna, a couple in their twenties who'd recently moved to London from Leicester, had joined the walking group to meet new people. 'We weren't sure quite what to expect,' Deanna said. 'We thought it might just be a load of old blokes in walking boots. And there's a few of those – Mal, for one . . .'

Mal, catching this, turned and said, mock angry, 'Watch it.' Deanna grinned at him; Paul, lifting his beer, said, 'Only messing, Mal.'

'He's so great,' Deanna said to Christina, who stared at her, taking in her sweet, earnest expression, her Fair Isle Christmas jumper with its pattern of woven snowflakes and stars. Paul, the boyfriend, was wearing a similar one, in navy blue. She wondered if they always dressed the same, like siblings, like twins, or if they'd just put on the jumpers as a festive touch. 'Paul or Mal?'

Deanna laughed. 'I meant Mal. But Paul's great too, of course.'

But mainly Christina talked to Mal; sat close to him at the table, their knees almost touching, aware of him, of where he was and what he was doing, even when they were each in conversation with someone else. In the moments when just the two of them were talking he sketched a few bare details for her, the outline of his life so far. Childhood in Durham, mother a miner's daughter, father a factory worker from Pakistan; a misspent youth roadying for bands, trying and failing as a drummer, finding photography, trying and failing at that. His ex-wife, Karen, Australian, now living back in Brisbane with their twelve-year-old daughter, Annabel. 'Brisbane?' she said. 'God, I'm sorry, that must be hard.'

'It is,' he said, and was then absorbed back into a conversation on his other side. *You intrigue me*, she thought as he turned away, the words arriving with a startling, shining clarity. *You make me want to find out more.* But she enquired no further, afraid that Mal would expect her to respond in kind; and she didn't want to, not here, not now, not when the sharp truth of things was receding so nicely, when she was doing such a good job of forgetting.

The trouble was that Mal wasn't, it appeared, that kind of man – the kind more than happy to drone on about himself for as long as anyone would listen. 'What about you, anyway, Christina?' he said after a while, fixing her with his steady, enquiring gaze. 'I'm prattling on here. Tell me about you.'

'Oh,' she said, looking down at her empty glass, 'there's really nothing to tell.'

'That's never true.'

'No.'

He watched her. 'Fair enough, Christina. Keep your counsel. Another round?'

She shook her head. The group had thinned now, there were only the two of them and Angie left, and a man whose name Christina couldn't remember, wearing novelty reindeer antlers and apparently, from the snatches of conversation she could overhear, quizzing Angie about the best way to overwinter geraniums. 'I've had enough, I think. I should be getting back.'

'Want Ziggy and me to walk you?'

The dog, hearing his name, looked up from his sleeping-place under the table, fixed her with liquid beseeching eyes.

'No. No, thank you, that's kind, but I'll be fine.'

Mal shrugged. 'Fair enough. Get home safely. And hey – thank you for coming. I'm glad you did.'

'I'm glad I did, too.'

She met his gaze, was able, despite her drunkenness, to hold it for one second, two, three. Then turned, waving at Angie and the other guy, and walked out. It might just have been the wine, the strangeness of the day, the week, the month, the year, but as she closed the door behind her she felt disappointment settle over her: perhaps she should have said yes, perhaps she should have let Mal walk her home, with all that might have meant. Nothing, probably – they were virtually strangers, she hadn't done that kind of thing in years, and what was he going to do with Ziggy, anyway, tell the dog to sit in the living room and wait? (What *did* a single person with a dog do in such a situation? Leave it at home, surely.) No, she had done the right thing in refusing – she wasn't ready for anything, wasn't sure how she ever would be, couldn't imagine how Ed could do it, just draw a line under everything that had happened and start again with someone new. The thought exhausted her, an exhaustion greater than the tiredness that dogged her now, that made her want to lie down on the ice-cold pavement and sleep. And she would, when she got home, wouldn't she: she'd draw the duvet up over her head and dive down into sleep, pillowy and obliterating, for as long as her mind and body would allow.

Ten

Jen was throwing a party for New Year's Eve at the Arrow Dance headquarters in Bermondsey. A disused railway arch over which trains heading in and out of London Bridge still rumbled and shook; it had been the cheapest place Jen could find, back in the late 1990s, though the area had come up quite a bit since then. The adjacent arches had been taken over as artists' studios, a bakery, a jewellery workshop, rehearsal rooms; all of them still somehow – by the grace of good fortune and Network Rail – guaranteed a peppercorn rent. A cobbled courtyard formed a communal meeting space; there were benches, and bunting, and a van dispensing freshly ground coffee, and tonight, patio heaters, fairy lights, a trestle-table bar, a band strumming away in fingerless gloves from a makeshift stage.

'You really don't have to come on Monday, Chris,' Jen had said a few days before. They'd taken Leila and Gabriel to *The Nutcracker* at the Coliseum. Jen had wangled free tickets, she knew the choreographer and several of the principals. Classical ballet wasn't her thing any more, not now, but she respected it, she said, as an abstract painter might admire a fine draughts-man. And anyway, Leila loved ballet as well as football, she took weekly classes, was becoming, in Jen's words, 'a proper little bun-head'. Afterwards they'd taken the children for tea at Brown's on St Martin's Lane; they'd been sitting there, the children apparently absorbed in their respective fudge brownie sundaes, when Jen had raised the subject of the party.

Christina had sipped her coffee and said, 'Of course I'll come.'

Leila had looked up from her ice cream. 'Come where? What's happening on Monday, Mum?'

'New Year's Eve, darling. You're spending it with Grandma and Grandpa, remember? You can watch the fireworks on the telly, if you're still sure you want Grandma to wake you up.'

Leila nodded; across the table, Gabriel did the same. 'We *do*,' Gabriel said, saucer-eyed, and Leila added, 'I might stay up all night. I might not go to bed at all.'

'Oh God.' Jen met Christina's gaze, gave a mock grimace. 'Watch out, Mum and Dad. Watch out world.'

Christina loved observing Jen as a mother, always had. She'd seemed to take to it immediately, to find from the earliest moments this lovely lightness around her children, this sense of ease. There were routines and boundaries, but Jen didn't seem as fixated by them as other parents were, as Emma was: with Alfie, Emma had followed a draconian book that insisted on set times for sleeping and waking, times that had seemed rarely to coincide with Alfie's own desires. But what did Christina know, really, of the challenges of early motherhood? And Jen had somehow managed to continue to work, to create, from just a few months after each of her children had been born; they'd been easy births, both of them, her body had soon reacquired its lithe panther grace. Christina knew it wasn't as simple as that – Jen was more of a swan than a panther, really, gliding along on the surface while her legs paddled wildly beneath. And nobody, least of all Christina, could imagine that Jen hadn't struggled with being abandoned by her partner just a few months after the birth of their second child: who wouldn't, it had been awful,

Christina would have liked, at the time, to get hold of Ariel by the lapels and perform a primal scream into his ear. Still would, probably, given the opportunity, though of course he was still the children's father; of course there was that, even if he did little more for them now than send extravagant birthday gifts, and occasional postcards from the exotic places he visited on tour.

'Are you really sure,' Jen had said to Christina a few months back on one of their Tuesday-evening sessions on the sofa, 'that you know what you're getting into, proposing to go for this embryo transfer? I mean, what if Ed agrees, and it works, and you *do* have a baby? Are you really prepared to do it alone?'

'You manage,' Christina had said, and Jen had nodded, but slumped back against the sofa, rubbing the skin between her fine arched brows.

'Only just,' she'd said. 'Don't think, for a second, that I'd have let any of this happen if I'd been actually given a choice. Oh, I don't regret the kids, of course – how could I – but *this . . .*' Jen had shaken her head. 'I'm only just holding it together, C. I promise you. It could all collapse at any moment.'

Jen's words returned to Christina now, standing alone in a corner of the courtyard, waiting for Emma and Pete to return from the bar. *I'm only just holding it together.* The same words she'd have offered Mal the other day if she'd been braver. She'd sent him a text after the Christmas drinks, typing his number into her phone from the business card he'd given her, asking when the next walk was scheduled for, whether she could come along. Information she could easily have acquired from the Facebook group – she'd been fishing, really, emboldened by wine and exhaustion, testing for something: what, she wasn't sure. But his reply had made her smile – *I've checked with Ziggy, and he says you're fine to join us for our annual New Year's Day Hungover Stroll as long as you bring treats (biscuits for him, a hip*

123

flask for me). Blackheath to Greenwich, pub at the end, promise it'll be worth it.

They'd exchanged a few more texts since. Christina had asked for the starting point of the walk (more details she could have got from Facebook, but he hadn't pointed this out). Mal had wondered what she was doing for Christmas; she'd told him, he'd told her (up to Durham to see his parents, his sister, his sister's kids). On Boxing Day, he'd asked how the festivities had gone. *Fine*, she'd written, *everything was fine*. And several hours later he'd sent back, *Don't give much away, do you, book thief?* Then a photograph: Mal in the Santa hat and a matching jacket, a cushion stuffed under his belt, his dark stubble overlaid with a home-made cotton wool beard. Three children arranged around him, boys of various ages, wearing matching grins; Ziggy between them, serenely dignified in his canine approximation of a Santa suit. Mal's accompanying caption read, *See how my nephews love to humiliate us? Ziggy hasn't quite recovered yet. I'm not sure I have either.*

Christina took out her phone now, scrolled to the photo, wondered what Mal was doing tonight and with whom. He'd seemed quite pally with that woman Angie at the drinks – the one who had the clothes stall, ran the gardening business. But no, she hadn't thought ... . But then she hadn't really been ... Had she been? Was she now? For God's sake; this was hardly the time. She was a mess, her life was in pieces, and surely he couldn't find her attractive, nobody could, she was three stone overweight and the bags under her eyes had acquired bags of their own. Surely he hadn't said what she'd thought he'd said. *Isn't she gorgeous?* (To be fair, why would Angie have said something like that if they had that sort of relationship?) *Yes, yes she is.* No, surely she'd imagined it, she'd been so tired that night: tired and emotional, as the saying went.

'Here you go, love.' Emma, glamorous in another floor-length gown and sheepskin-lined aviator jacket, brandishing a jug of what looked like sangria; Pete behind her, carrying the glasses, David trailing behind him. Christina hadn't known he was coming. He seemed to be everywhere Pete and Emma went these days, the tag-along, the third wheel. God, was that what she was turning into? Was that what her own life looked like now: single, childless, middle-aged, always clutching at the hems of others' busier, fuller, more successful lives? 'Winter sangria, whatever that is. Smells like rocket fuel. Pete, give Chris a glass.'

Christina slipped her phone into her pocket, let her mind return to other things: to the evening, to the party washing around her, over her; absorbing her, carrying her along.

Later, she would tell herself that it only happened because of the email, but this was an excuse, really; perhaps it would have happened anyway, perhaps it was always going to happen, perhaps, in the end, she'd had only the illusion of choice.

It was close to 1 a.m. when she read the email. The first hours of the new year, blankly rolling, unwritten, the party still in full exuberant flow. Pete and Emma had left just after midnight – Isla was at a party in Forest Hill, they were collecting her, Emma had stopped drinking after one glass – but Jen was still here, dancing with Dan (he hadn't come to the show in the end, fool that he was, but it seemed she was giving him another chance); and Ana, her pregnancy showing now, but clearly not tiring her too much, she'd hardly stopped dancing all night. And David – yes, David, in his black and white tessellated party shirt (it had grown colder as the night deepened, the party had mostly moved inside, removed their coats, danced on). David, fellow survivor, matching spare part; David, with whom, in the months since her marriage had ended, Christina had found herself increasingly paired, thrown together like statues when the music stopped.

They'd been talking, drinking, dancing; perhaps he'd been flirting with her, perhaps she'd been responding a little. Perhaps it had felt good to have that frisson, that feeling that something could happen if she wanted it to; but she didn't, she hadn't, she hadn't thought she did. And then she'd gone to the loo and looked at her phone and there, at the top of her inbox, it had been.

Sender: *ed.macfarlane@bigbrightideas.co.uk.*
Subject line: *Next steps.*
Hi Christina, it's New Year's Day here – and I guess it is in London too now, just, though you're probably out having fun somewhere. I hope you are and that you don't read this until the morning.

Anyway, it's been a while since we met at the BFI, since we talked. I wanted to give you that time, I wanted to honour the space I'm sure you needed. But it is a new year now – a new start for us all, perhaps – and we do need to discuss the next steps in progressing the divorce. Marianne is into the second trimester now: we've just had the twelve-week scan. I don't want to pressure you, neither of us do, but I'm sure you can understand that there is a certain degree of pressure intrinsic to this situation, which isn't, believe me, one I'd have chosen – I really would never have chosen to hurt or disrespect you, Christina, in any way – but is nonetheless the situation in which we all find ourselves. So the suggestion I'd like to make is this . . .

It was Ed's sheer reasonableness, perhaps, that tipped her over the edge; his measured tone – *honour the space* – and the facts he imparted so calmly, reminding her of the truth she could not ignore: it was over, it was really over, Marianne was into the second trimester, they'd just had their twelve-week scan. Ed was having a baby, and it wasn't hers. She'd known all this, of course, she'd known for weeks, but the email thrust it forward in her mind; she stepped out of the loo, stumbled downstairs, wanting only to find her coat, a taxi, a train, whatever, she just needed to get home and close the door, the curtains, the night. And David found her, gibbering incoherently at the poor exhausted teenager manning the cloakroom; helped her put on her coat, stepped out into the courtyard with her, asked her what was wrong, stood there looking so solid and calm and rational: so much like Ed, it seemed to her then in her distress, though she'd never seen any resemblance between them before, not in the least. She told David about the email, and he listened, and he said he was sorry, that he'd had no idea Ed had met someone; Emma and Pete had said nothing to him. 'That must be very painful for you,' he said, and she nodded, and then he offered to drive her home; he had his car, like Emma he'd only had one drink, OK maybe two but they'd been small ones, he was perfectly safe to drive.

David's car was low and sleek; the interior was tidy, spotless, smelling of leather and glacier mints. She wasn't drunk – she'd only had a few glasses of the sangria, a flute or two of prosecco at midnight – she was wildly lucid and clear, watching the grimy, sodium-lit south London streets. *That must be so painful for you.* Yes: it was pain she was feeling, fierce and searing, and the terrible sadness of it all, the unignorable truth that it was over, the marriage, the IVF, the fever-dream of children, her own children, her own family. It was this that made her turn to David, when he pulled the car to a halt outside the flat, and say, 'Come in.' He hesitated: was she sure? She was upset, he didn't want to . . . Christina took his hand. It could have been Ed's hand she was taking, or Mal's hand, or the hand of any man at all; she just didn't want to be alone, she couldn't be, not tonight, not now. She looked at him. 'Please. Come in.'

He did. He went inside with her, and she poured them each a glass of wine, and they stared at their glasses, and there was a second in which nothing happened, in which they stood and looked at each other, in which either of them might have made a move towards the landing, the door. But they didn't. The move they made was towards each other; they were kissing, they were touching, they were each making a choice.

Afterwards, lying together in the bedroom, David said, 'It gets easier, you know, Christina, missing them. I promise you.'

She wanted to say, *It's not Ed I miss, really, or only sometimes. It's being married. It's making plans. It's having someone there with you, your person, your decision made. It's the mother I wanted to be, the children we couldn't have. That's what I miss. That's what I can't ever get back.*

But she didn't say any of this, not aloud. She said nothing. She lay there in the darkness holding David's hand, and then, when she could feel him succumbing to sleep beside her, she let go.

Eleven

Her mobile woke her, drawing her up roughly from a deep, blackout sleep. She lay for a moment as it squealed, disorientated. The room was grey and shadowed, the curtains closed, but the light creeping in around the edges of the window was pale, diffuse: morning. A shape beside her in the bed, a head on the adjacent pillow (she had removed the hammer). David didn't move; the noise coming from his half-open lips was low, breathy, not quite a snore. The phone stopped ringing. Silence; Christina closed her eyes. Then, after a second or two, the ringing began again.

'Jesus.' She sat up, swung her legs down onto the carpet. David still didn't move. Where was the bloody thing? Not on her bedside table, where she usually left it charging; she fumbled among the litter of clothes abandoned at the bed's foot, found it in the pocket of her jeans. Still ringing; she was just in time. Aunt Dinah's number, the landline; breathlessly, she said, 'Hello? Dinah? Is everything all right?'

The voice that responded wasn't Dinah's. 'Christina? This is Ruth, from the swimming club. Listen, Dinah's been taken to hospital. I'm at her house now, I came to pick her up for our swim. I think it had only just started – honestly it was so lucky, we only decided yesterday that I'd come and meet her, encourage each other, you know, buddy up. And imagine if it had happened in the sea . . .' Her voice faltered, then rallied. 'I'm sorry, Christina, I'm rambling. They're saying she's almost certainly had a heart attack.'

Comprehension came slowly to Christina, drip by drip. New Year's Day: the annual cold-water swim. 'God. Oh God. Which hospital?'

'Queen Margaret's, Margate. Petrina and I are driving there now.'

Christina showered, made toast and coffee, propelled by adrenaline. The clock on the kitchen wall said half past nine. She'd slept poorly again, even worse than usual, confused by what had happened, by what she'd allowed to happen, by the motionless shape in the bed next to her; she probably hadn't succumbed to sleep until sometime after five, but she felt bracingly alert, all senses sharpened. In the half-light of her room she dressed, threw more clothes into a bag: who knew how bad things were, how long she'd be away? Still David slept. When she'd finished packing, put in her laptop and her toiletries, she woke him, pulled back the curtains, offered him a mug of coffee (black: she didn't know how he took it, didn't have the time or inclination to find out). He sat up, took the mug, blinked at her through sleep-shuttered eyes. His hair was sticking up at all angles, a cockatoo's crest. She felt nothing for him but a residual pity – how old he seemed in the brutal greyscale light of morning, how tired; she was sure that to him she looked just the same. What had either of them been thinking? Who cared – there wasn't time for any of that now.

'You need to go,' she said, and his face puckered, wounded. 'No,' she said, 'it's not like that. I don't mean it like that. I mean, I do, but . . . I can't think about that, David. My aunt's had a heart attack. I need to go right away.'

She left David in the flat to shower, dress; it didn't matter if he couldn't double-lock the door, there was nothing in there worth stealing anyway. Perhaps she'd call Mrs Jackson later, ask her to turn the Yale; she had her number, was pretty sure her neighbour still held a spare set of keys. Her phone was almost out of battery. She set it to charge on the cable in the car, put on the radio: Radio 3, in Dinah's honour, and to ease the rhythm of her pulse. A New Year's concert, live from Vienna: Strauss waltzes and polkas, incongruously rousing. She turned off the radio, let silence carry her along the near-empty roads, through the unlovely jumble of Catford and the straggling suburbs, the houses ageing in reverse, grand Victorian residences giving way to 1930s semis that had perhaps once been desirable but now seemed to crouch, cowed, before the traffic's relentless onward push. A looping bend, and then she was there, joining the A2, the road that would carry her east to Kent, to Dinah, and whatever was happening to her, whatever she would find.

Somewhere close to Rochester – crossing the bridge, the Medway broad and silver, boats moored on the mudflats, church spires rising above the tiered terraces and bungalows – her mother called, the bright chime of her voice flooding the car. She'd been at a New Year's dance the previous evening; Ray had taken her to dinner first, at the nice Italian in Carshalton Beeches. 'Hello, darling! Just calling to wish you Happy New Year. How was your evening? Did you go to the party in the end?'

'I did, Mum, but listen . . .' She told her mother about Dinah, and a brief silence fell across the car, filled, for Christina, with all the resonances the information was surely conjuring for Sue. Dad, hospitals, illness, bad news. It was all there for Christina, too. Quickly, she said, 'I don't know any more than that, at this stage. Perhaps it's . . . Well, this woman Ruth didn't make it sound as if it was critical. But I really don't know. I'll tell you more as soon as I'm there.'

'Should I come, do you think? Ray could drive me.'

Her mother hated motorways, always had: Dad had been the driver, one of the hardest things for her mother since his death, Christina knew, had been forcing herself to get back behind the wheel. 'Why don't you hold off for now? Let me get there, see what's happening, how she is, and then we can take a view.'

The sound of her own voice surprised her – sensible, almost calm. Soothing, rather than being soothed. It had been a long time, she thought, since she had been the one asked for help rather than asking for it. Her mother rang off, eliciting further promises to call as soon as there was any news. She drove on in silence, the hedgerows thickening, fields rolling out to either side. A text: she caught an image of the message, flashing up on the phone's screen, sitting in its little windscreen holder. Mal. *No show! Shame. Ziggy's disappointed. Big night? Hope all's well. Happy New Year.*

The walk. They'd been meeting at eleven; it was half past now, she'd forgotten all about it, she hadn't even let Mal know. Ah well. What could she do? All was not well; she'd tell him later, he'd understand.

Dinah was in surgery when she arrived: an angioplasty, the doctor said, to unblock the coronary arteries, restore the flow of blood. 'Is it bad?' Christina asked her, and the doctor looked back at her, unblinking, as if assessing the degree of truth to offer. She was young, early thirties maybe, her blonde hair pulled back into a low ponytail: a junior doctor, presumably all the important ones were in theatre right now, saving Dinah's life.

'It's not great,' she said, 'but it could have been much worse. We'll know more soon.'

Christina was shown to a waiting room, a bland magnolia holding pen whose plastic seating, muted television and battered, ancient magazines could have belonged to any NHS hospital, anywhere. Petrina and Ruth were there, bravely sipping vending-machine coffees, awaiting the news only Christina could be given. They looked up as Christina approached. 'Still in surgery,' she said, and they slumped. 'Do you both want to get home? It's so kind of you to have come, but I'm sure you've got things you need to be doing, families waiting. If you leave me your numbers, I'll call as soon as I have any news.'

The women looked at each other; there was a general burbled exchange of apologies, but yes, if Christina was sure she didn't mind waiting on alone, they'd get back for now.

'Let us know if you need anything,' Petrina said, 'anything at all.'

Ruth stepped forward, placed a hand on her arm. She was swathed in a black padded coat, her hands bristling with rings. 'She's strong, our Dinah. Keep us posted, love, won't you? We'll all be worrying, the whole group. None of us will rest until we know how she is.'

After they left, Christina went downstairs to find the coffee shop, take a breath; the doctor had said there'd be no news for another hour at least, and she hated hospitals. Most people did, but her hatred was localised, specific: the smell of them, the chlorinated airless stink of illness, death, misery. Happiness too, she supposed: the maternity ward was here somewhere, after all, and there was surely good news everywhere – people loving each other, people going into remission, people thanking their

133

doctors, God, whoever they believed in. But that had not been her experience, not recently; not ever, perhaps. After they'd lost their daughter, after the 'evacuation of retained products', surely the ugliest sequence of words in the English language, they'd placed her in a private room in the antenatal ward, not the postnatal; but she'd still been able to hear them, the cries of the newborns, those high, kittenish wails. She'd sent Ed home without her and lain there for a day and a night, facing the window, listening to the cries of other people's children, until they'd allowed her to go home too.

Outside, she called her mother; hung up, called Jen. She was still in bed (the children were with their grandparents until dinner time), blearily hung-over; Christina could hear Dan moving around in the background, yawning, turning on the shower. 'Christ, I'm sorry,' Jen said. 'Do you need anything? Do you want me to come down? I'm sure Mum could keep the kids another night. I'm just not totally sure I'd be safe to drive . . .'

'No, no. Thanks, but no, you don't need to do that.'

Her finger hovered over *Emma* in her address book – she ought to call, Emma would be offended if she knew Christina had told Jen but not her. But she hesitated, thinking of David, not wanting to lie to Emma by omission, knowing obscurely, instinctively, that Emma wouldn't like it if she knew, that she would have something to say. Scrolled instead to Mal's text, tapped out a message. *So sorry I didn't make it today. My aunt's had a heart attack. I'm at the hospital in Margate now.*

His reply came a quarter of an hour later; she was back in the ugly waiting room, a weak, milky coffee warming her hands. *Oh no. So sorry to hear that, Christina. Hope she's OK. Let me know if there's anything I can do.* An odd thing for a near stranger to say, perhaps, she thought, reading the message over – just one of those platitudes, those phrases people handed out, small ceremonies, meaningless offerings. But even as she thought this, it struck her that Mal wasn't like that – that he was, in his stillness, his watchful calm, entirely sincere. He meant this – he wanted to help, though he hardly knew her, they hardly knew each other at all – and the fact that he meant it cheered her a little, even as she sat there, in a hospital waiting room on New Year's Day, waiting for news.

Dinah lay propped on thin white pillows, her eyes closed, her hair, unplaited, falling in Medusa coils across the pillowslip. Greyer than Christina remembered it; she had rarely seen her aunt with her hair down, it was almost always caught in a plait or a bun or a swimming cap. She looked older, too, as everyone did under the unforgiving glare of hospital lights: the lines on her face more deeply etched, the skin around her eyes purplish, like bruised fruit.

'She's sleeping,' Christina said to the nurse, 'should I come back later?'

The nurse shrugged. Not indifferent, Christina thought, only busy. A small, compact woman, neat in her uniform, already turning towards the next patient, the next task. 'You can sit and wait if you like. She'll be sleepy for a while. The anaesthetic.'

Christina sat. The nurse drew the curtain as she left, shrouding the bed and its accompanying plastic chair in a sudden bluish intimacy, muffling the intrusive bustling business of the ward: the murmurs of patients, the beeping and whirring of machines, an incongruous peal of laughter from the nurses' station. Time slowed here, Christina knew, it clotted and stilled, and then accelerated in sudden unpredictable bursts: a machine's tempo shift, life ebbing, life restored. They'd been grateful, really, Christina and her mother – Dinah, too – when Dad had been released from the hospital, even though it had really been an admission that nothing more could be done for him. At least at home, and then in his room in the hospice, they'd been able to make him comfortable, to shield him from the noise and administration of others' suffering. But there'd be none of this for Dinah, at least not now. The news was good, the operation had gone well, though she was not, as the doctor had put it – not the junior from before; an older man, a consultant, filled with the confidence of experience and status – 'entirely out of the woods yet'.

Christina sat. After a while – it might have been five minutes, or fifteen – her aunt's eyes tugged open; she blinked at the ceiling a few times, then saw Christina, gave a thin, tight smile. 'Sorry,' she said, 'about all this fuss.'

'Don't be silly. I'm just . . . Well. Glad that it wasn't worse. How are you feeling?'

'Sore. Stupid. Old. Like a very stupid old lady.'

'You're not that old.'

'Christina.' Dinah's glare, blue and fierce, was reassuringly that of her familiar impatient self. 'Don't sugar-coat things. Of course I am.' Then, softening a little, she said through a wry half-smile, 'But you agree with stupid.'

Christina smiled back. Her relief was giddying; she was awash with it, light as air. 'Of course not. How could this be your fault?'

'There are risk factors, aren't there?' Dinah said. 'I don't eat well. I'm prediabetic. I live on sugar and tea. Iris was always trying to get me to eat better, but since she's been gone I just haven't been bothered. It never seems worth it, cooking for one.'

'I know what you mean.'

They were silent. Christina thought of Iris: a bird of a woman, small-boned, delicate, short black hair, fine silver bracelets dangling from slender wrists. A poet, latterly; she'd published a few volumes, small local presses, Christina had seen her read once or twice, enjoyed the lilt of her voice (she was Welsh, and every phrase she uttered emerged like a song), the words' soft, plangent music. They'd met, she and Dinah, when each was almost forty, only a few years younger than Christina was now; the poetry had come around the same time, as Christina understood it, and behind this, beyond this, Iris had trailed a life, a marriage, a whole previous existence she had preferred not to discuss. She and Ed hadn't gone to the funeral: the date had coincided with some essential aspect of their third round of IVF. So much had been lost, it seemed to Christina now, to a timetable, a schedule that had not been of their own choosing.

Her aunt's eyes were closing again. Christina stood, said softly, 'You need to rest. I'll be here again tomorrow. I'm staying at your house. Ruth gave me keys.'

Dinah nodded, her eyes still half-shut. Blearily, she said, 'Sorry again for the fuss.' And before Christina could protest or reassure, she was deeply asleep, tugged back below the surface by some unseen hand.

Twelve

The doctors planned to keep Dinah in until at least the weekend. Christina decided to stay – Margate was far closer to Whitstable than it was to London, after all, and the state of her aunt's house shocked even her, never a clean freak at the best of times. At home, weeks could pass before she noticed dust or finger-smears; this had driven Ed, who prized cleanliness far above godliness, to distraction. But even Christina baulked at the layers of grime encrusting the surfaces of Dinah's kitchen and bathroom. The oven was a horror show; dust lay everywhere in grim little piles; there were dead spiders curled in ceiling corners, caught in the webs they had spun.

Dinah was starting to look brighter. Christina took in books for her from the pile on her bedside table, Ruth and Petrina and others from the swimming club kept up a rotation of visits. Between her own trips to the hospital, she cleaned, working room by room, dusting and vacuuming, attacking metal and enamel with aggressive caustic products she bought from the supermarket on the high street, having found almost nothing of use in the cupboard under Dinah's kitchen sink. Guilt clawed at her – had she really never noticed how bad the place was getting? – but the work, steady and containable, offering imme- diate tangible results, soothed her, too. London receded; with it went David, Ed's email, the flat, her work, all the decisions she needed to make, the things that needed to be done. All that could wait. For now there was this, the scrubbing and the mopping, the waking alone in the single room at the back of the house to the high shriek of gulls, the driving along the grey, cloud-heavy coast to the hospital, the daily processing of the minutiae of her aunt's condition, prognosis, planned discharge.

Her mother came to visit, driven by Ray, who, having never met Dinah, absented himself for a tactful stroll. Christina led the way to her aunt's ward, navigating the warren of the hospital like an expert, parsing its index of bodily malfunctions – *oncology, fracture clinic, rheumatology*. Sue was subdued; she also loathed hospitals, Christina knew, for the same reasons she did herself. They spent an uneasy hour or so at Dinah's bedside. Dinah had slept poorly, was becoming increasingly frustrated, which a nurse told Christina to interpret as promising – the more unwell a patient was, she said, the less of a fuss they tended to make. Then Ray collected them from the car park, drove to the seafront, took them to a restaurant he'd researched online, on a square that even, on a grey weekday in January, had an air of France about it, something loose and sophisticated and European: cobbles and awnings and tables spilling out onto pavements, warmed by the lurid orange glow of electric heaters.

'It's good of you,' Sue said after they'd ordered, 'to come down and look after your aunt like this. Stay with her, I mean.'

Christina shrugged. Ray, across the table, sipped his non-alcoholic beer (he never drank and drove), watching them both with his mild, blinking gaze. 'Well, not exactly *with* her, not yet. I've been cleaning the place, getting it ready for her when she comes out.'

Sue's lips pursed. 'I'm sure that's taking some doing.'

'It is. But I'm quite enjoying it, really.'

'Haven't I always told you,' Sue said, 'that cleaning can be therapeutic? You know what I was like after your dad died. Cleaned the whole place from top to bottom, over and over again. Honestly, the house was spotless.'

'I know, Mum,' Christina said. 'It really was.'

Ray nodded. 'I was the same after I lost Yvonne. You could have eaten your dinner off our kitchen floor. My kitchen floor, that is.' He smiled, sheepish. 'Takes a while to get used to someone being gone, doesn't it? A very long while. And then, somehow, you do.'

Christina and Mal were texting. He'd been back in touch later on New Year's Day, asking how her aunt was doing; she'd replied, and then he had, and now a type of epistolary conversation was elapsing, a bright thread woven through the plain, homespun weft of each day.

His texts were witty, made her laugh; he sent links to articles – reading material, he said, for while she was sitting around in the hospital – and photographs. Ziggy lifting a paw, apparently waving; a wall in his back garden, awash with flowers: honey-suckle, he wrote, winter-flowering, he couldn't believe he hadn't killed it, it was his ex who'd had green fingers, he was useless with all that. She asked to see some of his other photographs, his work. He sent her a link to a website: weddings mainly, reportage-style, brides smiling into champagne flutes, mothers of grooms clutching their hats; and a few other subjects, his own projects: hands, caught in grainy close-up, so that puckers and wrinkles became geographical contours; seaside towns out of season, lugubrious beaches, widescreen skies. *If you like English seaside towns in winter*, she wrote, *you should come to Whitstable*.

Cursed herself afterwards for her clumsiness; she hadn't meant it to sound like an invitation, not really, or at least she didn't think she had. But Mal had parried, or failed to notice. *Been there many times. They don't call it South London on Sea for nothing, do they?* And then she'd been almost disappointed: realised that she had, on some level, been hoping for him to offer to come and visit, perhaps suggest a walk, Whitstable to Faversham or Canterbury. She had, she could admit, already pictured it: the two of them walking under a high, pale sky, Ziggy running out ahead. There was so little she knew about Mal, really. There was so much she wanted to know.

And then, one evening – Friday; Dinah's discharge was scheduled for the following morning, assuming she had another good night – Mal called. The squeal of her phone caught her by surprise. It was eight-thirty, she'd just finished dinner and washed up, was sitting reading in the living room, now pristine, every cobweb and dust ball chased away. *Aunt Julia and the Scriptwriter* by Mario Vargas Llosa, drawn from her aunt's bookshelves: she'd left the IVF memoir at home, forgotten it in her rush to pack a bag. Her phone was in the kitchen; in her scramble to retrieve it before the call was missed, she failed to register the name on the screen. 'Hello?' she said. 'Who is it?'

A brief silence; then, 'It's Mal. Sorry. Am I disturbing you? I guess you don't have my number saved.'

'Mal?' Christina stood a little straighter; in the dim glass of the kitchen window, robbed of its ancient dirt earlier by a bottle of Windolene and a microfibre cloth, her reflection smiled back. 'No, I do. Sorry. I didn't see who was calling. I ran for the phone.'

'How big is your aunt's house?'

Her smile strengthened; she took herself and the phone back to the living room, the sofa. Closed the book with her aunt's leather bookmark, embossed with a gold image of Hever Castle. 'Tiny. I'm just really, really unfit.'

Oh God: that was basically like telling him she was fat. Not that he needed telling; he'd seen that for himself, hadn't he? She heard him laugh. 'So am I. Despite all the walking. I'm basically a slob.'

'I don't believe that.'

She paused, he waited. There were, she knew, two paths open to her now. She could defuse the small talk, imply that she was busy, let the conversation fizzle and die. Or she could – and this was, she decided as she weighed the two, the option she favoured – respect the fact that he'd taken the step of phoning, respond in kind, ask at least some of the questions for which she wanted answers. She took a breath, and said, 'So, now you've called – which is very nice, by the way, hello – tell me more about it. The walking. Starting the club. You said it helped when you were having a tough time. Why? How?'

Mal laughed again, a little nervously, it seemed to her; perhaps he was nervous, perhaps she was too, perhaps it was perfectly normal for two middle-aged people who didn't know each other very well to be nervous speaking on the phone on a Friday evening, when one has made himself vulnerable to the other, without any guarantee about how she might respond. 'All right,' he said. 'Proper talking, Christina. Gloves off. But I'm warning you – if I'm answering your questions, you're going to have to answer some of mine.'

They talked for three hours; it might have been longer, had her phone not run out of battery, had she not dashed upstairs to plug it in and seen, as it spluttered back to life, that it was almost midnight. She was sleeping better here, in the single bed in her aunt's tiny back room, but tiredness still plagued her: she was exhausted, talked out. *Sorry about that – my phone died*, she texted; after a minute or two, his reply said, *No problem – figured it was that rather than me boring you. Though that was always a possibility. Anyway, I'll let you go now. Ziggy says it's past our bedtime. To be continued, I hope. Night night x.*

It was the first time Mal had put a kiss; she lay in bed wondering what it meant, what any of it meant. Scraps of their conversation returned to her, replayed, reframed. He'd been divorced for five years now – brutal, a total shitshow, she'd moved back to Australia with Annabel and he'd failed to stop her, just hadn't had any fight left in him. Missed his daughter every moment of every day; tried to speak to her as often as he could on FaceTime, to fly over when he could afford it, stay in a hotel nearby, but it wasn't the same, of course it wasn't. 'I lost it for a while after they left,' he'd said. 'If there's any advice I can offer you' – she'd told him, by then, about her own situation, or at least as much of it as she could bear to relay – 'it's to try to keep it as civilised as you can. Really, if you don't hate each other now, you'll only end up hating each other by the end.'

She'd nodded, though of course he hadn't been there to see. 'Funny,' she'd said. 'That's the exact word Ed uses too.'

'Which one?'

'Civilised.'

'Well, he's right. Though it's far easier said than done.'

'Sure is at the moment.'

'Well, of course. You've been through a lot together. But you don't hate him, do you? Not really. You hate what happened, but you don't really hate *him*.'

She thought about that now, weighed the truth of the statement. *You don't hate him, do you?* Ed, over there in America, with Marianne, expecting a child, the one thing she wanted, the one thing she couldn't have. There was no way Ed would agree to her going ahead with the final treatment now, no way she would ever ask him. So where did that leave her? She could return to the clinic, try again alone; but how long would that take, and how would she afford it? Useless to think of other options: she was forty-four this year, she would never get pregnant without medical intervention, barring a miracle, and even if she did meet somebody new, who would be crazy enough to go on that journey with her now, to start the whole thing from scratch? She wouldn't ask it of anyone; no, it was better to learn to accept that that part of her life was closed, that motherhood was no longer open to her, not in the way she ached for, as the flesh-and-blood mother of her own child. Impossible, perhaps, to explain it to someone for whom children had come easily, or who was happy without children – many were, of course; Christina knew this, it wasn't that she considered a childless life as somehow less than, as devoid of meaning, just that it wasn't the life she wanted, for which she had fought so hard. Nobody wanted to think about failure, did they, about trying for something with all your heart and energy and faith and falling short. Failure was a whisper, a coda, an afterthought.

'I get it,' Mal had said when she'd tried to explain this to him. 'It's a kind of grief. Grief for the children you wanted, for the life you can't have. I know I have Annabel, and she's wonderful, but I think I grieved for a long time, too, after they moved to Brisbane. For the dad I'd wanted to be, you know? For the life I'd thought we were going to have together, the three of us. The hardest thing, I think, after something like that – after losing everything – is trying to work out what comes next.'

Christina still couldn't believe that she had talked about these things with Mal, opened up in a way she rarely had with anyone other than Jen and Emma. It was the lack of history between them, the blank slate, that had made it possible, perhaps; or just something in the way he'd asked questions, listened so carefully, drawn her out. 'Have you thought about adopting?' he'd even asked her, not long before her phone had died. 'Or fostering? My cousin and her husband are foster-parents, up in Newcastle. It's amazing, really. They've had some great kids.'

Her voice, replying, had been careful, small. 'I've thought about it. Ed and I did talk about it. I'm not sure how it works, now that I'm . . . single. Soon-to-be divorced. And I've got to move out of the flat soon. The tenancy agreement's up this month.'

'Well. Even so, I could talk to my cousin, if you like. You could have a chat. Only if you'd like to.'

'Maybe. Maybe, thanks. That's kind.'

She lay there now in the darkness, thinking about how it would be to have that conversation: to open up again to some-one else she didn't know, to the cousin of a man who was himself more or less a stranger, but was perhaps becoming less of one, by the minute, by the hour, by the day.

Dinah was tired when she got home. The journey from the hospital – their slow passage from the ward to the car park, Dinah clutching Christina's arm; the drive, Dinah dozing in the passenger seat, Christina watching her speed, taking every bend and corner as gently as she could – had exhausted her, she wanted only to sleep.

'A bath first, perhaps?' Christina said. 'I could run it for you, if you like. Wash off the hospital.'

'Tomorrow.' Her aunt was firm. Christina carried her bag up-stairs (she'd brought a few of Dinah's things to the hospital from home). Under Dinah's direction, she drew out clean pyjamas from a drawer – man's pyjamas, white with a fine blue stripe, fraying at the cuffs – and stepped out onto the landing to give her time to undress.

'Are you sure you can manage?'

The voice that returned through the closed door was stern. 'For God's sake, Christina. I'm not dead yet. I'm perfectly capable of removing my own clothes.'

Christina smiled. At discharge, the nurse filling out the forms had called Dinah a character, said she'd kept them all on their toes. 'Oh, let's not beat about the bush, dear,' Dinah had said. 'I'm a cantankerous old crone, and we both know it.'

'Believe me,' the nurse had offered back, 'I've seen worse. Now take care, Miss Lennox, won't you? Eat well, limit your alcohol intake, and certainly no swimming in the sea. Not for a good while.'

'Will you miss it?' Christina said now, returning to the room, helping her aunt into bed, drawing the duvet up over her (fresh, smelling of fabric conditioner and clotted tumble-dryer heat; she had washed and dried all the sheets and towels in the house). 'Swimming, I mean.'

Dinah was settling into her nest of pillows. Her hair, tugged into a low, loose bun, was lank; Christina would help her wash it when she took her bath, if a shower felt like too much for her. She had washed Dad's hair once, when Mum had been sick with the flu; this was close to the end, when he'd still been at home, before he'd gone into the hospice. Sat him in a chair before the basin, tipped his head back, poured warm water from a measuring jug over his soft, still-dark pelt of hair; tried not to let the water trickle across his face, tried not to look at how sallow his skin was, how yellow and waxen: how unlike himself he was, as if a part of himself was already absent, elsewhere.

'Yes, I'll miss it,' Dinah said. 'But if I spent every day sitting around making a catalogue of the things I miss, I'm not sure I'd ever get out of bed. I'm not sure any of us would.'

Downstairs, Christina tidied the kitchen, emptied the ancient dishwasher. Put the kettle on for tea, then stood drinking it, leaning against the counter, watching a robin settle on a garden chair: his quick bobbing movements, his clawed feet gripping the wood. A sense of lassitude came over her, a mid-afternoon emptiness, blank, hollowed out. Her aunt was home, she had made a full recovery, the doctors were pleased with her, had pronounced her strong as an ox. Christina was reaching the limit of her usefulness; she'd stay until the following weekend, do the shopping and cooking, drive her aunt back to the hospital for the first of her cardiac rehabilitation sessions (Dinah was under strict instructions not to drive for another week). But after that, her return to London was non-negotiable: there were things to be done, she could ignore them no longer, and the knowledge of that, the sheer exhausting checklist of administrative processes, fell across her heavily now, drinking her tea, watching the robin rise and dart and disappear from view.

A walk: her father's answer to everything, Mal's too. She'd go down to the high street, get a few things from the supermarket, maybe a quick stroll by the sea. She found her coat, her bag, her aunt's spare keys. Retrieved her phone from upstairs, where she'd left it, on Dinah's chest of drawers, gentle, soft-footed, not wanting to wake her. Dinah was sleeping, her mouth half-open, emitting a low, grumbling snore. Christina closed the door as quietly as she could, padded back downstairs. Glanced at the phone's screen, unexamined since they'd left the hospital.

Two texts. One from Mal. *How's this for a plan? A walk tomorrow, Whitstable to Herne Bay. I've mobilised the troops. Meet at the harbour at 10 a.m.?*

Another from a number she didn't have saved in her phone. *Christina, it's David. How are you, and how is your aunt? I really hope she's doing OK. I'd love to see you again, if you would. A drink, maybe? Let me know when you're back in the city.*

Christina stood for a moment in the dim hallway. She'd hardly thought of David in the days since New Year's Eve: everything that had happened that night seemed dreamlike and insubstantial, not quite real. Surely David didn't think it could have been the start of something? Or perhaps he did; perhaps she had been selfish, thoughtless, allayed her own distress without paying the slightest attention to his own. She closed his text; she'd deal with it later, find some kind way to rebuff his suggestion, a way that left his dignity intact. Then to Mal she wrote, unable to keep the smile from breaking across her face, leavening the gloom, *Yes. Great plan. Thank you. I'll see you there.*

There were five of them down at the harbour in the morning. Mal, of course, taller and more substantial, somehow, than she'd remembered, his leather jacket exchanged for a thick padded coat, walking boots, a woollen hat, pulled low across his ears. 'I know,' he said as they exchanged greetings, shy suddenly after the intimacy of their phone calls, their texts, neither of them quite meeting the other's eye. 'I look like a dustman. Don't laugh.'

'I won't,' she said. 'No Ziggy?'

He shook his head. 'He's at home today. He'll be furious when I get back, but he's a bit lame – nothing serious, I don't think, but he had a thorn in his paw the other day, his foot still seems sore. I'm not sure he'd have gone the distance.'

'Poor Ziggy,' Christina said, and was then quickly absorbed into the business of introductions, or reintroductions. Angie was there, and Paul and Deanna, and another man named Stuart, older than the rest – in his sixties, Christina guessed, heavy-lidded, owlish, blinking at her from behind round wire-framed glasses. He stepped off briskly, leading the way. Mal fell into step with him and Paul and Deanna followed, leaving Angie and Christina to bring up the rear.

'You are honoured, love,' Angie said as they set off, passing the black-stained huddle of harbour buildings: a fish shop, an oyster restaurant, a kiosk dispensing freshly ground espresso. 'Mal doesn't often change the route at the last minute.'

Christina kept her gaze on Paul and Deanna: their twin out-lines, hers a foot shorter than his, both of them wearing proper walking gear, waterproof jackets and sprung-soled shoes. She must look an amateur in her winter coat and ancient trainers, the best she could find among the clothes she'd brought from London. But no matter. 'Where were you meant to be going?'

Angie turned to look at her; Christina, turning too, caught her quick, knowing smile. 'Stuart favoured Box Hill. He likes to take the lead. I think he's a bit put out.'

'Is he? I'm sorry. It was Mal who . . .'

Angie waved a hand. 'Sure, course it was. It's all good. Who doesn't love a winter walk by the sea?'

They continued past the beach huts, the rising grass-topped slopes; to their left, the tawny shingle stretched to meet the water, which was calm today, a stippled pewter sheet. Conversation came easily as they walked, keeping the formation they'd fallen into at the harbour; Mal made no move to turn back, join them, and Christina told herself that she wasn't disappointed, focused on talking to Angie, who had, she said, been one of the first people to respond to Mal's Facebook post asking if anyone locally was interested in joining a walking group. They'd already known each other from the market, and Angie had been having a rough time: her daughter (she didn't mention a husband, a partner, anyone else) had recently left home for university. The house had been so quiet without her, too quiet. The walking had helped: there was something, she said, about just putting one foot in front of the other, about setting yourself a target, however small – a five-mile walk – and completing it in friendly company.

'I can understand that,' Christina said. A pause, and then, 'What's she doing now, your daughter? Does she still live in London?'

Angie shook her head; her earrings chimed and jangled, twin silver pendants in the shape of icicles. 'Madrid. She did Spanish, went there for a year, fell in love. I miss her like crazy, but what can you do? I go out as often as I can.'

On they walked, out of Tankerton and towards Swalecliffe, the others moving on ahead, metres opening up between them. It wasn't long before Angie said, as Christina had known she would, 'What about you? Any kids?'

'No. No, sadly not. We . . . tried, my husband and I, for a long time. IVF. It didn't go our way, in the end.'

That was the sum of things, really, wasn't it? She was getting better at telling people; she was finding it easier to say the words aloud. She could feel Angie studying the side of her face. 'I'm sorry. That's rough.' Christina nodded, and Angie said, 'You're married, then?'

'I am. Not for much longer. We're separated. He lives in America now. We're divorcing. We just need to . . . get things off the ground. I have a solicitor, just for the financial side of things. We'll do the divorce ourselves – she's come up with this plan.' Christina sighed. 'To be honest, I don't think either of us has the money to do it any other way.'

Angie was quiet for a moment. Then she said, 'You still get on, then? Well enough to sort it out yourselves?'

'I think so. We don't . . . There aren't kids involved, of course, and we don't own a house, we spent all the savings we had on IVF. We kept our own bank accounts. He's been paying half the rent on our flat, just for now. I'll have to move out, that can't continue. But we don't . . . Financially, I'm not sure there's that much to sort out. The solicitor's just there, she says, to set it down on paper, present it to the court.'

'Emotionally, though, it's not that simple, is it?'

'I don't know. Maybe. He's met someone else already. She's pregnant, actually. So I . . . Well, it's not as if there's any question about whether it's over.'

'Fuck me.' Angie stopped walking, put a hand on Christina's arm. Her eyes, on Christina's, were fierce, sincere. 'That's hard, love. I'm so sorry.'

Christina shrugged. 'Thanks. But it's not . . . I'm OK. At least I think I am. It just feels as if everything's fallen apart, and I don't know how to put it back together. Nothing looks the way I thought it would. I'm forty-three, my marriage is over. I don't own a house, I don't enjoy my work any more, I don't earn enough to get a mortgage on my own.' She faltered, hating the sound of her own voice. Complaining, whining. Who wanted to hear all that? 'I mean, I know I'm lucky really, there are plenty of people far worse off than me.'

'Don't do that,' Angie said sternly. 'Don't feel you have to make excuses. Yes, you're not starving or living on the streets. But that doesn't mean you haven't suffered.'

Quietly, into the wind, Christina said, 'I lost two babies. One at seven weeks, one at twelve. I wanted them so much. I miss them. Is it crazy to miss something that was never really there?'

Silence. Angie reached across the space between them, took Christina's hand in hers. She felt the pressure of the other woman's rings against her skin. Her touch, so unexpected, seemed to transmit a tangible current, an electrical pulse. Angie squeezed her hand, let go. 'To be honest, Christina, children can be a fucking pain in the arse. You get fat, you never sleep, they take all your time and your money. My friends without kids are the happiest people I know. You have to laugh, love, in the end. You have to. What else can any of us do?'

Christina looked at her. Angie was grinning, tipping into laughter, and Christina laughed with her; they laughed together, there on the cliff path, between the sea and the sky, until the other walkers out ahead turned to watch them, staring, wondering aloud – Mal's voice, drifting along the path towards them, carried on the air – what could possibly have been so funny.

They caught the train back from Herne Bay. It was turning colder, an icy wind rolling in from the sea, and nobody had the energy for the five-mile return. Anyway, the others were going on to London; they'd all taken the train out together, mostly they tried not to drive to an out-of-town walk, saving petrol, doing their bit. Christina went with them; Whitstable was only one stop away, so she stayed standing by the doors while the others found seats. Mal stood with her.

'Sorry,' he said in a low voice, 'that we didn't get much time to talk.'

'That's all right. Thanks for arranging things, bringing the group out here. I had fun.'

He smiled. She noted, perhaps for the first time, that he seemed to smile with his whole face: eyes, teeth, even eyebrows.

It made him look younger, puppyish, even. An overgrown puppy with a grey-black beard. Well, they did say that owners looked like their dogs. 'I hoped you might. How's your aunt doing?'

'Very well, I think, considering. The doctors all said she'd been very lucky. She's tired. She looks older, too. Diminished, somehow. She has to make some changes. She's not allowed to swim, not for a while. Not in the sea, anyway.'

He nodded. 'She'll find that hard, I imagine. She sounds like a tough one.'

'She is.'

Christina could feel Angie watching them. Stuart was beside her, talking about tide times; across the aisle, Paul and Deanna lolled together, her head against his shoulder, eyes closing. Christina met Angie's gaze; the other woman smiled, as if in encouragement, and then looked away.

The train was drawing to a halt; the blur of tree and brick and pylon stilled, came into focus. 'This is me,' she said, reaching for the button, calling out her goodbyes. Mal stepped forward with her, as if he were also leaving the train; for a wild moment she wondered whether he was going to, but no, he only leant forward as she descended, said quietly, 'It was really good to see you, Christina. Can we talk again soon?'

'Yes,' she said. 'Yes, I'd like that.' Then the doors closed and the train moved off, carrying him, carrying all of them, away.

Thirteen

Dinah was rallying well; the doctors were impressed. Her GP called twice, checking in, and Christina drove her back to Margate for the first of her cardiac rehabilitation sessions. Gentle exercise – 'aerobics for fatties and the ancient', Dinah called it – followed by a group seminar on diet and heart health. 'The man's a child,' Dinah declared of the nurse leading the seminar, 'he's barely out of nappies.' Christina met him, collecting Dinah; he was, by her estimation, about twenty-five. A smooth-skinned, smiling man named Lesley – he wore a badge – of apparently infinite patience. 'Thanks for your participation, Miss Lennox,' he said brightly as Christina escorted her aunt from the room. Dinah gave a queenly wave, turned to Christina and said, not particularly quietly, 'Thank God that's over. Can we go somewhere for tea and cake now, please?'

Her aunt's diet, Christina was discovering, consisted primarily of cake, tea, toast and the occasional omelette: Iris had been the cook. Christina wasn't sure what Dinah had done about cooking in the decades before she'd met Iris; that portion of her aunt's life was obscure to Christina, defined only by broad brushstrokes, hardly more illuminating than a curriculum vitae. Her cleverness had carried her from the unhappy house in the Kentish fields – the angry father, the lost mother – to university, a first-class degree at Oxford and her PhD and research career at Canterbury; though for most of it she had travelled, exploring cultures and ways of living, doing what Christina supposed an anthropologist must do. The tiny house was stuffed with mementos from almost every continent – Christina had dusted most of them herself over the last week – though Latin America dominated. This was where Dinah had spent much of her time: she was fluent in Spanish and several indigenous languages. Iris had also loved Latin America, had spent some time living in Brazil and Argentina; they'd met at one of Dinah's public seminars, on male culture and identity in the Argentine Pampas. This, and Iris's exquisite cooking, and her gentleness – Dinah, in her company, had seemed to soften, her hard edges planed away – and her keen, clear-eyed intelligence formed more or less the limit of Christina's knowledge of Iris. She'd had the sense, from her earliest understanding of the woman whose role in her aunt's life was never formally ascribed – neither to her, nor, Christina suspected, to anyone else in the family, even her father – that this limit was deliberate, and that any associated silence was to be respected.

This Christina had always done. But something – perhaps sleeping each night, better than she had in London, in the room that had been hers when she stayed here as a child – was opening an unplumbed vein of curiosity about Iris, about her life with Dinah and her life before. The small white bookcase in her room; the box of toys, long vanished; the selection of children's books – *Grimms' Fairy Tales*, *Black Beauty*, *Anne of Green Gables*, old stories speaking comfortingly of the distant retreated past – now gone, replaced by weighty academic tomes. Dinah hardly ever talked about Iris now, as she still avoided, too, the subject of John. A new frustration was rising in Christina with each day she spent in such close proximity to her aunt, two lone women rubbing along in a shared space: was this really, she asked herself, how losses were to be borne, as absences, silences, gaps in a conversation, never to be filled? Was this how it would be, now on, with Christina, too? Was this why she hadn't yet replied to Ed's email: this blasted inherited reticence, this inability to name a thing for what it was, and in doing so dispel at least a portion of its power and its pain?

'Talk to her,' Jen said when they spoke late on Tuesday; Christina, feeling guilty about not having been able to do her usual school pick-up, had called to see how Jen had managed without her. Apparently Emma's Sarah had been able to step in, had insisted it was no trouble to drive on to Wilberforce Primary from Alfie's prep. 'Just open your mouth and ask. What's the worst that can happen?'

'She bites my head off, I guess.' Christina was semi-whispering; she was on the sofa in the living room, her aunt upstairs in bed, she suspected not yet asleep. 'Or worse. It's just not how things are in my family. We don't really talk about things. We've always been this way.'

'Yes, well' – Jen was wry – 'I'd say that's a fair part of the problem, wouldn't you? Though I envy it in some ways. All my lot ever do is talk. It's exhausting. If my mum asks me one more time when I'm going to sort my life out and find a proper father for the kids, I'm going to scream.'

'She's not still going on about that, is she?'

'She asked me on Sunday. First time in a while, to be fair. I almost told her about Dan, but it's still early days, as you know. And it's hard to call Mum out on it. Not when she and Dad do so much for me, for us. All the childcare. I couldn't do any of this without them, as you know. I just couldn't manage.'

'I know.' Christina was silent, contemplating the enormity of the logistical challenge that was Jen's life as a working single

157

mother of two. All that activity, that busyness, that jigsaw-piecing. Christina had too much time, Jen not enough. There had been times, through all the trying, the failing, that she had resented Jen for all that she had, despite Ariel's defection, despite the difficulty of it all; she had resented Jen for a while, almost as much as she had Emma, and the knowledge of it now flushed her cheeks, brought a knot to her throat.

'Have you spoken to Emma recently?'

Jen's tone was neutral, but Christina sat up straighter, her senses sharpening. 'Not since New Year. Why?'

She could hear Jen rolling a cigarette, the pinch and crease of smoking papers. In a minute, Christina knew, Jen would step outside into her scrappy London garden and light it, lean back against the wall and close her eyes, folding herself deep into the moment, that rare fragment of alone time in which she had nowhere to be but there, no other needs to answer but her own.

'I'd give her a call if I were you,' Jen said. 'Don't tell her I said anything. Just talk to her. Talk to your aunt, too. And David, maybe. Put the guy out of his misery: he's clearly thinking this one-night thing was going to be something more. As for Ed, well . . . You can make him wait a bit longer, perhaps, but why? What are you gaining? Nothing's going to change, is it? It's time to deal with things, C. You can't stay in limbo forever, treading water.'

Jen's words played over and over in her mind. *It's time to deal with things*, C. Trust Jen to speak plainly, to name things for what they were. Jen was always honest, sometimes brutally so:

it had been Jen who'd told her, in those dark weeks after Ed had left, that she agreed with him, that she didn't think going back for the final treatment was a good idea.

It had been a week or two after their day in central London, the cinema and the Savoy, distraction tactics while Ed had excised half their things from the flat: that time when Christina had stayed with Jen, and then with Emma, shuttling between the two. Her own flat was half-filled, silent, empty of life; she couldn't bear to stay there, not for more than a night or two at a time. It was Jen, eventually, who'd suggested she come over, spend the day with her – she'd dispatched Leila and Gabriel to Emma's; Sarah was taking the children to the city farm. Maybe they could go out and buy some stuff, Jen said, if Christina wanted to: try to reclaim the flat, make it her own. Christina had agreed, and they'd gone up to the Triangle together, chosen a few things – cushions; a set of wine glasses; a new duvet cover; a print Jen had insisted on gifting her, a bare monochrome image of a hand, fingers crossed, bearing the words *Things will get better*. But mainly, they'd sat in the garden – long neglected, overgrown – and talked. And that was when Jen had said it: that really, the marriage was over, the treatment was over, it was time to let go of it all; Jen knew how hard it was, but it was time. 'You couldn't have gone through another round,' Jen said. 'It would have broken you, C.'

Christina had wanted to say, *I'm already broken*, but she hadn't. Perhaps it wasn't true. She was coping: struggling, perhaps, but coping, as she always had. Another soft summer evening – it had been so fine, the previous summer, so incongruously lovely, so cruelly detached from the sour, overheated solipsism of her mood. The two of them sitting in the garden, drinking rosé out of her new tumblers, dark recycled glass, heavy in the hand.

Christina had nodded, and closed her eyes, knowing there was nobody else in the world – not her mother, not Emma, not even Ed, who had said many things to her by now, many things that had wounded her, as she had wounded him in turn – who would speak to her like this, who would dare to, and nobody else from whom she would tolerate the truth. For that was what it was, she'd known it then. It was all over, she had to let go, she had to move on. And she'd felt a kind of deep, wordless peace, sitting there in the garden. She remembered it now, all these months later: there'd been a resolution within her in that moment, an acceptance. Her idea, her mad, grief-crazed plan – speak to Ed, persuade him to let her go ahead alone with this last treatment – had come later, and Jen had disliked it, she knew she had. She hadn't actually put this dislike into words, but Christina had been able to read her doubt, her concern, in every gesture, in every word she hadn't said.

And so she heard, again and again, her friend's fresh honesty – *you can't keep treading water*. She thought of her father's stoicism, his brave acceptance. *It's all right, I'm comfortable*. She thought of her mother, scanning the pub for Ray, the smile creeping across her face as their eyes met. *We . . . get on, I suppose. Enjoy each other's company*. She thought of her aunt, pale in the hospital, eyes closed, hair spread across the pillow. She thought of endings and beginnings, of grief and loss; of the whole cycle of things, and the way change could start with something tiny, a seed, a thing as simple as a word spoken, a question asked, an answer given. Cogs moving within cogs, wheels turning. A key turned in a lock, and a door pushed open.

She texted David back.

Thanks for getting in touch. New Year's Eve was great, but I don't think it's such a good idea for us to meet up again. I'm sorry. I've been something of a mess, as I think you know – well, it was pretty obvious on New Year's Eve – and I'm not sure I thought things through. I don't know whether I was really thinking at all. If I led you to believe it could be something more, then I really am sorry. I know you've been through a lot, too. Take care, C x.

Then she deleted her message from the brief exchange between them, determined not to wait for his reply.

She called Mal. They'd texted a few times, but hadn't spoken since the walk on Sunday. It was Thursday now, early evening; Dinah was resting upstairs, the fish pie Christina had made for dinner warming in the oven. She was sitting on the bed in her tiny room, looking out through the small sash window over her aunt's yard, the back walls of the terrace beyond, all of it still and shadowed under the early winter dark.

'Good to hear from you,' he said. 'I'm still on the stall.'

'Oh. Sorry. Is this a bad time?'

'It's all right. No one's around. I'm packing up.'

'I just wanted to say hi. So, hi.'

'Hi.' She could hear him smiling. 'How's things? How's your aunt doing?'

'Well, I think, considering. The doctors seem pleased. She's doing this cardiac rehabilitation thing at the hospital. She can drive again from tomorrow. It's amazing, really, how well she's recovering.'

'That's wonderful. Really.'

'Yes. I'm back this weekend. Saturday, probably.'

'Right. That's good.' A rabble of sounds at his end: raised voices, cursing, a heavy thud. 'Sorry, it's a madhouse here. One of the guys is moving new stock in. Maybe we can talk later?'

'Sure. Whenever. That would be good.'

Hanging up, she found herself picturing Mal's face: the shabby glamour of it, the creases and puckers, the dark curls. The tall, solid shape of him, bending as he packed away the crates of books, did whatever he needed to do to close up for the day. What was this? She didn't know yet. Maybe it was nothing, just a friendship, two battered old tugs finding harbour in adjacent berths. But she was still smiling. She called her aunt, telling her it was time for dinner, and then went downstairs to serve.

Later, she wrote to Ed. Hit reply before she lost her courage, wrote down the words that came.

Hi. I'm in Kent at the moment: Aunt Dinah had a heart attack, she's all right now, thank God. I'm sorry for my silence. It's been a lot to take in.

I'll do it, Ed. I'll sort out the forms, get my solicitor moving on the financial side of things, such as they are. Her name's Joanna, she works with Emma. You said you had someone in mind at your end. Why don't you send me their details, and I'll pass them on?

She sat for a while, staring at her laptop screen, before hitting send. And then it was gone, bouncing out across the ether to California. As simple as two hands on a keyboard, a touchpad's slide and click.

Ruth and Petrina came for coffee early on Friday morning, bringing pastries and the briny salt-whiff of the sea: they'd been swimming, their faces were flushed, their hair still damp. Each went upstairs to dry it in turn while the other sat in the kitchen with Dinah, who was up and dressed, more or less her old formidable self.

'Shouldn't you be resting?' Petrina said. 'You didn't need to get up on our account. I thought we'd sit at your bedside, cheer you up.'

Dinah waved a hand. 'I'm fine. You can cheer me up down here.'

Christina made the coffee, laid out the paraphernalia, mugs and milk and sugar, and left them to it; she had work to do, clients' queries to answer, spreadsheets to feed. Not as much work as she needed – that was another task to administer, another crumbling foundation stone to shore. No reply from Ed yet.

The women's voices mounted the stairs, seeped up through the cracks in the floorboards; their talk was easy, spirited, punctuated by gusts of laughter. Dinah, at the heart of it, sounded younger, looser, almost girlish; Christina thought again of Iris, of how her aunt had softened in her partner's presence. Or perhaps it was in her absence that she had changed; perhaps it was her grief that had hardened her. She'd always been blunt, no-nonsense, at least about anything other than emotions – 'You don't get anywhere in the field,' she'd said many times, 'by beating about the proverbial bush' – but she had been tender, too. It was Dinah Christina remembered putting her to bed in this room when she'd stayed here as a child. (Where had her mum and dad been on those nights? She didn't know. Perhaps they'd taken the opportunity to go out for the evening by themselves, oysters and pints of porter at the Neptune.) Dinah, and sometimes Iris, too: the two of them, one tall and dark, the other slight and fair, reading to her, leaning down over the bed to say goodnight. But perhaps she had embellished the memory, or even invented it wholesale: she'd been five when Dinah had met Iris, old enough to read to herself; and it was difficult to reconcile that unfocused, sepia-tinted image with the woman her aunt was now.

Dinah was tired by her friends' visit. She insisted on sitting up after they left, reading García Márquez in her armchair, but when Christina came downstairs again at lunchtime she was asleep, her head thrown back, exposing her pale wattled throat. Christina left her to sleep, heated herself a bowl of soup, returned to her laptop, to the realignment of her clients' tangled financial affairs. Sometime after that – the hated middle of the afternoon – she went back down to make tea and found Dinah in the kitchen, a mug already in her hand.

'Sometimes,' she said as Christina came in, her gaze fixed on the garden, pale and steely in the fading winter light, 'I feel so very old. I mean, I really *feel* it. In my muscles, my bones. Everything is tired. Everything just wants to sleep.'

Christina turned on the tap, filled the kettle, returned it to its stand. 'The doctor did say you should be resting.'

The kettle steamed and clicked; Christina poured her tea, added milk, took the chair opposite her aunt, the chair she had started to think of as her own. Her aunt was silent, but her eyes were active, lucid. Christina followed her gaze outside but saw only the untended yard (Dinah had never shared her brother's love of plants), the leafless pergola, the table and chairs: a garden unused, wintering.

'I used to sit here for hours,' Dinah said, 'after Iris died. Whole afternoons, more or less, just sitting, letting my tea get cold. I never used to believe people when they said they'd done that, or saw people doing it in films. But I did it. I still do, sometimes.'

Iris. The air in the room seemed suddenly potent, charged. *Now*, she thought. *Do it. Now.*

'Tell me about her,' Christina said.

Dinah shifted to face her, her expression neither stern nor gentle, but somewhere in between. 'What do you mean? You knew Iris. Tell you what?'

'I don't know. It's staying here, I suppose. I feel like I know so little about her. She was roughly the age I am now when you met, wasn't she? She'd lived in South America – is that right? Who with? Was she married? I feel like she talked as if she'd been married once, but I'm not sure. Memory can be so funny, can't it? It plays tricks.'

For a long moment Dinah looked at her, not speaking. Christina replaced her mug on the table. Perhaps she had gone too far; perhaps there were reasons for her aunt's reticence, and Iris's; reasons over which she had no business trampling. 'I'm sorry, I don't mean to pry, I just wanted to . . .'

'No,' Dinah said. She gave a long exhale: a balloon deflating, a breath let go. 'It's all right. You're right. She was married before we met. She was married for fifteen years. It wasn't a secret exactly, Iris just didn't like to talk about it. You see, Christina, there had been a child.'

The words hung between them. *There had been a child.* Cogs turning in cogs, wheels within wheels. The books on the shelf. The toys in the box. Not, then, for Christina, but perhaps for . . . The slippage of focus, an image blurring, returning differently, reframed.

'Her name was Tamsin.' Dinah spoke quietly, with care. 'She was six. They were in Mexico at the time, a *finca*, somewhere

165

really quite remote. Meningitis. It came on suddenly, and it took too long for them to get her to hospital. Iris never forgave him, I think – her husband, I mean. Ex-husband. Francis, his name was. It wasn't his fault, of course, but it was his work that had taken him there. She was mad with grief, she said, for a long time. She never got over it. Of course she didn't. How could anyone?'

The afternoon was gathering around them, thickening into evening; they were almost in darkness, and Christina made no move to turn on a light. 'I'm so sorry. I never . . . I never knew.'

Dinah shook her head, a shadowy figure on the other side of the room. Christina couldn't quite see her face. 'Iris didn't want it talked about. She couldn't bear it. I think she felt . . . I don't know, guilty, somehow, that she'd gone on, managed to have another kind of life. A good one, even. We talked about it, at the end. About how she'd had to find a way to carry on, and I'd have to do the same, after she was gone. As your mother had to, after John. It's not the same, of course, as losing a child. Well, I wouldn't know – perhaps you do know something about it, Christina; with what you've been through, I imagine that you do. But everyone has to carry on. Somehow, despite it all, we survive.'

'Come with us tomorrow,' Ruth had said when she and Petrina were leaving. 'We'll be down on the beach at nine. Just a quick dip – no longer, not as a beginner. I have a wetsuit you can borrow. You'll love it, Christina – honestly, you will. There's nothing like it in the world.'

And so, persuaded, she was here: standing at the edge of the world (that was a song, wasn't it? Cass Wheeler – yes – her father had been a fan, had played her cassettes over and over in the car on their long drives north to Scotland and Norfolk, west to Wales), in a borrowed wetsuit, mustering the tattered remnants of her courage. Ruth and Petrina beside her, either side, all three of them with thick towelling dressing gowns over their suits and costumes. Around them, a dribble of other swimmers; behind, Ruth's husband Adam and daughter Ingrid, bearing a tray of home-made blondies and a thermos of hot chocolate laced with brandy; and Dinah standing with them, wrapped in a hat and a scarf and her warmest, thickest coat. In front, the lapping water, the lacework of breaking waves, the layered paintbox wash of sky and sea.

'Right,' Petrina said. 'Gowns off, hold hands. We'll go in together. Christina, the cold will hit you hard – you'll think you won't be able to bear it, but you will. We'll move forward together, gradually. If you feel that your body isn't acclimatising, or you're struggling to breathe, say so immediately, get out right away. In any case, Christina, don't stay in longer than five minutes. All right? Are you ready?'

She wasn't. She wanted to turn and run. Shakily, she said, 'All right.'

A gasp as the water hit her ankles: it took her a second or two to recognise the sound as her own. The freezing bite of it, the burn. On she moved, hand in hand with Ruth and Petrina. Around them, other women stepped forward, a chain of women, moving into the mouth of the sea. Women wearing wetsuits and swimming costumes, women wearing their bare beautiful skin. Was this why her aunt loved cold-water swimming so much, Christina wondered, with the sliver of her teeming, pulsing brain admitting any sensation other than the teeth of the water, rising, reaching to her thighs? Because it reminded you so forcefully that you were still alive, still here, still breathing? 'Now!'

Petrina shouted, and she and Ruth dipped below the surface of the water, tugging Christina down with them. The cold rose up, closing over her shoulders like a living, moving thing; and with it came a rising wash of joy, wild and giddying: she was breathing, she was here, she was alive, alive, alive.

Fourteen

The flat was hushed-breath silent in the early afternoon; the air inside felt strange, heavy, as if it had clotted in her absence. There was a fine patina of dust everywhere, on skirting boards and worktops and bookshelves. Weeks had passed, she realised, since she had last bothered to clean.

Christina laid her bag down in the hall and went from room to room, opening windows, admitting the fine, fresh winter air. Then, in a sudden fit of energy, she retrieved the hoover and a duster from the cupboard and patrolled the flat, wiping and vacuuming, setting to rights. Thinking, as she did so, of her father, of a game they had used to play on their return to Carshalton from holiday. Dad would say the house had been lonely without them, that it could only be placated if they greeted each room in turn. Solemnly, then, Christina would perform the ritual, her small hand grasped in his. *Hello bedroom! Hello living room! Hello garden!* Mum watching them, resting after the journey (she hated car rides, even as a passenger), a smile twitching the corners of her lips.

The bedroom was a mess, the duvet pulled back where she – they – had left it, two mugs of coffee mouldering on the bedside table. David could have tidied a little before he left, she thought unfairly: for God's sake, she'd slept with the man and rushed off in a panic, then not even been in touch. He'd replied to her text the previous evening, employing the same defensive technique he'd used all those years before. *Thanks for your directness, Christina, but there was really no need. I was suggesting we met up as friends – I don't think either of us is in a position to be looking for anything more, do you?* Oh, why was he bothering to lie? Why couldn't he just admit that he was sad, and vulnerable, and lonely, and maybe even that she'd hurt him a little, too? Why was the whole bloody world pretending, making excuses, wearing a borrowed face?

She tidied the bedroom, changed the sheets. Dragged the hoover around the carpet, and then out onto the landing. Paused before the smallest room, the closed door. Pushed it open, went in.

Three white walls, one grey. The mountain range. The crib. The chest of drawers filled with tiny clothes, still carrying their labels, still breathing out their brand-new stockroom smell. She closed her eyes and saw them: their missing daughter, their lost son. She had seen them often, after the second miscarriage: in dreams and in the daytime too. A small, dark boy, head turned away, chubby legs bare beneath his dungarees, running barefoot across the floorboards. A little girl with Christina's own colouring, racing to the bookshelf Christina had placed here, under the window. In the months after they'd lost her, she had spent long hours in this room, the door closed behind her, stretched out on the carpet, suspended between sleep and dream. She had told nobody this. Not Jen, not Emma, not her mother; not even Ed had known that she had lain here, while he was at work, while she was meant to be working, and watched their shadow-daughter play.

Read me this one, Mummy, the girl says. Her name is Laura, Livia, Ada, Lois, Claire. They have a list, haven't decided yet;

she favours Lois after Lois Lane, Ed likes Ada after Ada Lovelace. *Read me this.*

Bring it here, darling. Come and sit with me. Open the book to the first page, and let me read to you, let me feel your small, strong body alive and pulsing in my arms, let me breathe in the scent of your hair. Come to me, my daughter, my child. Come. I am waiting for you. I am here.

Christina opened her eyes. The room was silent, empty. No child. No ghost. Just four walls in a shabby rented flat, holding inside them the echo of what might have been.

'So have you given notice yet?'

Christina shook her head. 'Not yet. I'll email tomorrow.'

Emma was inscrutable behind her sunglasses. 'And then what?'

'Then' – Christina squared her shoulders, lifted her chin – 'I guess I'll start looking for another place to live.'

The sun was out today, low-slanting, dazzling: one of those rare English winter days in which grey is displaced by gold and scarves are loosened, coats left unbuttoned. *Meet me at Battersea Park at ten*, Emma had said by text. *Alfie has Mini Kickers. We can drop him off and get a coffee.* Christina had parked close to the football field, found Emma by the chain-link fence, waving to Alfie as he crossed the grass: a small figure in a miniature football kit, his little legs scissoring as he ran, joining a stream of other voluble, blue-shirted children. Christina, greeting Emma, had watched her friend turn, see her, not quite smile. They'd kissed on each cheek, as they always did, but stiffly; she'd felt a coldness from Emma then, a new awkwardness that overshadowed the slight unease she'd been aware of between them before. Christina could still feel it, walking beside her friend towards the café under the high, sparse trees.

'You know you can always stay with us if you need to,' Emma said.

The offer was kind, but her voice didn't match: Emma sounded flat, dull, as if she were reading from a script.

'Thanks,' Christina said, 'really, thank you. But what is it, Em? You're being weird with me. What's going on?'

Emma kept her gaze fixed on the path. 'Nothing.'

Christina stopped walking. She'd slept well the previous night inside her clean sheets, better than she had in weeks, even at Dinah's; she had woken after eight o'clock to find the sun shining and her mood responding, lifting. Ed had emailed back – she'd read his message after dinner, on her phone. He'd been fulsome in his gratitude, his relief. She could read guilt there, in his eagerness to thank her, to reiterate his faith in the fact that they could work this all out with such civility, such lack of fuss. Joanna had seen it, too: Christina had forwarded the email to her and she'd replied almost immediately, though it had been nine o'clock on a Saturday evening. (Did the woman have no life of her own?) *He feels guilty*, Joanna had written. *If you want to, we can make something of this*. Christina hadn't yet replied. Did she want to make something of it? No, not really; she just wanted things acknowledged, arrangements made, the truth of things no longer hiding in the darkness.

'That's not true, Emma,' she said now. 'Things have been weird between us for a while. Let's stop pretending. You're pissed off with me, I can tell. Why? Have I upset you? If so, I'm sorry, but I don't know what I've done.'

'You haven't upset me,' Emma said. She had only briefly slowed her pace to match Christina's pause; she stepped off

172

briskly again, forcing Christina to do the same. 'I'm not pissed off.'

'So what is it?'

Silence. A runner passed, sheathed in leggings, emitting a ragged, panting breath.

'David,' Emma said. 'What happened with you and David at New Year.'

Christina felt her cheeks flare. She crossed her arms, kept walking. 'What about it?'

Emma still didn't look round. 'He's depressed. I mean, really depressed, clinically so. He's taken a real hit since splitting up from Louisa. He's not been coping. He tried to kill himself last year, Christina. Took a load of pills, called Pete, didn't want anyone else to know.'

David, sitting up in her bed on New Year's Day, sleep-mussed and vulnerable. His message the other day, so brittle, so protective, a soft-bodied creature scuttling back into its shell. *Thanks for your directness, Christina, but there was really no need.*

She swallowed. 'That's awful, Emma. Really awful. But what does that have to do with me?'

Emma was gathering speed. 'You just don't notice things, Christina. Not any more. Not for a while. I know you've had the most terrible time – the IVF, the miscarriages, Ed, your dad, all of it, I'm so sorry all of it happened to you, I feel for you as deeply as anyone could. But . . .' Emma trailed off for a moment, and Christina could almost hear it: a decision, a choice made. 'It's all about you, isn't it? For a long time now, Christina, it's all been about you. The people around you – what we're feeling, what we're going through, what we need . . . None of us get a look-in.'

For a moment, Christina couldn't speak: she was winded, gut-punched, her throat dry, her heart drumming in her chest.

They passed a bench; she threw herself down onto it and Emma did the same, each of them sitting at opposite ends, a foot of empty space between them. They were silent, watching more runners as they passed: a woman in cropped leggings, lithe, not an ounce of excess fat anywhere on her spare, lean frame; a man wearing ear buds, nodding along to music only he could hear.

After a while, Christina said, 'You're not just talking about David, are you?'

'No. I'm not.'

Christina's breath was easing, her pulse steadying. There was relief, wasn't there, in saying what needed to be said. 'What is it, then, Em? What is it that I haven't noticed?'

'I'm sorry,' Emma said. Her voice was smaller now. She had removed her sunglasses, pushed them back from her face; her eyes, Christina saw for the first time, were tired, pink-rimmed. 'That wasn't fair of me.'

'Don't worry about it. Tell me.'

Another silence. A couple passed on a pair of municipal bicycles, heavy, red-framed: young, early twenties at most, the woman leading, her unhelmeted hair streaming out behind her; she was looking back at her partner, laughing, calling at him to catch up. When they'd moved on, Emma said, 'We've been trying for a long time, now. A year, maybe a bit more. You re-member that when we had Isla, we thought we'd stop at one. It was so hard making it work around our jobs, and then with the New York transfer and everything, we really thought she was it. You know all this. And then along came Alfie – our surprise – and then, well, I didn't expect to feel what I started feeling, which was . . .'

Christina felt her hesitation. 'Don't spare me. What?'

Emma shot her a look – wild, wide-eyed, her usual compos-ure chased away. 'This kind of panic. I can't describe it. Feeling that this was it, that we'd never have another baby after Alfie, that time was running out. It felt like that, I guess – something ending, walls closing in, a kind of suffocating. I never expected to feel it. I think Pete was shocked, how strongly I felt. We started trying, but it's not . . . Well, it hasn't happened. It's not happening. It was so easy, so simple, the other times. I'm sorry, C . . .'

'You don't have to be sorry. *I'm* sorry.'

'For God's sake, C, let's both of us stop apologising.'

Emma was smiling now, and Christina smiled with her. She reached across the bench, took her hand. 'Does Jen know?'

'I only told her the other day. I've been worried about Isla. I didn't want her to know anything about it – not until there was something to tell her, anyway – but she came upstairs one day and heard me crying, sobbing my fucking heart out in the upstairs bathroom. She was furious. She said that I'm too old, that she didn't want a baby around again, screaming like Alfie did, keeping us all awake. She said it was disgusting, that I must be going mad. I wonder if she's right, you know, C. I seriously wonder if she's right.'

Isla in the spare room all those weeks ago. *They ruin everything, don't they?* Jen on the phone. *Don't tell Emma I said anything. Talk to her.* 'You're not mad, I promise you. It just feels like that sometimes. It's stronger than you can ever imagine. The desire. The lack.'

Emma nodded. Her hand, in Christina's, was smooth, her palm cool.

'Have you seen anyone yet?'

'Not yet. No.'

'You should talk to Dr Ekwensi. I'll put you in touch. She's brilliant, you'd love her. And her results are great. I mean, don't let me put you off.'

175

'Oh, C.' Emma shuffled across the bench, erasing the distance between them. She laid her head on Christina's shoulder; her hair, in its stiff bun, tickled Christina's neck. 'Are you sure you wouldn't mind? There are other clinics. Would it be too painful, either way?'

'No. Well, maybe, but like you said, it's not about me, is it? It's been all about me for too long.'

'I didn't mean it.'

'You did. And you were right.'

Emma offered no answer. They were silent, sitting close together, Emma's head still resting on Christina's shoulder. A dog passed, a collie, snuffling the verge; Christina thought of Mal, of Ziggy, and her smile returned, despite everything, despite it all.

The estate agent's name was Jason, a twenty-something in a light grey suit, his trousers exposing several inches of bare skin between their hems and his sockless brogues. He stood to greet her, like a schoolboy pulled to attention by the presence of a form teacher. They'd all had to stand, at Christina's school, every time a teacher had entered the room. Her mum and dad had thoroughly approved, and perhaps Christina had too, in a way – she'd liked her school, even enjoyed its arcane rules, which had become a kind of comfort, a road map through the chaos of adolescence. She couldn't imagine that secondary pupils at any but the most fusty, old-fashioned institutions were expected to stand for their teachers now. Could she picture Isla doing such a thing? No, no more readily than she could picture her turning off her iPhone, donning a ballgown and dancing a debutante's waltz.

Jason's handshake was firm. They both sat down. Jason faced her across the desk, or at least his body faced her – his head was turned to his computer, which was angled towards him and away from her, like a bank manager's, like that of a person with something to hide.

'So, Christina,' Jason said. 'The bad news is, we don't have much in this area within your budget.'

Could there be good news? She waited; he beamed; it seemed there could.

'The good news is that if you could consider going a little further afield – South Croydon, perhaps, or Thornton Heath, or even out to Purley – there are a couple of one-bedrooms that could work for you, if you can stretch the budget just a tad.'

This was not news to Christina, good or bad. She'd done her research, had been doing it, on and off, since the summer, ever since her marriage had, in the legal lexicon in which Joanna was educating her, 'irretrievably broken down'. She knew that the best she could afford to rent, alone, on her current income, was a first-floor bedsit in Thornton Heath, or a one-bedroom ex-council flat off Purley Way, close to the industrial estates she and Ed had once frequented at weekends, buying compost and toolboxes and flat-pack furniture with a pleasure that, it seemed to her now, had been faintly ironic, like two children playing house, designing the semblance of an adult life. She let Jason flick through the listings on his screen – he angled it towards her now, secrecy dispelled – making polite noises at appropriate intervals. Yes, that living room did look a good size. Yes, she didn't necessarily have to have a bath; a shower would do. Yes, it would be so convenient to be so close to Ikea. She thanked Jason. She told him she would think about it all. And then, as she was turning to leave – he didn't stand to see her out; she had the feeling that she had disappointed him – she saw it:

the cottage on the high, steep lane, close to Mal's market (she thought of the market, now, as his). Its photograph, preserved in a digital colour print; the little row of cottages, pressed cheek by jowl. Each house was small, she knew (she'd looked online): mostly two bedrooms, a couple of them with three, but each worth at least half a million. Here was the price of this one, right here, below the photograph, above the floor plan, the breathless description. *A rare opportunity to buy a glorious period cottage, replete with original features.* Asking price: £630,000. A fortune to anyone, surely; all right, perhaps not to Emma and Pete. But yes, a fortune to her.

'Is this still on the market?'

Jason looked up; he'd returned to his computer, forgotten her. A deep line appeared on the smooth, unclouded skin of his forehead. 'That's not a rental. That's for sale.'

'I know. I was just . . .' What was she doing? Dreaming, imagining. The line on his forehead deepened. 'Can I take this? I have a friend who's looking to buy.'

He smiled without warmth. The line vanished. 'Be my guest.'

The market was mysterious in the dusk: a place of layered shadow, dark corners, bare bulbs hanging from high rafters, casting the strange, assorted objects – a pair of dressmaker's dummies, set together as if in conversation; crates of records; a wall of clocks, each telling a different time – in pools of syrupy amber light. Angie's stall was closed, a rail of coats barring the entrance. Christina stood there for a moment, running her hands over a brocade collar, an astrakhan sleeve. No fur, she noted with approval; though of course it was different with vintage clothes, refusing to wear an animal that had died half a century before was hardly going to bring it back to life.

'Angie's gone for the day,' somebody said. She looked up, saw the man with the old framed photographs, stiff-backed Victorians, the high, proud, glinting dome of the Crystal Palace. He was wearing the same army-issue anorak as before. Beside his low stool he had a thermos, a foil-wrapped packet of sandwiches; a book lay open on his lap. 'I can give her a call if you like, tell her you're interested.'

Christina stared at the man, confused, then realised he meant the coats. 'Oh, it's OK. I was just having a look. I've come to see Mal. Is he here?'

The man nodded, returned to his book. 'As far as I know.'

She went upstairs, aware with each tread of a lightness, a sense of anticipation: he was there, she was about to see him, in a moment Mal would turn and see her, and there they would both be. She found him crouched, bending low over a box of books; it was Ziggy, again, who saw her, lifted himself from his belly, gave a brief, informative bark. Then Mal looked up and smiled, and she smiled back.

'Hello,' he said.

'Hi.'

Mal straightened, giving a low groan, a hand moving to the small of his back. 'Sorry about the old man noises. My back's not what it used to be.' Her smile strengthened, concealing her embarrassment, his too: his implication, the idea of the uses to which his back, young and healthy, might once have been put hung between them until he laughed, dispelling the moment. 'To what do I owe the pleasure, Christina?'

She shrugged; she had no excuse, hadn't thought to prepare one. Had simply wanted to see the house on the lane again from the outside – imagining, dreaming; *a rare opportunity to buy a glorious period cottage* – and then thought of Mal and Ziggy, as she did quite often now, the two of them haunting the edges of her mind. 'I was in the neighbourhood.'

He laughed again; it was, she felt, becoming a joke between them, these stock phrases, these deliberate clichés. It gave her pleasure, this idea of a shared joke, of knowing him well enough to have a kind of history, however raw it was, however lightly sown. 'Of course you were. Well, it's good to see you. I'm just packing up.'

'Let me help.'

Mal looked at her, his smile still lifting the corners of his lips. 'You don't need to do that.'

'No, I want to. Let me.'

He put a CD on as they worked, sorting the piles of books into the boxes and crates he kept beneath the trestle tables: something with synths and drums, very 1980s-sounding, a man's voice rising above, high and soft and sad.

'The Blue Nile,' he said. 'Are you a fan?'

She shook her head. 'Sorry. I'm not much of a music buff. But I like what I hear.'

She lingered over some of the books as she handled them: a few novels she'd always meant to read; a couple of hardbacks on gardening. These she flicked through, thinking of Dad. 'The triumph of hope over experience,' he'd called it, gardening, laughing at himself: the belief that somehow you could trump nature, or at least bend it to your will; that a day spent weeding wouldn't need to be repeated the following week, when new weeds sprang back in defiance. Here, between these covers, was her father's hope, his optimism: hard work and order, the trowel and the hoe, the obedient, gleaming rows of plants. Verbena and buddleia. Dahlias and asters. Alliums and geraniums and silver sheaves of grass.

'Take them,' Mal said. 'If you want them, they're yours.'

'Thanks, but I shouldn't. I've given notice on the flat. I'll need to start packing soon.'

He put down the book he was holding. 'You're moving? Where to?'

'I don't know yet. My mum's, initially, probably. Or my friend Emma's, in Clapham. From there, who knows?'

She'd been aiming for bright, brave; hope over experience. But perhaps the slight tremble in her voice had given her away: he was still looking at her, and now he leant over, placed a hand briefly, gently, on her arm.

'That's big,' he said.

Their gaze, matching, linked, was suddenly too much; she broke it, looked away, back to the book she was holding – *The Gardening Year* – placed it in the box on the floor. 'Yes. But it has to be done. I never loved the flat – it was always just a means to an end. I can't afford the rent, not alone, not on what I earn. That's another thing I need to sort out. More work, or different work. More money. But step by step, I guess.'

Mal nodded. The band played on, singing of crowded streets and downtown lights. Ziggy, standing sentry, barked at a passerby: the glass man, Christina saw, looking up, Sinclair, with his catalogue of dolls. Perhaps she should follow his example, find a hobby, start crocheting or doing découpage, whatever that was.

'All right, Sinclair?' Mal said, and then, turning back to her, 'Yes, Christina. Step by step. Steady as you go.'

'What would you do, then,' he said, 'if you could do anything at all, start over? What would you choose to do?'

Christina looked down at her glass, as if the answer might be contained within an inch or two of straw-coloured Sauvignon. They were in the Wheatsheaf – Mal's suggestion, offered as they'd left the market together, stood for a moment in the street under a pall of sudden awkwardness. *We could get a drink, if you like.* Now here they were, at the same corner table that had hosted the walking group's Christmas drinks. Mal was known here; the landlord, Eddy (Mal had introduced them), had greeted him warmly, asked if he and Ziggy wanted the usual. A pint of Guinness for Mal; two bowls for Ziggy, one of water, the other of biscuits in the shape of bones.

'I don't know,' she said, pathetic. 'I really don't.'

'Come on, you must know. Take a moment. Really think about it.'

She took a moment. She thought. She had always envied them, the people who seemed so certain about what they did, for whom work was a centrifuge, a guiding force: Jen, with dance; Emma, with law, which she freely admitted she actually loved, not just for the money, which was prodigious, but for the order of it, its stark patterning of right and wrong. Her parents, with their teaching; Dinah, with anthropology, with her research. Ed had been divided; she knew he'd have loved to have made it as a stand-up – fronted a podcast or, in his most feverish dreams, a TV quiz – but he'd managed to reassign his loyalty to tech. Her own career, such as it was, seemed to her now to be entirely the product of happenstance: she'd been good at maths, Jen and her fellow creatives had needed someone who wasn't afraid of numbers, it had all grown from there. She'd never dreamt of being an accountant; did anybody? Not as far as Christina knew; at Wright and Marshall, they'd mostly been just like her, maths-literate people killing time until something more interesting came along. Or, in the case of many of the young women – Christina included – children, maternity leave, going part-time, or perhaps not coming back at all. Well, that wasn't an option now. Mal was right, it was time to think again, it had been for a long while.

'Gardening,' she said suddenly, the thought surprising her, voicing itself almost before she'd allowed it to take root. The hours she'd spent in the back garden at Carshalton with Dad, under his tutelage, digging and weeding, matching the stroke of her small fork to his larger one. She'd taken good care of each of the gardens she'd had since leaving home. There hadn't been that many – most of the flats she'd rented since university had been on the first floor or above, the cheaper floors. But there'd been a biggish plot behind the Mansion in Levenshulme, one she'd tended, cleared, filled with lavender and herbs: cheap plants as they'd be leaving, as the garden wasn't theirs to keep. And this flat, the one she was leaving now, the one she'd lived in for longer than anywhere aside from her parents' house – six years; could it be normal, in your forties, never to have lived in one place for longer than that? She'd looked after the garden there, too, until it had become too much for her, until everything in her life had narrowed to one single objective, one tiny pinprick of light.

'Gardening.' Mal's echo drew her back.

'Yes.' She nodded. 'If I could do it all again, I'd be a gardener. Or garden designer. Landscaper. I don't know. One of those. I'm not quite sure of the difference.'

His pint was almost done. 'So do it.'

'What, just like that? Forget accountancy, and retrain?'

'From what you've said, it sounds like work's pretty thin on the ground anyway, and what you have you're not enjoying. But no, I'm not saying you should just jack it all in – we've all got to eat. But retrain while working, yes. Why not? You're, what, forty . . . ?'

She laughed; they hadn't actually admitted their ages, had they, in all these weeks of deepening conversation. 'Forty-three.'

'A youngster! Plenty of people start new careers later than that. Look at me – I've been a drummer, a roadie, a bookseller, a photographer, a fishmonger . . .'

His eyes were dancing. She laughed again. 'A fishmonger?'

'All right, no, that was a joke. I hate fish, can't stand the stuff. But God, I've done a lot of jobs. More than I could even list. We don't all get on one path and stick to it. And to be honest' – Mal lowered his voice, cast his eyes dramatically around him, as if the walls might be listening – 'most of the people who do aren't really happy. They're just afraid.'

'Afraid of what?' She knew her own answer, but she wanted his.

He looked at her. 'Of change, of course. Of what might happen if they stepped out of the little box they've made for themselves and looked around.'

She considered the image: pictured herself in miniature, a tiny doll-person emerging from a high-sided crate, standing blinking in the dazzle. 'It's not that easy for most people, Mal. You talk like it's so easy.'

'I never said it was easy. I know it's not.'

He drained his glass; she lifted hers, took a sip. Across the bar, two women of about her mother's age began laughing, throwing back their heads, their glasses of red wine brimming in their hands. Christina watched them, smiling, thinking of Mum: happy again, it seemed, despite everything, despite losing Dad, the man she'd loved without wavering for forty-seven years.

'At least talk to Angie,' Mal said. 'Perhaps you could help her out a bit, get a feel for the work. Sometimes the thing we love isn't the thing we want to get paid for.'

'Yes. That's a good idea. Maybe I will.'

He stood. 'Same again?'

She nodded. 'All right. Why not?'

Fifteen

Jen suggested they meet at the lido for a swim; she was a member, went several mornings a week after dropping the children at breakfast club. Another of the myriad activities she seemed able to tick off her dizzying daily list before Christina had even got out of bed.

She'd invited Christina to join her many times, urging her, through the years of IVF, to exercise, distract her body and her mind, offer them some other focus. Christina had always demurred: the idea of plunging willingly into freezing water seemed horrifying, a kind of showy masochism; but this time, thinking of that icy dip at Whitstable, she said yes. Driving down to the lido in the silvery rising morning (they were meeting at eight), she had a sense of herself as somehow different, transformed, her old self sloughed off like a snake's skin. 'Sometimes clients feel better,' Joanna had said on the phone a few days before, 'just to have made a decision, to have set the wheels in motion. Do you?' *Yes*, Christina said to herself now, silently, edging along in the school run traffic, *a little. Perhaps I do.*

They changed in adjacent cubicles. Jen was voluble, fired by caffeinated energy; she'd been up for hours, the boiler was broken again, the children had all had to pile into bed with her. 'I've called Ali about fifteen times,' she said, her voice travelling under the partition, 'but, as always, he won't answer his bloody phone. And the agent's no use either. Honestly, Chris, it's too much.'

Christina agreed: of course it was, Ali was a terrible landlord, why didn't she try withholding the rent for another month, see whether that motivated him?

'I guess I should,' Jen said. They were together in the main changing room now, stuffing their clothes into their bags: Jen long-limbed and sleek in her black halterneck costume, her stomach, as she bent to zip her holdall, folding itself into a neat, unpadded crease. Christina, beside her, felt pale and ungainly. The body she inhabited now still surprised her; sometimes, catching sight of it in a mirror, she needed a half-second or two to recognise it as her own.

Jen hoisted her bag onto her shoulder. 'Dad's going to come and take a look later today. If he can't fix it, he's got a guy who can. Dad'll pay, and we'll take the money off the rent. Bloody Ali. He really is the end.'

The pool wasn't busy, just a couple of swimmers in the fast lane, cleaving the water, their crawl strokes elegant, controlled. The slow lane was empty, the water navy, mirroring the sky: fading inky night-colours, drifting masses of grey cloud. Jen went first, clambering to sit on the tiled rim with practised ease, offering only the smallest of tight, high gasps as she lowered herself in. She stood for a moment in the shallows as Christina dithered, childishly afraid. 'Come on, C. It's worse thinking about it.'

'I know.' Christina approached the ladder, swung round, descended rung by rung. And there it was: the water's freezing grasp, her body's recoil. The cold, the pool, her body, the struggle between opposing forces as Christina immersed herself, struck off from the side.

'That's it.' Jen's voice was dimmed by the water. 'Keep moving, OK? You'll soon warm up.'

Christina swam, finding her rhythm, measuring the distance between one end of the pool and the other with each stroke. The cool slap of the water; pushing off from the tiled edging with her feet. The way that sound was muffled and obscured, and the frantic rhythm of the world seemed to slow and still, until all that was left was her body, and the water, and the regular, measured movements of her arms and legs.

'Amazing, isn't it?' Jen said when they paused together for a moment in the shallows. Christina, enjoying the iced breath of air on her face and arms – she was warmer now in the water than outside – nodded. 'Yes.'

They had coffee together afterwards in the café; Jen had a slow morning, she said, nothing on until an Arts Council meeting at midday. Christina smiled, admitting that most mornings, these days, were slow. 'Are you serious,' Jen said when they'd ordered, found a table, 'about this gardening thing?'

'I don't know. Maybe. This woman Angie's offered to have me along on a few jobs, let me get a feel for it. She retrained – we had a chat, she was telling me about it. She used to be some kind of secretary, I think, a paralegal. She had kids, got divorced, decided to start again.'

Their order came. Christina took her cup, thanked the waitress. The coffee, with its leaf-shaped patterning of milk, looked almost too good to drink, but she did, letting the bitter liquid slide down her throat. 'It just feels like such an effort. Everything does. The flat, the divorce, work. It's like I'm razing my whole life to the ground.'

Jen was watching her carefully over the rim of her cup. 'I know, darling. It's scary. Step by step, eh? Step by step.'

Christina smiled, thinking of Mal. *Steady as you go.* He'd offered to help her move. She'd refused, insisted that she could manage. Emma and Jen had also offered, but she'd refused them too, knowing it was difficult for them to arrange time away from the children, from the crowded, regulated channels of their family lives. But Mal had kept on asking until she'd relented, admitting that she was struggling, dragging her feet; there wasn't so much to deal with, not really, but the thought of it exhausted her, the putting everything in boxes, filling a van, driving it to storage in Mitcham, near her mother's (she was going there, at least at first; it seemed too much to stay with Emma, really, with all that she had going on). Then unloading it, going through all the physical business of removal, of taking leave. 'I have a van,' Mal said. 'I can drive you. Really, Christina. Let me help.' And so she'd agreed, relief settling over her, relief and gratitude and confusion. She still had no idea what this was, or could become: a friendship, blunt in its simplicity, or something more, something complex and slippery and tricky to define.

'I have news,' Jen said now, impishly grinning. 'I slept with Louis again.'

Christina laid down her cup. 'How did *that* happen?'

'Well' – Jen was sensuous, self-mocking – 'it involved company drinks on Friday, and too many mojitos on an empty stomach. Annie from next door was looking after the kids – she was so weird with me when I brought Louis home, you know what a puritan she is, I think she thinks single motherhood is basically like taking the veil. I chucked him out right after – I didn't want the kids waking up, coming in. They'll use any excuse to get into bed with me these days.' Jen was rolling her eyes, but Christina knew she didn't really mind; she'd admitted before that she liked having the small, snuffling shapes of her children either side of her in the bed, allowing her to forget, at least for a night or two, that otherwise she slept alone. 'This was *before* the boiler broke. I wouldn't have left them freezing in their beds just to have sex with a guy who looks like Michelangelo's *David*.'

Christina laughed, carried on Jen's exuberant wave. 'He does! But what about Dan?'

Jen sipped her coffee; her nails, gripping the handle, were lacquered hot pink. 'I don't know. It's kind of fizzling, I think. He's starting to bore me. What do you reckon? Does he bore you?'

'Maybe a bit,' Christina said. The women met each other's gaze and laughed, the sound floating up to the ceiling, bursting against the rafters, seeping out through the window to the pool, the swimmers, the high, still morning air.

It was too wet to take Leila and Gabriel to the playground after school; it had been raining all day, falling steadily, in heavy, permeating sheets.

Christina walked them home, waving to Bev on the crossing, exchanging smiles with the parents she recognised. It would be further to come, of course, once she was installed in Carshalton, and from there to wherever she was going to go: Purley, Coulsdon, maybe even leave London altogether, move to Whitstable; she'd get more for her rental money there, and she'd be on hand if Dinah needed her. Jen had asked whether she'd like to give up her Tuesday pick-ups, insisted she could make other arrangements. Perhaps eventually, Christina conceded, she might have to, but for now she was holding firm: she enjoyed her hours with Jen's children, their energy and strangeness. Once, after a class presentation on space travel, Gabriel had emerged from the

school gates wearing the astronaut's helmet he and Jen had fash-
ioned out of papier mâché and silver foil and refused to remove
it, even in the bath. The feel of their small hands in hers. They
were holding on now, one on each side, the umbrella Christina
had brought with her from the car furled, dripping from her
wrist. Both children were better dressed for the weather than
she was, in her useless sodden trench: they had waterproofs on
over their uniforms, hoods pulled up. Gabriel splashed happily
through each puddle they passed, lifting his little legs high, a
pony's trot.

'Gabriel, you're making me *wet*,' Leila said, a high, affronted
whine; she was listless, dragging her feet in her black school
shoes, her long hair in a low ponytail, loose strands damply
framing her face. Asked how her day had been, she'd offered
only a sulky 'fine': some trouble had begun, Jen suspected,
among Leila's group of girls, alliances fractured and redrawn.

'You're already wet, stupid,' Gabriel said, kicking the next
puddle with what could only have been calculated deliberation,
soaking Leila's legs in their black tights; the resulting argument,
and Christina's careful arbitration, carried them all the way
home.

The flat was warm, at least: Jen's dad, true to his word, had
been round about the boiler, got someone in. Jen must have
left the heating on all day; the air was stuffy, thick with the
sour smell of washing drying on the radiators, the milk from
the children's breakfast cereal curdling in bowls beside the sink.
Christina dispensed snacks – cups of water, slices of apple and
cheese – and then the children settled together on the sofa,
their earlier dispute forgotten, watching television.

Christina boiled the kettle for tea, washed up the breakfast
things, wiped down the surfaces. Jen did what she could, but she
was naturally untidy (her room in the Mansion in Levenshulme

had been a horror show, a layered drift of clothes and books and mugs of ancient stewed tea) and there was no money for a cleaner. Jen had admitted, too, that, like Christina, she could hardly stir herself to clean, that the flat never rewarded her efforts. It wasn't a bad place, or wouldn't have been if Ali had maintained it properly: a garden flat like Christina and Ed's, though basement rather than ground-floor, and damp, as all Victorian basements were. Mould regularly sprouted in Jen's wardrobe, blackening the shoulders of her dresses and shirts; she had to wash everything at 60 degrees. Black spores were creeping up the walls of the children's bedroom, too. Jen had re-painted several times – Christina had helped her – but it always seemed to come back.

'I've got to find us somewhere better,' had been Jen's constant refrain since Ariel had left; the flat had, like Christina and Ed's, been a stopgap, a way station en route to somewhere else. And now Jen, too, was stuck. The rent was affordable – at least Ali hadn't put it up since they'd moved in – and there was no way Jen could manage a London-sized mortgage: her income was erratic, scattergun, for all her critical success. Her parents had offered to help with a deposit, but even that wasn't enough. As Jen had said to Christina many times (they both tended to avoid discussing money with Emma), she could ogle as many Rightmove listings as she liked, but there was no way she was going to be able to afford to buy any of them unless she married a rich man or moved out of London – something, in each case, she hadn't yet been able to bring herself to do.

The kettle clicked. Into the sequence of familiar activity – pouring hot water, pressing down on the teabag before remov-ing it, adding milk – came a thought, an image, clear and lucid as a photograph, a still frame. The two of them, Christina and Jen, together in a kitchen – not this one, peeling and shabby, nor the one in Christina's flat, but another, light and airy, white units, bare brick. The children sitting at a long table, eating; Jen and Christina with them, drinking wine. Where had that been? They'd been on holiday a few times together over the years; perhaps it had been that cottage they'd rented in Norfolk, Burnham Market – yes, perhaps that was it. But then, where was Ed, where were Emma and Pete, Alfie and Isla? Christina didn't know. She blinked the image away, carried her mug through to the living room, curled up on the sofa between Leila and Gabriel, engrossed in their cartoon; Gabriel sank into her, his gaze not leaving the television, and she put her arm round him, drew him close.

Dinah was driving again; she had managed to get herself to her last cardiac rehabilitation session and had been cleared for light exercise, including swimming; not in the sea, naturally – the risk of cold-water shock – but in the local indoor pool. 'As if that counts,' she said irritably to Christina on the phone; but she'd been several times already, with Ruth, with Petrina: the members of the swimming group were going with her, taking it in turns. 'That's kind,' Christina said, and Dinah agreed. 'I don't know what I'd do without them,' she said, her usual asperity dispelled. 'Or you, Christina. I'm far luckier, really, than I deserve.'

The weekend before Christina was moving out, Dinah summoned her to lunch: it felt like that, a summons, cutting through Christina's weak protest, her reluctant assertion that she really ought to spend the day packing up the flat.

'Your mother's coming too,' Dinah said. 'You can drive her.'

'Mum's coming?'

Dinah was brisk. 'Yes. Be here for one o'clock. I'm going to attempt a chicken. You have been warned.'

Christina phoned her mother right away. 'What is this? You're now best friends?'

'It's just lunch,' Sue said. 'And no, not exactly, but she is my sister-in-law, Christina. We've known each other for longer than you've been alive.'

'And disliked each other just as long.'

'No. You're exaggerating. And anyway, things can change, can't they? I thought you'd be pleased.'

She was pleased, really: it had long pained her, the coolness between her mother and her aunt; she suspected it had pained her father, too, though he had never said as much, had always remained scrupulously loyal to them both. Perhaps they would never have been close – they were very different women; Christina had known this even as a child – but by the time she was in her teens, Christina had suspected an additional source of friction, at least on her mother's side. She had, with the clarity that sometimes accompanies the shift towards adulthood – parents no longer shadowy adjutants but individuals with their own histories, their own flaws – begun to understand that her mother's career as a teacher had been a compromise. Sue had been brilliant at university, had considered an academic career of her own. But then she'd met John, and he'd been set on teaching, and she'd decided to align her ambitions with his. 'I never regretted it,' Sue had told Christina many times, 'not for a moment.' But Christina wondered, all the same, whether her mother's lack of warmth towards Dinah had been more rooted in jealousy than dislike. Sue had liked Iris: they'd been easy with one another, even affectionate; when Iris had died, her mother had felt the loss deeply, openly. Perhaps it was this – Dinah's loss, and then Sue's own – that had softened things between them; perhaps, in their respective widowhood, they'd no longer seen the point of carrying a grudge whose origin was now so distant, its piquancy obscure.

Her mother was waiting on the doorstep when Christina pulled up outside, to save her the trouble of trying to park: the narrow Sunday-morning street was thick with cars. 'I've sorted you a permit,' Sue said as they pulled off. 'Three months, for now. Do you think that will be long enough?'

Christina's grip tightened on the wheel. 'I don't know, Mum. I can hardly think more than a day ahead.'

Sue nodded. She was holding the handle of the passenger door, as she always did, as if Christina were about to veer off down the suburban street at ninety miles an hour. 'Of course, darling. I was only wondering. Anyway, we'll see, won't we?'

Christina caught something darting, secretive, in her mother's tone; she glanced at her, then back to the road. 'See what? What do you mean?'

'Just that, darling. We'll see.'

Christina gave up, put on Classic FM, asked her mother how Ray was and how the rehearsals were coming along: the dance group had a performance planned for a few weeks' time in aid of a local children's charity. Ray and Sue were dancing a Viennese waltz. 'It's ever so difficult,' Sue said. 'Keeping the frame, you know – a good stiff back – and the footwork . . . I keep losing track, getting totally muddled. I must have stepped on Ray's toes a thousand times.'

'I'm sure he doesn't mind.'

Sue smiled. She was wearing her navy striped top and a pink raincoat. Her face was immaculate, her nails French-manicured, neat and buffed. 'No. He doesn't seem to. He's stepped on mine a few times, too.'

It was half past one by the time they reached Dinah's: there was traffic on the M2, speed restrictions, the usual frustrated coastwards pace. Rich, savoury smells greeted them as Dinah opened the door, a grubby apron knotted over her jumper and skirt. 'You're late,' she said. 'It's almost ready.'

'Smells good, Dinah,' Sue said, stepping into the hallway, leaning in to kiss her sister-in-law on the cheek. 'Can I do anything?'

'Yes. You can come and tell me whether this bloody bird is cooked through.'

Christina laid the table while her mother and her aunt busied themselves with the food; alongside the chicken, which Sue pronounced sufficiently cooked, there were roast potatoes, carrots, broccoli, gravy. 'Only Bisto,' Dinah said, placing the jug on the table. 'Iris used to make her own. I've no idea how. And the potatoes are frozen, I'm afraid. Well, they were. With any luck, they're not any more.'

'It all looks wonderful,' Christina said.

'Well.' Dinah sat, still in her apron, pushing a damp strand of hair back behind her ear. 'I've been making a few changes, as you know. Making a bit more of an effort to eat properly. It's been pure laziness, really. This isn't anywhere near Iris's standards, but it's something.'

Sue, across the table, sipped her wine; she had brought a bottle of Chenin Blanc with her, insisted on them each having a glass, even Christina, though she would stop at one, mindful of the return drive. Her mother was drinking more these days – Ray's influence, Christina assumed, but it suited her, as Ray himself did, too: Sue seemed softer, more at ease. More like the woman she'd been years before, before Dad's illness. 'It really is, Dinah,' Sue said. 'Thank you.' She lifted her glass. 'To making changes.'

'To making changes,' Christina murmured in reply; she took a sip, replaced her glass, was just spearing a slice of chicken with her fork when her mother said, 'Now, Dinah? Shall we tell her now?'

'Tell me what?' She put down her fork. Dinah and Sue were looking at each other, smiling, like children carrying a shared secret, itching for its release. 'What is it? What's going on?'

Her mother spoke first, and then Dinah, the two of them in easy dialogue, passing the baton back and forth. What was going on, they said, was this. They had decided, between them, to give Christina a sum of money. Dinah had more in savings than she knew what to do with: she had lived frugally all her life, and Iris had left her everything of her own; and of course she'd never had children, there was nobody to leave it all to but Christina.

'Don't talk like that,' Christina said, 'please don't.' But her aunt waved her protest away; there was nothing like an experience like hers, she said – being blue-lighted to hospital, convinced that that agonised half-hour was her last – to make you rethink your arrangements.

'Let's be frank, Christina,' Dinah said. 'You need the money. You spent everything you had, the two of you, trying to become parents, trying to make it happen.'

Christina nodded, a lump forming in her throat, blocking speech.

'At least this way,' Sue said, 'we'll both see you get the use of the money during our lifetime. At least this way you could buy somewhere. It won't be a fortune, but between us, we should be able to come up with enough for a deposit.'

'But you, Mum? Do you mean you're going to . . .'

Two spots of high colour had appeared in her mother's cheeks. She had never found talking about money easy, Christina knew.

Dad had dealt with everything; after his death, Christina had sat down with her mother over several days, poring over the accounts, helping her take the measure of what was left. Not so much, really: they'd been careful, yes, but Dad's care had eaten into most of it, the only significant asset was the house.

'Sell the house, Christina? Yes. I think it's time. I've a little in savings. Dinah will advance you the majority of what you need, and once the house is sold I'll pay her back.'

Christina shook her head. 'No, Mum. You can't sell the house just to help me. It's too much. I won't let you.'

Her mother looked at her. Her eyes – the same shade of blue as Christina's own: pale at the centre, around the pupils; almost navy at the edge – were clear, decisive. 'I wish you'd let us help you sooner, Dad and I. You know your father wanted to. You were so set on doing everything yourselves, paying your own way, and then with his illness, well . . .' She trailed off; Christina waited, let her take her time. 'I know how hard it all was for you both, what a toll it took. I don't mean just financially, of course, but that was a part of it, wasn't it?' She took a sip of wine, returned her glass to the table. 'And this isn't just for you, darling. I need you to know that. I want to sell. It's not easy, being in that house, not any more. The house is full of your father. He's everywhere. And he always will be, in here.' Sue tapped her temple. 'But I'd like to get somewhere new, somewhere smaller.'

'With Ray? Isn't it a bit . . .'

Her mother interjected gently, firmly. 'No. Not with Ray. Somewhere just for me.'

Christina, out of questions, sat in silence for a moment. Nobody had eaten much while they talked; the three plates were still half-full, and now Dinah and Sue returned to eating. The low clink of glasses, the scrape of a knife, the rustle of Dinah's napkin as she unfolded it, smoothed it across her lap.

Christina looked at her plate, which seemed now transformed, as the whole room did, the room and everyone in it, blazing in a bright, dazzling light. Her gaze was blurring, fracturing. She swallowed. 'Thank you. Really. I don't know how to . . .'

'Don't.' Dinah shook her head; Sue, across the table, did the same. 'You don't have to say anything. We want to do this for you, and we're doing it, and that's all there is to say. Just eat up, Christina. It's getting cold.'

Sixteen

She moved out a week later, on a Sunday in early February; the sky grey, heavy-bellied, threatening rain.

Mal came early, just after nine. Christina went down to meet him, to move the wheelie bins she'd placed in the street overnight, marking a space directly in front of the house. She watched him park, manoeuvring the van expertly into the narrow gap; it was red, larger than she'd expected, with the Parcelforce livery still visible on the side, though the adhesive letters had been removed. He grinned at her through the open window, waving a thermos. Ziggy was on the seat beside him, sitting straight-backed on a scratchy tartan blanket; she caught the mingled smells of coffee and lemon air-freshener and damp dog.

'I've brought supplies. Thought you might have packed the kettle.'

'Not yet.' She smiled. 'But thanks. Really, Mal. Thank you for this.'

He nodded, opened the driver's door. 'You're all right. It's Ziggy you'll need to make it up to. He usually gets a long run on Sundays.'

'Of course.' She leant forward, offered Ziggy her palm through the open door; he sniffed it, gave it a rough, tugging lick. Beside her on the pavement, Mal laughed. 'I think you're forgiven.'

It was, she realised as Mal followed her inside, the first time he'd seen the flat; embarrassment crept over her as she led him to the living room, where she had stacked most of the boxes. Dust on the skirting boards, cobwebs lacing the upper reaches of the ceiling: places she'd missed, things she'd failed to notice, as it seemed to her now, standing in the echoing emptied room, she had missed so many things, through all her years of single-minded wanting, hoping, failing.

'Nice place,' he said. 'High ceilings. Lots of space.'

Christina looked at him. It was a long time since anything about the flat had seemed nice to her, but perhaps it was, really, such things were always relative. She knew where Mal lived, though she hadn't been there yet: one of the small 1980s terraces in the centre of the Triangle, ex-council; Karen and Annabel had lived there with him, he'd kept it in the settlement. She'd walked past a few times, admired the neatness of the little houses, their clean, modern lines; but perhaps their place had been a compromise, too: perhaps they'd imagined they'd move on to other, better things. Perhaps everyone did, until they stopped moving, or set off alone in another direction altogether.

'I suppose so,' she said. 'It was always a stopgap.'

Mal nodded. 'You were happy here once, I'm sure.' He lifted the thermos. 'Now why don't you find us a couple of mugs, and we'll make a start.'

There wasn't so much to get through, not really: the sofa, the kitchen table and chairs, the bed, which she'd dismantled herself earlier that morning. Mattress, bedding, boxes of clothes, a few pictures and clocks sheathed in bubble wrap and brown paper. Kitchen things, books, the contents of her office. A couple of bookcases, some rugs she'd rolled and taped, a box she'd labelled 'miscellaneous' into which she'd thrown anything that didn't fit elsewhere. Suitcases to go in the boot of her car, with clothes and toiletries, work stuff, everything she'd need while she was staying at her mum's. Garden tools, a few potted shrubs. They carried it all out, moving from one room to the next, filling Mal's van, filling Christina's car, working in easy synchronicity until both the thermos and the flat were almost empty.

'Anything in there?' Mal said; they were on the downstairs landing, outside the bathroom, the door to the box room standing ajar.

Christina took a breath. She'd spent an afternoon here during the week, sorting, clearing. The clothes and toys she'd given to Emma; there were regular second-hand sales of baby stuff among the school mums, Emma had promised to deal with it all. As she was preparing to leave – she'd come round after work one evening in the Range Rover – Emma had reached into a bag and taken out one of the pristine newborn sleepsuits, a brown rabbit with long soft ears. 'Keep something,' she'd said gently. 'You'll regret it if you don't.' She had them now, tucked into her overnight bag like relics from another age.

The larger furniture – the cot, the changing table, the wardrobe – Christina had put on Freecycle. The set had been claimed almost immediately, by a young pregnant woman and two men, one of whom Christina presumed was her boyfriend; they'd come to collect it that same evening, the woman standing beside the van as the men had manoeuvred the furniture out onto the street. Stroking her swollen stomach; beaming, waving at Christina as she'd thanked her. 'You're welcome,' Christina had shot back brightly from the front door as they'd slammed the van doors shut, 'you're welcome.' Thinking of Marianne – four months, she must be now, or almost five. Not thinking of Marianne. Stepping back into the flat, closing the door behind her, not thinking of anything, reminding herself to breathe.

'Nothing,' Christina told Mal now. 'Nothing at all.'

His dark eyes were shrewd and shining under the bare, un-sheltered bulb. He nodded. 'All right. I think we're all done. I'll give you a minute to check, shall I?'

When Mal was gone, Christina pushed open the door. Pale carpet, still holding the small indentations of the nursery furni-ture; three white walls, one grey; the stencilled mountain range. She hadn't had to redecorate – their contract didn't require it, and anyway Jason had said the landlord was doing the place up, preparing to sell.

'Interested?' he'd asked her over the phone; she'd told the agent she was planning to buy, that she would now be able to stretch to a deposit after all. His colleague Adam in sales was already flooding her inbox with email listings; the little cottage opposite the market was already under offer, and too expensive anyway, even with her mother and Dinah's help. So far she'd seen nothing else she liked or could afford. 'I'm sure he'd be keen to discuss a price.'

'No,' she'd said. 'No, it's time for me to move on.'

Christina remembered that now, standing alone in the centre of the room. A tiny room, no more than a few metres square, with a high barred window admitting a grainy, insufficient light. Just a room, just four walls holding their allocated quantity of air.

I think we're all done. Christina put a hand to a stencilled mountain, tracing the shape of it with her finger: its ascent, its apex, its downward slope. And then she nodded, crossed the carpet and stepped back out onto the landing, closing the door behind her.

It was lunchtime by the time they'd finished at the self-storage place in Mitcham; after lunch, in fact, closer to half past two.

Sue called, asking what time she'd be arriving: was Mal coming with her, did she want her to make them something to eat? Her mother was, Christina knew, desperate to meet Mal, from whose willingness to help with the move Sue was drawing a far blunter inference than Christina herself. Christina had not allowed herself to interrogate Mal's reasons for helping her too deeply; much easier, far less frightening, to ascribe it to his general kindness, his broad-based desire to help when help was needed. She wasn't used to this. Ed had been many things – she had loved him fiercely once; that she could not, would not, deny, even now – but kindness had never been supreme among his qualities. Or perhaps that wasn't fair; he'd done his best: it was circumstance, really, not lack of care, that had warped their marriage, bent it out of recognition.

'I'll call you back, Mum,' she said into the phone. 'Let me see what Mal wants to do.'

He was beside the van, resettling Ziggy on the passenger seat. He looked up as Christina approached.

'My mum called. She's asking if you'd like lunch. If we both would. Are you hungry? Do you need to get back?'

He watched her, in that still way of his, considering. 'That's kind of her. I am hungry, and I don't need to get back, not right away. But if I don't give Ziggy a run, I'm afraid he might destroy your mum's house, and I'd really rather he didn't. Not on a first meeting.'

Christina nodded, smiled. Her own reservations were broader: she didn't want to bring Mal and her mother together, not quite yet. She couldn't quite picture them in the same room, didn't want to subject him, subject the two of them, whatever this was, to the inevitable post-meeting dissection. *Well, he seems nice.*

Tell me again why he and his ex-wife got divorced. She took the child back to Australia? Oh, the poor, poor man. And he's a photographer, is he, as well as a bookseller? Well, I always did think you were more suited to a creative type.

'We could go to Morden Hall Park,' Christina said. 'It's not far. There's a café. I can buy us lunch.'

She looked at Ziggy, who stared back at her, tongue lolling from his mouth. He seemed to be smiling.

'All right,' Mal said. 'Thank you. Sounds good. You lead the way.'

They had tea and sandwiches at the National Trust café, sat outside feeding Ziggy dog biscuits from a paper bag. The day was still damp, but not cold; they kept their coats on, unbuttoned, and then struck out across the park, crossing a white iron bridge over a broad, still stream.

'How do you feel?' he asked her as they skirted the wide-open swathe of grass beyond, Ziggy racing out ahead.

'About what?' she said, watching his profile, his clear, emphatic features, his lion curls.

'About leaving. About having left.'

'I don't know.' It was true: she was as empty as the flat had been when she closed the front door and locked it, posted the keys back through the box with a card for Mrs Jackson, saying thank you and goodbye. Empty and hollowed out. Tired, too: she'd slept poorly again, lain there most of the night among the bags and boxes, waiting for morning. Heard that noise in the garden again sometime in the darkest portion of the night – that shuffle, that scrape – and thought of the hedgehog, of the shelter she'd never made, of all the things that had never come to be.

'I think it'll take a bit of time to sink in. It'll be strange, staying at my mum's.'

'Stranger than being at your aunt's?'

She shrugged. 'Perhaps. I'll be back in my old room, which is weird in itself. And Dad's gone, of course, and now Mum's planning to sell.'

'Everything's changing around you,' he said. 'It does, you know. Nothing stays the same.'

'Yes. That's one thing I do know.'

They walked on, passing another pair of dog walkers, an older couple with grey hair, stylish in bright waterproofs and spotless wellington boots. Ziggy sniffed around their red Labrador, and they all stood together for a moment as the two dogs performed their elaborate dance of greeting.

'Lovely collie,' the woman said. Looking at Christina, she added, 'Have the two of you had him long?'

Christina felt her cheeks flush. 'Oh, he's not . . . We're not . . .' Beside her, shrouding her embarrassment, Mal said, 'Since he was a puppy.'

When the couple and their dog had moved on, the air between them seemed different, thicker, charged. They rounded the grass, pursuing Ziggy into a copse of trees. Neither of them spoke for what seemed a long time. They entered the copse, the trees narrowing around them, filtering the light. She measured the rhythm of her breathing, and his. She watched the path, the jostling trunks: silver birches, narrow and tapered, casting their leafless sculpted shadows. Ahead, the path led out of the thicket, back to open grass; they walked on, not speaking, not needing to speak, Ziggy rising to his feet to follow on.

Christina's old room was at the back of the house, overlooking the garden. Sometime in her teenage years, she'd had her dad paint it a deep red; her mother had hated it, calling it the colour of blood and rust, but Dad had been broadly supportive, in his usual easy-going way. 'The Victorians used deep colours like these, Sue,' he'd said when he was done, when they'd all stood there admiring it (in Christina's case) or loathing it (in Sue's). 'It'll be lovely in the evening. Intimate. A little cocoon.' And it had been. She'd found an old floor lamp with a glass shade in a junk shop, placed it next to a cracked leather armchair a neighbour had been planning to send to the tip, and spent long hours here, cradled between these blood-red walls, doing whatever teenage girls did: reading, writing in her diary, spending entire evenings on the phone to friends whose names now sounded obscure to her, like words from a language she no longer knew.

The red paint was long gone; her parents had redecorated soon after Christina had moved to Manchester, and again during Sue's frenzied re-envisioning of the house a decade or so ago. Now the walls were a pale green, the carpet beige, the curtains printed with a repeating pattern of abstract leaves. The bed was a small double, Christina's ancient single long since dispatched. On the wall opposite her mother had hung a framed photograph of a Scottish landscape: looming reddish hills, glassy mirrored loch holding the reflection of the sky.

'The agent says I should redecorate,' Sue said; she had helped Christina upstairs with her bags, which now occupied most of the space between the bed and the window. 'Paint everything white or grey. He says it's much easier for people to project their lives onto a blank canvas.'

Christina followed her mother's gaze around the room. She had spent some weeks staying here after Dad had died, not wanting her mother to be alone. Ed had come for a night or two at weekends, but mostly it had just been the two of them; crying sometimes, separately and together, but more often just sitting watching television, or moving around the house, entering one room and leaving it again, forgetting the reason for doing so, wondering whether there had ever been a reason for doing anything, really, other than habit, other than necessity.

'People want a home, don't they?' Christina said. 'Not some kind of show house.'

Sue looked at her. Under the glare of the electric light – it was already dark outside – she seemed tired, strained, older than she had in recent months, under Ray's rejuvenating influence. 'Perhaps you're right.' She crossed the carpet, stood beside Christina, laid a hand on her arm. 'Are you all right, darling? Really? I know today must have been difficult.'

'Not so difficult, really. I never liked that place much. Neither of us did.'

'No. I know.' Sue's hand remained on her arm; then, after a second or two, withdrew. 'I'll leave you to get settled, then, shall I? There's a cottage pie in the oven. Just the two of us tonight, I thought. There's something I'd like to watch at nine. You could watch it with me if you like. Or we could sit and talk, if you prefer, if that's what you feel you need . . .'

Conversation, real, deep-diving conversation, didn't come easily to her mother, Christina knew, and never had; Sue was someone who preferred to skate along on the surface of things, and there was something beautiful in that, it seemed to Christina now, something healing and beautiful and good.

'No, Mum,' Christina said now. 'I'm tired of talking. Let's watch your programme. That sounds perfect to me.'

Time at her mother's passed slowly, with an ease, a stillness, that reminded Christina of the time she'd spent in Whitstable with

Dinah, though of course her mother was not in need of her care.

Perhaps it was less about being needed, and more about having company; she allowed herself to acknowledge, now that she'd left the flat behind, all that she'd disliked about living alone, the silence and the long, unpunctuated evenings and the strange, unattributable night sounds. The hammer she'd kept under her pillow.

She slept better in her childhood home, beneath the picture of the loch. Her dreams were formless, unremembered; working at her laptop at the dining-room table by day, her mind felt clearer than it had in weeks. She made more lists, enjoyed a small rush of satisfaction with each completed task. So many remained, written and unwritten – find somewhere to live; sort out work; finalise the divorce; call the clinic, decide on her next steps. Work out what, if anything, was going on with Mal, or might happen. What she wanted. Who she was, or wanted to be. What was going to happen next.

Joanna rang with news: not about the divorce, but about a friend and former client, a film producer looking for part-time help with the company accounts. 'Can I give you her name?'

Christina, sitting in her mother's dining room in the middle of the afternoon, said, 'Yes. Thank you. Why not?'

The woman's name was Daphne Smart; she emailed right away, suggested a meeting for the following day at her Soho offices. Christina dug out a decent shirt and trousers from the bottom of her suitcase, took the Tube to Tottenham Court Road. Daphne's building was on Berwick Street, a narrow, brick-fronted town house. On the first floor a languid teenager, hardly older than Isla, greeted Christina with a slow half-smile.

'Ms Smart won't be a moment,' she said, returning her attention to her screen.

Christina sat and waited, tried not to fiddle with her phone, tried not to acknowledge the anxiety tugging at her sleeve: how long had it been since she'd last gone to a job interview, twenty years? Though Daphne hadn't called it an interview, had she: *a chat*, she'd written. *Come in for a chat.* That was worse, wasn't it? She was bound to say the wrong thing, and what was she wearing, she must be twice the size of that skinny thing behind the desk, surely Daphne would be the same, skeletal, fashion-conscious, red-lipsticked, formidable, really the best thing she could do for everyone was turn round and go back downstairs, get on the Tube and forget this had ever happened, slink back to her mother's house and stay there until . . .

'You must be Christina.' A large, round-faced woman looming above her, in leather trousers and an oversized floral shirt. 'I'm Daphne. Joanna says you're just the woman I need.'

Christina stood. 'I hope so.'

Daphne's handshake was strong, her smile broad, if not quite extending to her eyes. 'Now, is it Christina, Chris, or Chrissy? You can never be sure . . .'

'Chris is fine. Or Christina. Whatever you prefer.'

'Well.' Daphne let go of Christina's hand. 'I'll go for Chris, if I may. So. Come on through.'

They crossed into a diminutive workspace – exposed brick, pot plants on shelves, four desks, heavy with papers and files. A meeting room behind sliding glass doors. Framed posters – films and TV shows, actors grinning telegenically at the lens. Only one of the desks was occupied: a man, youngish, his hair long at the front and close-shaved at the sides. He jerked to his feet as they entered; she thought, again, of school, of the rows of girls scrambling to attention behind their desks.

'Rhys,' Daphne said, striding out across the varnished floor-boards. 'My right-hand man. Rhys, this is Christina. Chris. I'm hoping she might be the woman to sort out the bloody money.'

'Good to meet you,' Rhys said, extending a hand. She shook it, smiled, let go and followed in Daphne's wake.

Their chat ranged across Christina's CV, hastily compiled the previous afternoon. Daphne wanted to know why Christina had left Wright and Marshall, of course; Christina had considered this, prepared a safe, anonymous answer. *Freedom. Building my own client base. A new challenge.* But here between these glass walls, facing Daphne across a concrete-topped table, she found herself unable to offer anything but the truth. She took a breath. She said, 'It just seemed like the right time to make a change. My husband and I were going through IVF. My ex-husband, I should say: we're in the process of divorcing, hence Joanna. I was having to take so much time off work – for the appointments, you know – and we thought the stress wasn't helping.'

Daphne retained her half-smile, her gaze not wavering from Christina's face. 'And did it work?'

'Did what work?'

'The IVF.'

Christina looked at the table. 'No. Not in the end.'

'How many rounds?'

She lifted her gaze to meet Daphne's. 'Five.'

Daphne sat back in her chair. 'We had four. Total night-mare. The last one worked, thank fuck. But we're not together any more, either, as you may have gathered from Joanna. Our daughter's twenty now. A lifetime ago, but I can still remember every moment of that bloody treatment. And the times it didn't work . . . Well. I was a mess.'

Christina nodded. They held each other's gaze. A phone rang in the other room; Rhys answered, a high, trilling voice. 'Medusa Productions. Rhys speaking.'

'Why Medusa?' Christina said.

Daphne smiled again. There was more warmth in her eyes now; Christina noted their colour for the first time. Dark brown, almost black. Rather beautiful. 'Why do you think?' she said. 'Because she was strong as hell. Like me, darling. And, I think, like you.'

It was almost three o'clock when Christina left the Medusa office. She and Daphne had talked through lunchtime, through phone calls and two courier deliveries and Rhys knocking on the door to say that he was off to Pret, would they like him to bring them anything? *Yes*, Christina had answered silently, her stomach gnawing. 'No,' Daphne said, without a glance in her direction. 'No, I think we're fine.'

The job was hers. Two days a week – three, perhaps, at busy times: year's end, certain more demanding projects – for almost two-thirds of what she currently earned. She'd keep her current clients, squeeze her work for them into the rest of the week. Numbers, dear logical numbers, rolled through Christina's head in busy shifting sequences. Her income rising, exceeding outgoings, leaving a glorious gap between the two.

Berwick Street was quiet; she lingered for a moment under the overhanging shadow of a pavement awning. There was a restaurant a few doors down – Italian, tiled frontage, a window table, an empty chair. She entered, sat, ordered penne alla Norma and a glass of prosecco. Texted Joanna. *Thanks so much for the introduction – I seem to have got the job!* Sat drinking her wine, watching the city go about its day. Across the road, a man in skinny jeans and low-heeled boots stepped out from a shop carrying two enormous helium balloons: 3 and 0, the blue foil digits seeming to float off towards Broadwick Street on a pair of disembodied denim legs.

She smiled, at the man, the balloons, at her own shadowy mirror image. How long had it been since she'd come into town and sat alone in a restaurant, enjoying nothing more than the pleasure of her own company? She couldn't think how long. Aloneness, for so long, had seemed the ultimate failure, the worst fate. And yet here she was, alone, and here the city was, all around her. The beauty of it, its beating heart. The slanting winter sun lowering over Soho, and her here to see it, attuned to the moment, to the city's endless, shifting possibilities.

The following week, she spent two days working with Angie in the back garden of a house in Streatham, recently acquired by a young couple with a child of about Gabriel's age. The previous owners had let the garden run wild: the borders were barely visible under great tangles of bindweed, high, angry nettle stems. Angie lent Christina a pair of elbow-length gloves and set her to work.

She did so steadily, tearing the weeds up by their roots, enjoying the accompanying pull on her muscles and joints, the strain of the physical labour and the focus of it, the way everything else fell away, leaving only this: a patch of ground, a recalcitrant stalk, the damp mushroom smell of bare earth. Angie talked as they worked; she was blunt, curious, no-nonsense. 'Can't be doing with bullshit,' she said, leaning on her spade, reaching behind her ear for the first of many hand-rolled cigarettes. 'You'll take me as you find me, all right? And I'll do the same with you. So first off, tell me, what's going on with you and Mal?'

Christina fiddled with the handle of her dad's old hoe. 'Well, I really don't . . . I mean, I'm not sure I . . .'

Angie laughed. She had a great laugh, full and husky, Marlene Dietrich by way of Pat Butcher. 'It's all right, love. Tell me to get lost. It's none of my bloody business, is it?'

Friday was cold and wet. Rain trickled down the open neck of Christina's waterproof, her mum's, borrowed from the back of the hall cupboard; there was no way her useless trench would cope with a day outdoors. Even her mum's wasn't really up to the job – purchased more for a quick shopping trip to Wimbledon, she suspected, than for standing around all day pulling up nettles in a downpour. Angie was stoical in a voluminous waxed coat. 'Not quite so much fun in the wet, is it, love? At least this way you'll see whether you're really cut out for this sort of work. If you're serious about gardening, you're going to need to invest in some proper gear.'

At lunchtime, Angie decreed that they head to a pub on the High Road for an hour, though strictly no booze, she never drank while working. Over burgers and Coke, Christina told her about trying to set her life in order; about her tick-list, about trying to work her way through everything that needed to be done. Angie listened, her head on one side. 'I'm not sure life works like that, love, really, does it?' she said. 'You can't tick it all off a list, one by one. You've just got to get up in the morning and see what happens.'

'Sure.' Christina had cleared her plate; she laid down her knife and fork, sat back in her chair. The pub was busy for a weekday lunchtime. It was one she'd never been in before, though she'd driven past many times, noted its handsome facade. The place was huge, cavernous, occupying the entire ground floor of an Edwardian mansion block. Angie had greeted the woman behind the bar by name – they'd been at school together, she'd told Christina as they ordered – and Christina had nodded, and thought about how strange it was to spend so many years in a city alongside so many other lives: all these circles spinning within circles, never touching, never intersecting. Her life with Ed, their marriage, had been narrow, it seemed to her then, so focused on one desire, one tiny beating pulse. And she'd felt, for a moment, a dizzying sense of possibility: she could do anything, be anyone, it was all there for the choosing.

'I'm learning to do that,' she said now. 'Abandoning control.'

Angie nodded; from her pocket she withdrew her papers and tobacco, began rolling another thick-waisted cigarette. Christina thought of Jen, imagined the two of them getting along, smoking together, laughing, sharing a dirty joke. 'Oh, you bet. No use trying to control anything. Though the house and the divorce – yes, that you have to move along. Can't sit around waiting for that to get sorted.'

'No.'

'Do you want to know what I did after my hubby and I split up? The first one, I mean?'

'Of course. Yes.'

Angie squinted at the papers, took a pinch of tobacco, lined it neatly up along the crease. 'Couldn't afford a place of my own, could I? Not with two kids and a secretary's wage. And my useless ex wasn't planning on giving me a penny, not until I made him. Or until the court did, anyway.'

Christina lifted her glass, took a sip. 'So what did you do?'

'Moved in with my best friend. Pooled our resources. She was single at the time, too. Her son Raf was the same age as my Daniel. We got a house together in Sydenham. Had a great time –

the best. Far more fun than either of us had had living with the kids' dads. Sharing the childcare, the chores. The kids got on great most of the time. One big, happy, noisy family. Stayed there two years. Broke my heart, really, when we moved out.'

'Why did you?'

Angie had finished rolling the cigarette. She tucked it behind her ear. 'She met someone. Moved in with him. And I had another fella by then.' She shrugged. 'It wasn't forever, but it was great while it lasted.'

Christina nodded. 'It sounds like it.'

Angie took up her Coke, drained it. 'Not everyone's in tidy little boxes, Christina, living their rigid little nuclear lives.' Her blue eyes were clear, unwavering. 'Things are messier than that. And that's all right, as far as I'm concerned. I like the mess. I learnt to like it. I had to. So do you.'

Seventeen

The idea came to Christina slowly, by degrees.

It was there – some version of it, as yet nameless, shadowy and indistinct – when she got back to Carshalton on Friday, damp and aching, too tired to do anything but sit in the bath her mum ran for her, and then crawl into bed. It was there on Saturday, when she drove down to Whitstable to see Dinah, went with her for a walk along the beach, sat for a while in Petrina's house on Marine Parade with the other women from the swimming club, drinking tea and eating home-made ginger biscuits. It was there on Sunday morning, which she spent helping Sue tidy and clean the already ordered and spotless house: the agent was coming on Monday with a photographer. On Sunday afternoon, Ray came to collect Sue for their dance rehearsal, and the idea was still there then, asserting itself, becoming clearer, assuming a tangible form.

Still Christina left it alone, allowed it to take root, didn't yet speak its name aloud; all through the week, with its spreadsheets and emails, a call from Joanna to say that all was progressing well, that she expected to have a draft of the settlement approved by the other side within the week. 'Told you I'd keep things simple, didn't I?' she said. 'Though actually, Ed's side are being about as co-operative as could be. Great motivating factor, guilt.'

Christina was working at the dining-room table; from the kitchen, where her mother was making a batch of lentil soup, snatches of Classic FM floated through to her: massed voices, sweeping violins. The two of them, Christina and Ed, here one year for Easter: Handel's *Messiah* on the radio, Ed leaping up from the table, waving his arms around, pretending to conduct; her father standing too, opening and closing his mouth, aping the deep bass growl. Christina and Sue laughing; all four of them laughing together, until the men, flushed and grinning, had fallen back into their chairs and the meal had carried on. That had been in the very early days, before they'd started trying for a child: the time when they'd simply loved each other, and believed that this was, that this would be, enough.

'It's not just guilt,' she told Joanna. 'Ed's a good guy.'

There was a short pause. Faint strains of office noise at the other end: a woman's voice, the bleat of a telephone.

'Would that all my clients were like you, Christina,' Joanna said. 'Would that they were. Though I suppose if that were the case, I'd be earning a lot less than I do.'

It was still there after that, the idea: stronger even, clearer, its outline more resolutely defined. That evening, while her mother and Ray were downstairs practising their waltz (the performance was the following weekend), Christina took her laptop up to her bedroom and spent a while with a new spreadsheet, inputting figures, arranging and rearranging numbers until they made sense, until they assumed a bright, clear, lucid form. Then she closed the spreadsheet and opened a property website, put in the numbers, the requirements, waited for the search results to load.

Houses were out of the question, they were too expensive, wildly so, the cottage opposite the market had been a fantasy; but a flat – a flat could work. A split-level flat, ideally, with three bedrooms, a garden; the children could share for a while longer, they did already, at least this way they'd know the boiler wouldn't break down, that mould wouldn't be climbing the walls. Christina could set up her desk in her own room: she didn't need much space, not really, the separate office in the old flat had been a luxury, one she couldn't afford if she – they – were buying, if they were finally going to stop throwing away all this money on rent, paying other people's mortgages. Here was a place; she sat looking, clicking from photograph to photograph. A maisonette, spread over the ground and first floors of a Victorian house, creamy plasterwork and soft yellow brick; she knew the road, a good one, broad pavements and high, waving trees. The residents closed it to traffic a couple of times a year, let their children play outside. A garden, a white kitchen, painted wooden floors. The flat looked good; it looked like a home. But if not this one, then there would be others. What mattered was the principle. What mattered was the plan.

She called Jen. It all depended on Jen, of course. Christina told her what she was thinking, let the idea take shape, step out of her mind to be examined, considered, appraised.

'Wow,' Jen said. The boiler had broken down again – her dad's fix had only been temporary. She'd plugged an electric heater on in the kids' room for an hour or two, she'd said, before putting them to bed; the rest of the flat was freezing, she was sitting on the sofa now in her coat and scarf. 'Wow. I hadn't even . . . Well, Christina. Wow.'

'Just think about it, all right?' Christina said. 'Talk to your parents. Think about it, Jen. This could really work, for all of us. But of course you need to think about what's right for you and the kids. And there's a lot we'd need to sort out, I guess, legally, financially. We could ask Emma for advice. That's if we can even get a mortgage. But I reckon we could.'

She could almost hear Jen working things through already, catch the whirr and click of the wheels turning in her friend's brilliant, beautiful mind. The mind that took dancers, the shapes and angles of their bodies, and moved them, line by line, curve by curve, around the stage. The mind that had forced itself to face the fact that the father of her children was leaving, that Ariel wasn't coming back, that it was just her and them now, that she would have to do it all alone. Perhaps Christina had never understood it, not really, not properly, until now: how Jen had adapted to circumstance, how she had swallowed her resentment, that sour, embittering taste. You had a choice, in the end, didn't you: you threw up your hands in despair or you got to work and carried on.

Emma and Pete had had their first appointment with Dr Ekwensi.

'What did you think?' Christina said. They were in Emma's kitchen, at the island, the remains of a Chinese takeaway spread out before them: a lone spring roll, two cold dim sum, a congealing tangle of chow mein. The pendant lights dimmed, casting the room in blocks of light and shade; beyond the black panes of glass, the walled garden stage-lit by sunken uplighters.

'We liked her.' Emma nodded in emphasis, lifted her glass. 'She didn't patronise us. She just laid out the facts as they are.'

'And what are they?' Jen said.

Emma was silent for a moment; around them the house creaked and stirred. Pete was out with colleagues, the children were asleep upstairs – all of them, Leila and Gabriel too; Emma had suggested a sleepover, it was half-term, she and Jen were thinking of taking them to one of the museums. The Science

Museum, perhaps, if Alfie wouldn't be too disappointed not to see the blue whale at the Natural History. Jen was going to stay over; Christina hadn't quite decided yet whether to do the same.

'Well,' Emma said. 'It's not exactly good news. I mean, I'm forty-four.' She spoke carefully, not meeting Christina's eye. 'The chances are not in our favour. Dr Ekwensi was clear about that. I asked for a percentage, but she didn't want to give us one.'

'No,' Christina said. 'She prefers not to. She says they work with people, not statistics. "Nobody's fertility journey is a plot on a graph."'

Emma met her eye then, smiled. 'Yes. That's exactly what she said.'

Christina returned the smile, though her throat was tight. She picked up her wine, took a sip. 'Of course. And what else? She must think it's a good sign that you already have children. That it bodes well.'

Emma's expression, under the dim light, was gentle, concerned. Jen, across the island, was watching Christina steadily. 'Are you sure it's OK to talk about this? I don't want to . . . Well. Upset you. Bring things up.'

Christina shook her head. 'No. You don't have to protect me. Really. This is about you.'

'All right.' Emma nodded. 'Yes, she thinks the fact we already have children is a good sign – but of course I was much younger then. She said – how did she put it? She said that, since then, "there will inevitably have been a significant reduction in the quality of my ovarian reserve". Of course they still need to do all the tests, check Pete over too – we haven't booked in yet – but she was pretty clear about that. We were expecting it, of course. It wasn't a surprise.'

Jen leant forward, reached for the bottle. 'So have you booked in?'

'Not yet.' Emma was still, her hand resting on the stem of her glass. She looked away, to the doors, the garden; Christina followed her gaze, watched the play of artificial light on stone, the pockmarked expanse of London brick, looming still and monochrome in the darkness. 'We're taking some time to think, to talk. She suggested we do that. She said she wanted to be honest with us about how hard it was likely to be if we went ahead. She said' – Emma turned to Christina – 'she said she knew we'd had some indirect experience of how difficult things can be. And that really, the most important question we need to ask ourselves now is, how much do we want this? Is it possible that, with two children already, our family is complete?'

Silence accompanied the question. After a moment, Emma added, 'She didn't say so, but I came away feeling that she thought we were demanding too much. Being greedy. I'm asking myself, now, whether she might be right.'

Jen shook her head. 'She wouldn't have been judging you, I'm sure. They must see plenty of couples looking for help with a third child, even a fourth.'

'Maybe. Perhaps I'm projecting. Perhaps I'm the one who feels we're asking for too much, but it doesn't feel rational, it doesn't feel like something I can control. Pete hasn't said anything, but I can tell he's not as driven by the whole thing. I think, if it were just up to him, he'd leave things as they are. I don't know. Perhaps we should. Perhaps I just need to find a way to let this go.'

Christina said nothing. She could still see Dr Ekwensi, elegant in a fitted navy dress, her nails a glossy scarlet, leaning across her desk. Christina not looking at her, not looking at Ed, staring at a loose knot in the carpet's tightly woven weft. *I don't think it would be a good idea to rush into another transfer, not right away. Why don't you both take some time to think, to recover. Especially you, Christina – your body's been through so much. We can keep this last embryo in storage. Why don't we say you'll take three months off, and then I'll have the reception team get in touch, see if you'd like to book in to see me again, start moving things forward? And if anything changes in the meantime – anything at all – just drop us a line.*

The doctor's words struck her differently now. *If anything changes in the meantime.* Had she known, then? Had Dr Ekwensi seen it, the toll it was taking; the way they'd barely looked at each other, she and Ed, the way each had sat in their separate chair, not touching, hardly speaking, separate, two satellites caught in simultaneous orbit, so many miles apart? She must have seen it a hundred times, a thousand times – what happened to them, the crying couples, the unsuccessful couples, the couples for whom it didn't work, the mysterious magic of assisted conception, of full-term pregnancy. She must have suspected. She must have known, even when they hadn't yet been able to admit it to themselves. That it was over. That they were done: with the treatment, and with each other. That it would only be a matter of time until they had understood this for themselves.

'What about you, Chris?' Emma said. 'Are you going to go in and see her? Have you thought any more about what you're going to do?'

'Not really. It exhausts me, the whole idea of starting again from scratch. And the cost, of course. I know there are other options. Mal has a cousin who does fostering, he said he could put us in touch with her.' She watched her friends exchange glances at the mention of Mal. Ignored them; took a sip of wine and said, 'But I'm hardly in a position to take on a vulnerable child, not now, not while I don't even have a place of my own.

I don't know . . . I'm tired of trying, of fighting so hard for something. It's like you said, really, Emma. If it's not meant to happen for me, having a child, my own child, then I'm thinking maybe I should just let it be. Accept it. It's not everything, in the end, is it?'

'Of course not,' Jen said softly. Across the island, Emma nodded, and said, 'No.'

Christina decided to stay the night. She sent her mum a text, borrowed a pair of pyjamas from Emma. In the spare room, she and Jen talked in low voices; they'd decided, by mutual instinct, not to mention the idea to Emma yet, not until it had shifted from an idea to a plan. Jen had spoken to her parents; they'd expressed reservations, found the whole thing a bit out of the ordinary. 'Is this really,' her mum had said, 'a thing women *do?* If they're not together, I mean – not, you know, a couple? Isn't it a bit weird?' But Jen thought they'd come round. They understood that things were different now, that it was difficult to buy unless you earned a fortune, especially without a partner. 'Dad agrees that we should formalise the financial side of things,' Jen said, 'make clear how much we're each putting in as a deposit, just in case, well . . .'

Christina was climbing into bed beside her. 'In case we break up?'

Jen laughed. She was in her *My Mum's a Rock Star* T-shirt and black leggings, her hair loose. Time seemed, to Christina, to have shifted in reverse: it was years since they'd shared a bed, decades even, not since the Mansion in Levenshulme, when they'd sometimes stayed up so late talking in each other's rooms that they'd all fallen asleep, Emma too, the three of them abandoned to the obliterating slumber of the young, the stoned, the frequently inebriated. Woken in the morning in the stale, overheated room, each drooling on another's shoulder, the bedside light still brightly shining.

'That's the thing,' Jen said. 'It's safer, as I see it, than buying a house with a boyfriend, even a husband. I reckon friendship's more solid than anything else, really, in the end. I'm not going anywhere. I'm not going to walk out because I decide I can't stand the way you grind your teeth when you sleep. I'm not going to leave you for someone else.'

Christina was settling on the pillow. She shifted onto her side. 'We don't know that for sure, though, do we? I might drive you mad leaving the cap off the toothpaste. I do that, you know. And I'm rubbish at cleaning, so lazy, I just don't notice the dirt. Or you might meet someone you actually like, decide to move in with him. Get married, even.'

Jen snorted. 'Ha. Not if I can help it. I'm done with Louis now. I don't want to be *that* woman – the creepy old choreographer lusting over her dancers. And Dan too. Far too complicated. Casual hook-ups only, please, at least until the kids are old enough not to care who I'm with. If that day ever comes.' She shifted onto her back. 'Anyway, you're just as likely to meet someone, Chris. It looks to me like you already have.'

'It's not like that with Mal.'

'It is, though. Maybe not now, not while you're licking your wounds, rebuilding things. But it will be eventually.'

'You haven't even met him.'

'No. But I can tell. And I will do soon, won't I? You can't keep him locked up forever.'

'Ha. Maybe. We'll see.'

Christina reached for the switch. They lay silently until Jen said, her voice formless in the darkness, 'I'm not worried, Chris.

I think we should talk to someone – a broker, whatever, find out what we can afford, and then start looking. It's a brilliant plan. We both need somewhere to live, neither of us can afford to buy on our own. Gabriel and Leila love you, and it would be amazing to have you around. It doesn't have to be forever. Nothing is. The only difference between us and a married couple is that we're prepared to admit that right from the start. And we don't have sex with each other. Mind you,' she added, 'that probably makes us *more* like a married couple. Am I right?'

Christina laughed. 'In my experience, yes.'

Mal had been away for a week: a cousin in Durham had been getting married, he'd agreed to do the photographs. He called one evening, a day or so after his return. Christina was sitting with her mother and Ray watching television; they had an encyclopedic knowledge of Netflix, enjoyed watching each new TV drama together almost as much as they did dancing. The two of them at their performance – Christina had gone along to watch – moving easily, deftly around the floor, Ray's hand firm on Sue's waist, her gaze fixed on his. Sue flushed and grinning when they finished, catching Christina's eye as she took a bow; and she'd seen it then, how happy he made her, how much her mother had needed this. Christina had smiled back until her face was aching; afterwards, she'd clasped her mother in her arms and said into her ear, 'You were wonderful. I'm so happy for you, Mum. It's so great that you've met Ray.'

She smiled again as she answered Mal's call. 'Hi,' she said into the phone, getting up from the armchair, her mother staring at her from the sofa, her eyes knowing, bead-bright. 'Just give me a moment.'

Upstairs in her old room she settled on the bed, legs outstretched; asked Mal about the wedding, which had been a three-day affair, a civil ceremony and a Muslim one, hours of feasting and dancing and general excess. 'I must have about three thousand photos to upload,' he said. 'And my cousin will want to go through every single one of them – that I can guarantee.'

She asked how Ziggy had coped with the journey – not too badly, Mal said, he was used to the van, didn't get too restless as long as he could poke his muzzle out of the window from time to time and have the odd run around. He told her that he'd seen his other cousin at the wedding – the one who did fostering – and she would definitely be happy to have a chat, if Christina wanted.

'Thank you.' Christina, propped up against the headboard, watched the framed landscape, the still water, the drifting cloud, the red flanks of the hills. 'Thank you, Mal, but I don't know. Let me think about it. It's not practical right now anyway, not without a place to live. I can't quite work out what I think about anything at the moment.'

Mal was silent; in the elapsing seconds her words began to acquire a deeper, more pointed resonance. 'Of course,' he said. 'You should take all the time you need.'

Was she imagining his slight coolness? Perhaps; perhaps it was in her mind, all of it, there was nothing tangible to make of any of it, was there, just nuance and interpretation, just the dance and parry of new acquaintanceship, of feelings for which she didn't even quite yet have a name. Or perhaps she did. Perhaps she was just too afraid to say it. Afraid of what it could mean, really, to shape this, frame it, make it real. To begin again, with all the mess and vulnerability such a thing entailed. Fitting your form, with all its peculiarity and strangeness, its anticipated joys and unforgotten pain, to the shape of another. Handing yourself over and saying, *Here I am. This is me. Be careful with me, won't you? There's only so much breakage I can take.*

For a while, they talked of other things: her new job, her plan to buy a place with Jen. He said this was the best idea he'd heard in a long time. 'Living alone's not all it's cracked up to be. Take it from me.'

Another silence rooted and grew between them after that. Christina was just about to open her mouth to break it – to say something, anything, to dispel the awkwardness, the sense of things unacknowledged, things unsaid – when he broke it for her. 'Hey, do you fancy a walk on Sunday? I was thinking of heading up to Ditchling Beacon. Not with the group, this time. Just me. And Ziggy. And you, if you'd like to come.'

Her eyes rested again on the Scottish landscape print. Her father, striding out across the heather in his walking boots, Christina trotting to keep up. Dad stopping to wait for her, turning, his voice carrying to her along the rutted path. *Keep going, love. Just put one foot in front of the other.* And she had, hadn't she: she'd kept going, she'd caught up, and they'd walked on together, covered miles, her father guiding, her small hand folded inside his.

'Yes,' she said. 'Yes, I'd like that very much.'

Mal's route carried them away from Hassocks, past 1930s semis and executive pillared homes, along a railway line to a vertiginous sloping field, rising to meet a stretch of cloudless Sussex sky.

They took a moment's rest at the stile, Ziggy waiting, his haunches lowered to the ground, his unsettling human eyes looking from Mal to Christina and back again. He had been herding them along, darting between them, his breath clouding the late-winter air. A fine day: bright, a coolness to the air, but a softening one. A high, restless wind carrying the rising sap of spring.

'Just a minute, Zig,' Mal said. 'We're not all as fit as you.'

'I'm certainly not.' The hill loomed, solid, implacable. 'Not sure I can make it up there, Mal.'

He shook his head. 'If I can, you can. It's a bit of a hike, but it's worth it, I promise. There's a surprise at the top. Come on. You go first, set the pace.'

Nothing else for it, was there, other than to turn back and retrace their steps. 'OK. Here goes.'

Step followed step. The pull and scream of muscle and ligament, the accelerating thud of heart and pulse. Ground covered, inch by painful inch. Her lido swimming sessions with Jen – more or less weekly now – hadn't done much yet to address the fact that it had been years since she'd done any proper exercise. She thought of Ed, in America, taking up running, pounding the sidewalks; did Marianne go with him, or did they consider it too much of a risk? Marianne was surely showing by now. Sometimes, at night, perhaps she felt the baby shift and move.

No. She blinked the image away. That was Ed's life, Ed's story. This was hers: this moment, the only true thing anyone could ever hold onto, ever carry in their hands. She knew that now. If she had learnt anything at all, in almost half a century of living and breathing and loving and trying and failing, it was that. She walked on. The slope was levelling. Mal, a pace or two ahead of her, turned, smiled, his great crown of hair waving in the wind like a flag. 'There. What do you make of those?'

They had reached the crest of the hill. Before them a pair of windmills, facing away, towards the ridge: the closer one huge, white, a lighthouse in a sea of grass; the further one smaller, more modest, painted black. None of the sails were turning. Incongruous, out of time, a vision from the flatlands of Holland, the Fens of three centuries before.

'Told you it would be worth it,' Mal said, his voice lifted and fractured by the wind.

She couldn't speak; the wind stole into her throat and swallowed her reply. Below them the country rolled towards the horizon. Fields and hedgerows, roads and copses, the grey peak of a church spire, the glint of distant scurrying cars. The sky was a high ceiling painted a blue that was more than blue, that contained all the blues there had ever been and could ever be. The space of it; all that unfathomable space. Not a person visible around them, before or behind, just them, the two of them, and these motionless windmills, and the dog racing off to bark impotently at the cows, staring and chewing behind their high wire fence.

'Are you all right?'

She nodded. 'Just catching my breath.'

Mal returned the nod. They stood with their backs to the mills, side by side, looking back down to the path they had traced. She watched the view, the layers of grass and tree and sky. She was still watching when she felt him bridge the space between them, reaching for her hand. The sudden warmth of his skin; warmth flooding to her face, though she didn't turn, didn't look at him, didn't dare. Ziggy darted in front, a streak of black and white crossing and recrossing the field, then throwing himself to the ground, tongue lolling, brown button eyes looking from Mal to Christina and back again.

'Come on,' Mal said. 'Let's carry on.'

'All right,' she said, and they turned and walked towards the windmills and the track, their hands still joined, neither wanting to let go.

Eighteen

It was late spring when they moved in, almost summer. The end of May; Christina had just turned forty-four.

She had celebrated her birthday with a picnic on the beach at Whitstable. A low-key affair: shop-bought sandwiches, tubs of hummus and guacamole, bags of crisps. Emma and Pete had brought a bottle of champagne, Jen a carrot cake she and the children had made, clumsily, wonderfully, iced with the words *Hapy Birtday Auntie Cris!* Ruth and Petrina came from the swimming club; Dinah sat in regal splendour on a deckchair borrowed from Petrina's front garden. Sue and Ray brought balloons, plates and napkins, flasks of tea; Ray set up a pair of windbreaks, strung brightly coloured bunting between them. The sun shone all day, dipping only intermittently behind drifts of cloud. Isla, in denim cut-offs, flirted determinedly with Ruth's grandson Ben. The younger children ran between the groynes, splashed in the surf, demanded ice cream. Late in the afternoon, Angie arrived on foot with a contingent from the walking group; they'd planned a celebratory route from Faversham. Mal was already there: he'd driven Christina down in the van. He spent much of the afternoon sitting with Dinah, discussing the relative merits of García Márquez and Isabel Allende; he was a fan of both, he'd read almost everything they'd written, though not in Spanish, he was sorry to say. 'Well,' Dinah said in the hallway when they dropped her home, looking from Mal to Christina, a sly smile tugging at her lips. 'I do hope I'll be seeing the two of you here together again soon.'

It was no use explaining to Dinah, or to Sue, that they weren't quite a couple: that they were taking things slowly, so slowly, infinitesimally slowly. 'No pressure,' Mal had said that day, on the train back from Sussex. 'No expectation. There's no rush, is there?' No, she'd said, and she'd laid her head on his shoulder, where it had seemed to fit so neatly, so easily. He'd bent his head to rest on hers, and together they'd watched the window, the scurrying fields, the speeding cloud, the lowering winter sun.

The purchase of the flat had taken months: there'd been the mortgage to sort, the legal arrangements to put in place. They'd made an offer on one flat, lost it after the seller decided to pull out; then another had become available, a flat that had previously been under offer, and they'd moved quickly, secured it before anyone else had even had a viewing.

It was the flat Christina had seen that day when the idea had still been forming: the Victorian maisonette, white stucco, a garden big enough for a swing set, a slide. It had to be a sign, didn't it: that first flat, available again, theirs for the taking. Jen had brought the children to see it and they'd run from room to room, wheeling and swirling like gulls. Leila and Gabriel would take the biggest bedroom, the one at the back, looking out over the garden; there was room for bunk beds, toys, a pair of small desks. Jen was going to take the smallest of the three bedrooms – she didn't need as much space as Christina, she said, all her work things were at the studio.

Christina's room was at the front, overlooking the street; her window framed a cherry tree, then wildly blossoming, flooding the open window with its heady, vivid perfume. Room for a desk, a bookcase; she'd work in here part of the week and the rest she'd spend at Medusa. There'd be work to do in the evenings, too: she'd found a course, Gardening for Beginners, at a place in Chelsea; she'd keep doing the odd day with Angie, was considering taking an RHS qualification if all went well. Angie was supportive, said she could use the help. 'You're a natural,' Angie said, and Christina felt the truth of it: her father's daughter, at home in mud-spattered boots, at peace among roses and dahlias and the gnarled, spreading roots of trees, taking mess and chaos and restoring it to order and calm. Taking control, where so little else in life would allow itself to bend to your will.

The first night in the flat, too tired to cook, Christina and Jen bought fish and chips from a place on the Triangle. They perched on boxes in the living room to eat, squeezing sachets of ketchup and mayonnaise. Gabriel and Leila ate with them, wiping their oily fingers on paper napkins, and then ran out to explore the garden; Darcey the cat, furious at her sudden uprooting, stalked the flat, sniffing out each corner, then followed the children outside.

They sat together, Christina and Jen, in the fading light – they hadn't yet found the lamps among the vanfuls of boxes, cases, furniture – raising glasses of champagne. A gift from Sue and Ray; there was another from Jen's parents in the fridge. Mal would be round the following day to help with the unpacking, Jen's parents too; and Emma, Pete and the kids were coming in the evening for an informal housewarming, bringing pizza. But for now, for tonight, it was just the four of them: Jen, Christina, Leila and Gabriel. A family of sorts; not the one either of them would have planned for, expected, but yes, a family, the one they had chosen, for now, for as long as it lasted, for as long as they wanted it to last.

'Well,' Jen said. 'We've really done it. We're here.'

Christina raised her glass to Jen's. The children's cries floated in through the open door. *Mum, come outside! There's another cat here! He's stripy! Aunty Chris, Darcey's getting really cross!*

'Yes,' Christina said, as their glasses chimed. 'Here we are.'

The email from Ed came in July.

Christina was in the garden when she read it: her garden, their garden, the first she'd ever owned. She was neatening the borders, plugging the gaps with grasses and shrubs; Angie was teaching her to choose plants for their shape and colour, perennials, plants that would return, not bloom for one season and then wither away. The swing set was already installed; they'd found one on Freecycle, Mal had gone to collect it in his van. Jen adored him, the kids did too; turned out he was great at football, which impressed Leila, and he'd given Gabriel a boxed collection of Paddington Bear books from his stall (both Gabriel and Leila were passionate about Paddington). Mal was round most weekends, though he'd not yet stayed the night.

'Honestly, Chris,' Jen said, 'you're allowed to move on, you know. You're officially divorced.'

'I know,' Christina said. The decree nisi had come through in June, the court order settled not long afterwards. A sense of calm had come over her after that; it was done, it was over, there was nothing more to be said. It seemed to her now that everything – the years of treatment, the end of her marriage; the trying, the wanting, the failing, the sadness, the loss – had been conducted in such a frenzy. There was no need to hurry any more, was there? There was no need to rush.

She was pausing from her work in the garden, sitting at the table with a glass of water, when she drew her phone out of her pocket, and there it was: an email from Ed. The first she'd had in – well, she couldn't think how long. Months. They'd been scrupulous, throughout the divorce process, to keep conversation to the lawyers. She'd thought about sending him a text on the day the divorce came through, but her fingers had hesitated, unable to choose the right words. So she hadn't bothered to say anything in the end, and neither had he.

Dear Christina, I hope you're doing well.

Our son was born last month. We named him Max. He's a wonder. Everything has changed. Everything is different. I'll say no more than that. I know it will be difficult for you to hear, and I'm not getting in touch to upset you.

I've been doing a lot of thinking – about what happened between us, what didn't happen. About how much we both wanted a child, and how heartbroken we both were, how much we retreated from each other. How different things might have been if we'd been successful, if we hadn't lost the pregnancies, or hadn't needed IVF at all. I've been seeing a therapist for a while – very Californian, I know. I suppose I've been feeling guilty about how things turned out. You might say I deserve to, but I'm not sure you believe that, not really. You were kind throughout the whole process, kinder than I could ever have imagined, ever deserved. I tried to be kind, too. I think we managed to keep our dignity, didn't we?

I think we managed to be 'civilised' (and yes, I know, I'm
cringing, too, but it's true).

Anyway, I've been talking to my therapist, and she's helped
me come to a decision. One I probably should have made
some time ago. One Marianne agrees with, too.

Christina, if you still want to do that last transfer, I'd
like you to go ahead. If it works – if our child is born – things
will be complicated, I know, but we'll figure something out.
I can write to the clinic, make my decision official. I can do
whatever I need to do.

I want you to have this chance, Christina. I'm a father
now. I know what it means, how profound it is, that
experience, that shift in everything, every pore in your body,
every thought in your head. The way it feels as if you are
missing a protective layer of skin. If you still want to be a
mother, and this is the best way for you to try to achieve that,
then hear me: I won't stand in your way.

Christina read the email over three times then laid her phone
on the garden table, face down. She slid onto a chair. Closed
her eyes, held them to the sun. Patterns danced against her
closed lids. She saw the room they'd left behind, each of them
in turn, first Ed, then her: the mountain range, the empty cot.
She opened her eyes. The afternoon was fierce, blazing; the
apple tree in next door's garden mapped its lacework of leaves
against the sky. She would carry them with her always, their
ghost children. And perhaps, now, another: a child of flesh and
blood, of sun not shade. Perhaps. She would decide, she would
make up her mind when she was ready. It was up to her now;
everything was up to her; she needed only to make a choice and
step towards it, out from the shadows and into the light.

ACKNOWLEDGEMENTS

Sincere thanks to Dr Ippokratis Sarris; Suzanne Todd of Withers LLP; Liz Barron and Morgann Runacre-Temple for their expert help with various aspects of my research for this novel. Any errors of understanding are entirely my own.

Thanks to my agent Judith Murray and my editor Federico Andornino for your support and belief at every stage of the writing process. Thanks also to Virginia Woolstencroft and everyone at Weidenfeld & Nicolson and Greene & Heaton.

I am also enormously grateful to Dr Sarris and to his colleague Mr Nitish Narvekar of King's Fertility and King's College Hospital, London, for navigating our own 'journey'; and to all my family and friends for bearing with me, both creatively and personally.

And most deeply of all, I am grateful to Andy and Caleb, for everything.

ABOUT THE AUTHOR

Laura Barnett was born in 1982 in south London. She studied Spanish and Italian at Cambridge University, and newspaper journalism at City University, London. As a freelance arts journalist, features writer and theatre critic, Laura has worked for the *Guardian*, the *Observer* and the *Daily Telegraph*, amongst others.

The Versions of Us, her debut novel, was a no. 1 bestseller and has been translated into twenty-three languages. She is also the author of *Greatest Hits* and *Gifts*.

CREDITS

Weidenfeld & Nicolson would like to thank everyone at Orion who worked on the publication of *This Beating Heart*.

Agent
Judith Murray

Editor
Federico Andornino

Copy-editor
Linden Lawson

Proofreader
Jenny Page

Editorial Management
Rosie Pearce
Kate Moreton
Jane Hughes
Charlie Panayiotou
Tamara Morriss
Claire Boyle

Audio
Paul Stark
Jake Alderson
Georgina Cutler

Contracts
Anne Goddard
Ellie Bowker
Humayra Ahmed

Design
Nick Shah
Steve Marking
Joanna Ridley
Helen Ewing

Inventory
Jo Jacobs
Dan Stevens

Finance
Nick Gibson
Jasdip Nandra
Elizabeth Beaumont
Ibukun Ademefun
Afeera Ahmed
Sue Baker
Tom Costello

Marketing
Brittany Sankey

Production
Claire Keep
Katie Horrocks

Publicity
Virginia Woolstencroft

Rights
Susan Howe
Krystyna Kujawinska
Jessica Purdue
Ayesha Kinley
Louise Henderson

Operations
Sharon Willis

Sales
Jen Wilson
Victoria Laws
Esther Waters
Frances Doyle
Ben Goddard
Jack Hallam
Anna Egelstaff
Inês Figueira
Barbara Ronan
Andrew Hally
Dominic Smith
Deborah Deyong
Lauren Buck
Maggy Park
Linda McGregor
Sinead White
Jemimah James
Rachael Jones
Jack Dennison
Nigel Andrews
Ian Williamson
Julia Benson
Declan Kyle
Robert Mackenzie
Megan Smith
Charlotte Clay
Rebecca Cobbold

'The beautiful love child of David Nicholl's *One Day* and Kate Atkinson's *Life After Life*' The Times

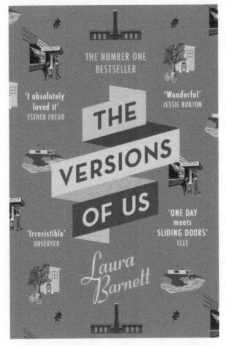

A no. 1 *Sunday Times* bestseller
A Richard & Judy book club pick

What if one small decision could change the rest of your life?

Eva and Jim are nineteen, and students at Cambridge, when their paths first cross in 1958.
As we follow three different versions of their future – together, and apart – their love story takes on different incarnations and twists and turns to the conclusion in the present day.

READ AN EXTRACT NOW

1938

This is how it begins.

A woman stands on a station platform, a suitcase in her right hand, in her left a yellow handkerchief, with which she is dabbing at her face. The bluish skin around her eyes is wet, and the coal-smoke catches in her throat.

There is nobody to wave her off – she forbade them from coming, though her mother wept, as she herself is doing now – and yet still she stands on tiptoe to peer over the milling hats and fox furs. Perhaps Anton, tired of their mother's tears, relented, lifted her down the long flights of stairs in her bath chair, dressed her hands in mittens. But there is no Anton, no Mama. The concourse is crowded with strangers.

Miriam steps onto the train, stands blinking in the dim light of the corridor. A man with a black moustache and a violin case looks from her face to the great swelling dome of her stomach.

'Where is your husband?' he asks.

'In England.' The man regards her, his head cocked, like a bird's. Then he leans forward, takes up her suitcase in his free hand. She opens her mouth to protest, but he is already walking ahead.

'There is a spare seat in my compartment.'

All through the long journey west, they talk. He offers her herring and pickles from a damp paper bag, and Miriam takes them, though she loathes herring, because it is almost a day since she last ate. She never says aloud that there is no husband in England, but he knows. When the train shudders to a halt on the border and the guards order all passengers to disembark, Jakob keeps her close to him as they stand shivering, snowmelt softening the loose soles of her shoes.

'Your wife?' the guard says to Jakob as he reaches for her papers.

Jakob nods. Six months later, on a clear, bright day in Margate, the baby sleeping in the plump, upholstered arms of the rabbi's wife, that is what Miriam becomes.

✻

It also begins here.

Another woman stands in a garden, among roses, rubbing the small of her back. She wears a long blue painter's smock, her husband's. He is painting now, indoors, while she moves her other hand to the great swelling dome of her stomach.

There was a movement, a quickening, but it has passed. A trug, half filled with cut flowers, lies on the ground by her feet. She takes a deep breath, drawing in the crisp apple smell of clipped grass – she hacked at the lawn earlier, in the cool of the morning, with the pruning shears. She must keep busy: she has a horror of staying still, of allowing the blankness to roll over her like a sheet. It is so soft, so comforting. She is afraid she will fall asleep beneath it, and the baby will fall with her.

Vivian bends to retrieve the trug. As she does so, she feels something rip and tear. She stumbles, lets out a cry. Lewis does not hear her: he plays music while he's working. Chopin mostly, Wagner sometimes, when his colours are taking a darker turn. She is on the ground, the trug upended next to her, roses strewn across the paving, red and pink, their petals crushed and browning, exuding their sickly perfume. The pain comes again and Vivian gasps; then she remembers her neighbour, Mrs Dawes, and calls out her name.

In a moment, Mrs Dawes is grasping Vivian's shoulders with her capable hands, lifting her to the bench by the door, in the shade. She sends the grocer's boy, standing fish-mouthed at the front gate, scuttling off to fetch the doctor, while she runs upstairs to find Mr Taylor – such an odd little man, with his pot-belly and snub gnome's nose: not at all how she'd thought an artist would look. But sweet with it. Charming.

Vivian knows nothing but the waves of pain, the sudden coolness of bed sheets on her skin, the elasticity of minutes and hours, stretching out beyond limit until the doctor says, 'Your son. Here is your son.' Then she looks down and sees him, recognises him, winking up at her with an old man's knowing eyes.

PART ONE

Puncture
Cambridge, October 1958

Later, Eva will think, *If it hadn't been for that rusty nail, Jim and I would never have met.*

The thought will slip into her mind, fully formed, with a force that will snatch her breath. She'll lie still, watching the light slide around the curtains, considering the precise angle of her tyre on the rutted grass; the nail itself, old and crooked; the small dog, snouting the verge, failing to heed the sound of gear and tyre. She had swerved to miss him, and her tyre had met the rusty nail. How easy – how much more *probable* – would it have been for none of these things to happen?

But that will be later, when her life before Jim will already seem soundless, drained of colour, as if it had hardly been a life at all. Now, at the moment of impact, there is only a faint tearing sound, and a soft exhalation of air.

'Damn,' Eva says. She presses down on the pedals, but her front tyre is jittering like a nervous horse. She brakes, dismounts, kneels to make her diagnosis. The little dog hovers penitently at a distance, barks as if in apology, then scuttles off after its owner – who is, by now, a good deal ahead, a departing figure in a beige trench coat.

There is the nail, lodged above a jagged rip, at least two inches long. Eva presses the lips of the tear and air emerges in a hoarse wheeze. The tyre's already almost flat: she'll have to walk the bicycle back to college, and she's already late for supervision. Professor Farley will assume she hasn't done her essay on the *Four Quartets*, when actually it has kept her up for two full nights – it's in her satchel now, neatly copied, five pages long, excluding footnotes. She is rather proud of it, was looking forward to reading it aloud, watching old Farley from the corner of her eye as he leaned forward, twitching his eyebrows in the way he does when something really interests him.

'*Scheiße*,' Eva says: in a situation of this gravity, only German seems to do.

'Are you all right there?'

She is still kneeling, the bicycle weighing heavily against her side. She examines the nail, wonders whether it would do more harm than good to take it out. She doesn't look up.

'Fine, thanks. It's just a puncture.'

The passer-by, whoever he is, is silent. She assumes he has walked on, but then his shadow – the silhouette of a man, hatless, reaching into his jacket pocket – begins to shift across the grass towards her. 'Do let me help. I have a kit here.'

She looks up now. The sun is dipping behind a row of trees – just a few weeks into Michaelmas term and already the days are shortening – and the light is behind him, darkening his face. His shadow, now attached to feet in scuffed brown brogues, appears grossly tall, though the man seems of average height. Pale brown hair, in need of a cut; a Penguin paperback in his free hand. Eva can just make out the title on the spine, *Brave New World*, and she remembers, quite suddenly, an afternoon – a wintry Sunday; her mother making *Vanillekipferl* in the kitchen, the sound of her father's violin drifting up from the music room – when she had lost herself completely in Huxley's strange, frightening vision of the future.

She lays the bicycle down carefully on its side, gets to her feet. 'That's very kind of you, but I'm afraid I've no idea how to use one. The porter's boy always fixes mine.'

'I'm sure.' His tone is light, but he's frowning, searching the other pocket. 'I may have spoken too soon, I'm afraid. I've no idea where it is. So sorry. I usually have it with me.'

'Even when you're not cycling?'

'Yes.' He's more a boy than a man: about her own age, and a student; he has a college scarf – a bee's black and yellow stripes – looped loosely round his neck. The town boys don't sound like him, and they surely don't carry copies of *Brave New World*. 'Be prepared and all that. And I usually do. Cycle, I mean.'

He smiles, and Eva notices that his eyes are a very deep blue, almost violet, and framed by lashes longer than her own. In a woman, the effect would be called beautiful. In a man, it is a little unsettling; she is finding it difficult to meet his gaze.

'Are you German, then?'

'No.' She speaks too sharply; he looks away, embarrassed.

'Oh. Sorry. Heard you swear. *Scheiße*.'

'You speak German?'

'Not really. But I can say "shit" in ten languages.'

Eva laughs: she shouldn't have snapped. 'My parents are Austrian.'

'*Ach so.*'

'You *do* speak German!'

'*Nein, mein Liebling.* Only a little.'

His eyes catch hers and Eva is gripped by the curious sensation that they have met before, though his name is a blank. 'Are you reading English? Who's got you on to Huxley? I didn't think they let any of us read anything more modern than *Tom Jones*.'

He looks down at the paperback, shakes his head. 'Oh no – Huxley's just for fun. I'm reading law. But we are still *allowed* to read novels, you know.'

9

She smiles. 'Of course.' She can't, then, have seen him around the English faculty; perhaps they were introduced at a party once. David knows so many people – what was the name of that friend of his Penelope danced with at the Caius May Ball, before she took up with Gerald? He had bright blue eyes, but surely not quite like these. 'You do look familiar. Have we met?'

The man regards her again, his head on one side. He's pale, very English-looking, a smattering of freckles littering his nose. She bets they gather and thicken at the first glance of sun, and that he hates it, curses his fragile northern skin.

'I don't know,' he says. 'I feel as if we have, but I'm sure I'd remember your name.'

'It's Eva. Edelstein.'

'Well.' He smiles again. 'I'd definitely remember that. I'm Jim Taylor. Second year, Clare. You at Newnham?'

She nods. 'Second year. And I'm about to get in serious trouble for missing a supervision, just because some idiot left a nail lying around.'

'I'm meant to be in a supervision too. But to be honest, I was thinking of not going.'

Eva eyes him appraisingly; she has little time for those students – men, mostly, and the most expensively educated men at that – who regard their degrees with lazy, self-satisfied contempt. She hadn't taken him for one of them. 'Is that something you make a habit of?'

He shrugs. 'Not really. I wasn't feeling well. But I'm suddenly feeling a good deal better.'

They are silent for a moment, each feeling they ought to make a move to leave, but not quite wanting to. On the path, a girl in a navy duffel coat hurries past, throws them a quick glance. Then, recognising Eva, she looks again. It's that Girton girl, the one who played Emilia to David's Iago at the ADC.

She'd had her sights set on David: any fool could see it. But Eva doesn't want to think about David now.

'Well,' Eva says. 'I suppose I'd better be getting back. See if the porter's boy can fix my bike.'

'Or you could let me fix it for you. We're much closer to Clare than Newnham. I'll find the kit, fix your puncture, and then you can let me take you for a drink.'

She watches his face, and it strikes Eva, with a certainty that she can't possibly explain – she wouldn't even want to try – that this is the moment: the moment after which nothing will ever be quite the same again. She could – *should* – say no, turn away, wheel her bicycle through the late-afternoon streets to the college gates, let the porter's boy come blushing to her aid, offer him a four-bob tip. But that is not what she does. Instead, she turns her bicycle in the opposite direction and walks beside this boy, this Jim, their twin shadows nipping at their heels, merging and overlapping on the long grass.

|||||||

Pierrot
Cambridge, October 1958

In the dressing-room, she says to David, 'I almost ran over a dog with my bike.'

David squints at her in the mirror; he is applying a thick layer of white pan-stick to his face. 'When?'

'On my way to Farley's.' Odd that she should have remembered it now. It was alarming: the little white dog at the edge of the path hadn't moved away as she approached, but skittered towards her, wagging its stump of a tail. She'd prepared to swerve, but at the very last moment – barely inches from her front wheel – the dog had suddenly bounded away with a frightened yelp.

Eva had stopped, shaken; someone called out, 'I say – look where you're going, won't you?' She turned, saw a man in a beige trench coat a few feet away, glaring at her.

'I'm so sorry,' she said, though what she meant to say was, *You should really keep your damn dog on a lead.*

'Are you all right there?' Another man was approaching from the opposite direction: a boy, really, about her age, a college scarf looped loosely over his tweed jacket.

'Quite all right, thank you,' she said primly. Their eyes met briefly as she remounted – his an uncommonly dark blue, framed by long, girlish lashes – and for a second she was sure she knew him, so sure that she opened her mouth to frame

12

a greeting. But then, just as quickly, she doubted herself, said nothing, and pedalled on. As soon as she arrived at Professor Farley's rooms and began to read out her essay on the *Four Quartets*, the whole thing slipped from her mind.

'Oh, Eva,' David says now. 'You do get yourself into the most absurd situations.'

'Do I?' She frowns, feeling the distance between his version of her – disorganised, endearingly scatty – and her own. 'It wasn't my fault. The stupid dog ran right at me.'

But he isn't listening: he's staring hard at his reflection, blending the make-up down onto his neck. The effect is both clownish and melancholy, like one of those French Pierrots.

'Here,' she says, 'you've missed a bit.' She leans forward, rubs at his chin with her hand.

'Don't,' he says sharply, and she moves her hand away.

'Katz.' Gerald Smith is at the door, dressed, like David, in a long white robe, his face unevenly smeared with white. 'Cast warm-up. Oh, hello, Eva. You wouldn't go and find Pen, would you? She's hanging around out front.'

She nods at him. To David, she says, 'I'll see you afterwards, then. Break a leg.'

He grips her arm as she turns to go, draws her closer. 'Sorry,' he whispers. 'Just nerves.'

'I know. Don't be nervous. You'll be great.'

He *is* great, as always, Eva thinks with relief half an hour later. She is sitting in the house seats, holding her friend Penelope's hand. For the first few scenes, they are tense, barely able to watch the stage: they look instead at the audience, gauging their reactions, running over the lines they've rehearsed so many times.

David, as Oedipus, has a long speech about fifteen minutes in that it took him an age to learn. Last night, after the dress, Eva sat with him until midnight in the empty dressing-room, drilling him over and over, though her essay was only half finished, and she'd have to stay up all night to get it done. Tonight, she can hardly bear to listen, but David's voice is clear, unfaltering. She watches two men in the row in front lean forward, rapt.

Afterwards, they gather in the bar, drinking warm white wine. Eva and Penelope – tall, scarlet-lipped, shapely; her first words to Eva, whispered across the polished table at matriculation dinner, were, 'I don't know about you, but I would *kill* for a smoke' – stand with Susan Fletcher, whom the director, Harry Janus, has recently thrown over for an older actress he met at a London show.

'She's *twenty-five*,' Susan says. She's brittle and a little teary, watching Harry through narrowed eyes. 'I looked up her picture in *Spotlight* – they have a copy in the library, you know. She's absolutely *gorgeous*. How am I meant to compete?'

Eva and Penelope exchange a discreet glance; their loyalties ought, of course, to lie with Susan, but they can't help feeling she's the sort of girl who thrives on such dramas.

'Just don't compete,' Eva says. 'Retire from the game. Find someone else.'

Susan blinks at her. 'Easy for you to say. David's besotted.'

Eva follows Susan's gaze across the room, to where David is talking to an older man in a waistcoat and hat – not a student, and he hasn't the dusty air of a don: a London agent, perhaps. He is looking at David like a man who expected to find a penny and has found a crisp pound note. And why not? David is back in civvies now, the collar of his sports jacket arranged just so, his face wiped clean: tall, shining, magnificent.

All through Eva's first year, the name 'David Katz' had travelled the corridors and common rooms of Newnham, usually uttered in an excitable whisper. *He's at King's, you know. He's the spitting image of Rock Hudson. He took Helen Johnson for cocktails.* When they finally met – Eva was Hermia to his Lysander, in an

14

early brush with the stage that confirmed her suspicion that she would never make an actress – she had known he was watching her, waiting for the usual blushes, the coquettish laughter. But she had not laughed; she had found him foppish, self-regarding. And yet David hadn't seemed to notice; in the Eagle pub after the read-through, he'd asked about her family, her life, with a degree of interest that she began to think might be genuine. 'You want to be a writer?' he'd said. 'What a perfectly wonderful thing.' He'd quoted whole scenes from *Hancock's Half Hour* at her with uncanny accuracy, until she couldn't help but laugh. A few days later, after rehearsals, he'd suggested she let him take her out for a drink, and Eva, with a sudden rush of excitement, had agreed.

That was six months ago now, in Easter term. She hadn't been sure the relationship would survive the summer – David's month with his family in Los Angeles (his father was American, had some rather glamorous connection to Hollywood), her fortnight scrabbling around on an archaeological dig near Harrogate (deathly dull, but there'd been time to write in the long twilit hours between dinner and bed). But he wrote often from America, even telephoned; then, when he was back, he came to Highgate for tea, charmed her parents over *Lebkuchen*, took her swimming in the Ponds.

There was, Eva was finding, a good deal more to David Katz than she had at first supposed. She liked his intelligence, his knowledge of culture: he took her to *Chicken Soup With Barley* at the Royal Court, which she found quite extraordinary; David seemed to know at least half the bar. Their shared backgrounds lent everything a certain ease: his father's family had emigrated from Poland to the US, his mother's from Germany to London, and they now inhabited a substantial Edwardian villa in Hampstead, just a short tramp across the heath from her parents' house.

And then, if Eva were truly honest, there was the matter of his looks. She wasn't in the least bit vain herself: she had inherited her mother's interest in style – a well-cut jacket, a tastefully decorated room – but had been taught, from young, to prize intellectual achievement over physical beauty. And yet Eva found that she *did* enjoy the way most eyes would turn to David when he entered a room; the way his presence at a party would suddenly make the evening seem brighter, more exciting. By Michaelmas term, they were a couple – a celebrated one, even, among David's circle of fledgling actors and playwrights and directors – and Eva was swept up by his charm and confidence; by his friends' flirtations and their in-jokes and their absolute belief that success was theirs for the taking.

Perhaps that's how love always arrives, she wrote in her notebook: *in this imperceptible slippage from acquaintance to intimacy.* Eva is not, by any stretch of the imagination, experienced. She met her only previous boyfriend, Benjamin Schwartz, at a dance at Highgate Boys' School; he was shy, with an owlish stare, and the unshakeable conviction that he would one day discover a cure for cancer. He never tried anything other than to kiss her, hold her hand; often, in his company, she felt boredom rise in her like a stifled yawn. David is never boring. He is all action and energy, Technicolor-bright.

Now, across the ADC bar, he catches her eye, smiles, mouths silently, 'Sorry.'

Susan, noticing, says, 'See?'

Eva sips her wine, enjoying the illicit thrill of being chosen, of holding such a sweet, desired thing within her grasp.

The first time she visited David's rooms in King's (it was a sweltering June day; that evening, they would give their last performance of *A Midsummer Night's Dream*), he had positioned her in front of the mirror above his basin, like a mannequin. Then he'd stood behind her, arranged her hair so that it fell in coils across her shoulders, bare in her light cotton dress.

'Do you see how beautiful we are?' he said.

Eva, watching their two-headed reflection through his eyes, felt suddenly that she did, and so she said simply, 'Yes.'

VERSION THREE

//////

Fall
Cambridge, October 1958

He sees her fall from a distance: slowly, deliberately, as if in a series of freeze-frames. A small white dog – a terrier – snuffling the rutted verge, lifting its head to send a reproachful bark after its owner, a man in a beige trench coat, already a good deal ahead. The girl approaching on a bicycle – she is pedalling too quickly, her dark hair trailing out behind her like a flag. He hears her call out over the high chime of her bell: 'Move, won't you, boy?' Yet the dog, drawn by some new source of canine fascination, moves not away but into the narrowing trajectory of her front tyre.

The girl swerves; her bicycle, moving off into the long grass, buckles and judders. She falls sideways, landing heavily, her left leg twisted at an awkward angle. Jim, just a few feet away now, hears her swear. '*Scheiße*.'

The terrier waits a moment, wagging its tail disconsolately, and then scuttles off after its owner.

'I say – are you all right there?'

The girl doesn't look up. Close by, now, he can see that she is small, slight, about his age. Her face is hidden by that curtain of hair.

'I'm not sure.'

Her voice is breathless, clipped: the shock, of course. Jim steps from the path, moves towards her. 'Is it your ankle?

Do you want to try putting some weight on it?'

Here is her face: thin, like the rest of her; narrow-chinned; brown eyes quick, appraising. Her skin is darker than his, lightly tanned: he'd have thought her Italian or Spanish; German, never. She nods, winces slightly as she climbs to her feet. Her head barely reaches his shoulders. Not beautiful, exactly – but known, somehow. Familiar. Though surely he doesn't know her. At least, not yet.

'Not broken, then.'

She nods. 'Not broken. It hurts a bit. But I suspect I'll live.'

Jim chances a smile that she doesn't quite return. 'That was some fall. Did you hit something?'

'I don't know.' There is a smear of dirt on her cheek; he finds himself struggling against the sudden desire to brush it off. 'Must have done. I'm usually rather careful, you know. That dog came right at me.'

He looks down at her bicycle, lying stricken on the ground; a few inches from its back tyre, there is a large grey stone, just visible through the grass. 'There's your culprit. Must have caught it with your tyre. Want me to take a look? I have a repair kit here.' He shifts the paperback he is carrying – *Mrs Dalloway*; he'd found it on his mother's bedside table as he was packing for Michaelmas term and asked to borrow it, thinking it might afford some insight into her state of mind – to his other hand, and reaches into his jacket pocket.

'That's very kind of you, but really, I'm sure I can . . .'

'Least I can do. Can't believe the owner didn't even look round. Not exactly chivalrous, was it?'

Jim swallows, embarrassed at the implication: that his response, of course, *was*. He's hardly the hero of the hour: the repair kit isn't even there. He checks the other pocket. Then he remembers: Veronica. Undressing in her room that morning – they'd not even waited in the hallway for him to remove his jacket – he'd laid the contents of his pockets on her dressing-table. Later, he'd picked up his wallet, keys, a few loose coins. The kit must still be there, among her perfumes, her paste necklaces, her rings.

'I may have spoken too soon, I'm afraid. I've no idea where it is. So sorry. I usually have it with me.'

'Even when you're not cycling?'

'Yes. Be prepared and all that. And I usually do. Cycle, I mean.'

They are silent for a moment. She lifts her left ankle, circles it slowly. The movement is fluid, elegant: a dancer practising at the barre.

'How does it feel?' He is surprised by how truly he wants to know.

'A bit sore.'

'Perhaps you should see a doctor.'

She shakes her head. 'I'm sure an ice-pack and a stiff gin will do the trick.'

He watches her, unsure of her tone. She smiles. 'Are you German, then?' he asks.

'No.'

He wasn't expecting sharpness. He looks away. 'Oh. Sorry. Heard you swear. *Scheiße.*'

'You speak German?'

'Not really. But I can say "shit" in ten languages.'

She laughs, revealing a set of bright white teeth. Too healthy, perhaps, to have been raised on beer and sauerkraut. 'My parents are Austrian.'

'*Ach so.*'

'You do speak German!'

'*Nein, mein Liebling.* Only a little.'

Watching her face, it strikes Jim how much he'd like to draw her. He can see them, with uncommon vividness: her curled on a window seat, reading a book, the light falling just so across her hair; him sketching, the room white and silent, but for the scratch of lead on paper.

'Are you reading English too?'

Her question draws him back. Dr Dawson in his Old Court rooms, his three supervision partners, with their blank, fleshy faces and neatly combed hair, mindlessly scrawling the 'aims and adequacy of the law of tort'. He's late already, but he doesn't care.

He looks down at the book in his hand, shakes his head. 'Law, I'm afraid.'

'Oh. I don't know many men who read Virginia Woolf for fun.'

He laughs. 'I just carry it around for show. I find it's a good ice-breaker with beautiful English students. "Don't you just love *Mrs Dalloway*?" seems to go down a treat.'

She is laughing with him, and he looks at her again, for longer this time. Her eyes aren't really brown: at the iris, they are almost black; at the rim, closer to grey. He remembers a shade just like it in one of his father's paintings: a woman – Sonia, he knows now; that was why his mother wouldn't have it on the walls – outlined against a wash of English sky.

'So do you?' he says.

'Do I what?'

'Love *Mrs Dalloway*?'

'Oh, absolutely.' A short silence. Then, 'You do look familiar. I thought perhaps I'd seen you in a lecture.'

'Not unless you're sneaking into Watson's fascinating series on Roman law. What's your name?'

'It's Eva. Edelstein.'

'Well.' The name of an opera singer, a ballerina, not this scrap of a girl, whose face, Jim knows, he will sketch later, blending its contours: the planed angles of her cheekbones; the smudged shadows beneath her eyes. 'I'm sure I'd have remembered that. I'm Jim Taylor. Second year, Clare. I'd say you were . . . Newnham. Am I right?'

'Spot on. Second year too. I'm about to get in serious trouble for missing a supervision on Eliot. And I've done the essay.'

'Double the pain, then. But I'm sure they'll let you off, in the circumstances.'

She regards him, her head to one side; he can't tell if she finds him interesting or odd. Perhaps she's simply wondering why he's still here. 'I'm meant to be in a supervision too,' he says. 'But to be honest, I was thinking of not going.'

'Is that something you make a habit of?' That trace of sternness has returned; he wants to explain that he's not one of *those* men, the ones who neglect their studies out of laziness, or lassitude, or some inherited sense of entitlement. He wants to tell her how it feels to be set on a course that is not of his own choosing. But he can't, of course; he says only, 'Not really. I wasn't feeling well. But I'm suddenly feeling a good deal better.'

For a moment, it seems that there is nothing else to say. Jim can see how it will go: she will lift her bicycle, turn to leave, make her slow journey back to college. He is stricken, unable to think of a single thing to keep her here. But she isn't leaving yet; she's looking beyond him, to the path. He follows her gaze, watches a girl in a navy coat stare back at them, then hurry on her way.

'Someone you know?' he says.

'A little.' Something has changed in her; he can sense it. Something is closing down. 'I'd better head back. I'm meeting someone later.'

A man: of course there had to be a man. A slow panic rises in him: he will not, must not, let her go. He reaches out, touches her arm. 'Don't go. Come with me. There's a pub I know. Plenty of ice and gin.'

He keeps his hand on the rough cotton of her sleeve. She doesn't throw it off, just looks back up at him with those watchful eyes. He is sure she'll say no, walk away. But then she says, 'All right. Why not?'

Jim nods, aping a nonchalance he doesn't feel. He is thinking of a pub on Barton Road; he'll wheel the damn bicycle there himself if he has to. He kneels down, looks it over; there's no visible damage, but for a narrow, tapered scrape to the front mudguard. 'Doesn't look too bad,' he says. 'I'll take it for you, if you like.'

Eva shakes her head. 'Thanks. But I can do it myself.'

And then they walk away together, out of the allotted grooves of their afternoons and into the thickening shadows of evening, into the dim, liminal place where one path is taken, and another missed.

WANT EVEN MORE LAURA BARNETT?

'Barnett has that rare talent, like Curtis Sittenfeld or Kate Atkinson, of building up the mundane aspects of everyday life until they acquire meaning' *The Times*

Cass Wheeler has seen it all – from the searing heights of success, to earth-shattering moments of despair.

A musician born in 1950, Cass is now taking one day to select the sixteen songs in her repertoire that have meant the most to her. And behind each song lies a story. The dreams, the failures, the second chances.

'Barnett excels herself in this mesmerising ballad of a book . . . An absolute must read' *Stylist*

AVAILABLE NOW

Help us make the next generation of readers

We – both author and publisher – hope you enjoyed this book. We believe that you can become a reader at any time in your life, but we'd love your help to give the next generation a head start.

Did you know that 9 per cent of children don't have a book of their own in their home, rising to 13 per cent in disadvantaged families*? We'd like to try to change that by asking you to consider the role you could play in helping to build readers of the future.

We'd love you to think of sharing, borrowing, reading, buying or talking about a book with a child in your life and spreading the love of reading. We want to make sure the next generation continue to have access to books, wherever they come from.

And if you would like to consider donating to charities that help fund literacy projects, find out more at **www.literacytrust.org.uk** and **www.booktrust.org.uk**.

THANK YOU

*As reported by the National Literacy Trust